gkdp.net

To Gunin-

thanks for your work for the NAACP!

U N A
QUEEN OF TROUBLE

Mary Ellen Campagna

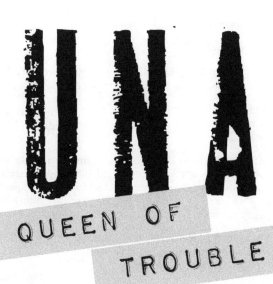

UNA

QUEEN OF
TROUBLE

MARY ELLEN CAMPAGNA

Gold King Diversity Publications
https://maryellenannecampb.wixsite.com/website
maryellenannecampbell@gmail.com

ISBNs
978-1-7378131-0-1 (softcover)
978-1-7378131-1-8 (eBook)

Printed in the United States of America

Cover and Interior design: 1106 Design
Illustrations: Linda Bostic Smith
Website: James E. Jones

INTRODUCTION

This novel is dedicated to the memory of my dear friends, Evelyn Davis Bethel and her sister Helen E. Davis, African American activists who spent decades fighting for racial justice and civil rights in Southwestern Virginia. It is also dedicated to Joan Trumpauer Mulholland, a white civil rights activist during the 1960s and one of the famous Freedom Riders. *Una* is inspired by two earlier novels by Mary Ellen Campagna titled *Unalet P. Zipley (2005)* and *The Journal of Sammy Gales, an unlikely witch (2019)*; however, *Una* is an entirely *new* reading experience.

I want to acknowledge and thank my friends, Megan Mizak, Sandra Carter, Angela Devore-Greene, Linda Bostic Smith, Rosa Pogue, Regina York, and James E. Jones for their creative help and support. I also want to thank Dr. Carolivia Herron, my professor one summer at Hollins University, for her wisdom. And I thank poet

Nikki Giovanni for her kind words expressing enthusiasm for the earliest version of *Una*.

Una is a fictional coming-of-age novel; however, some of the stories are based on true historical events that occurred in Roanoke, Virginia, and parts of South Carolina. Some names of people and places have been changed for the privacy of certain individuals and institutions.

This book follows MLA guidelines for capitalization of *black* and *white*.

"All men are caught in an inescapable network of mutuality, tied in a single garment of destiny."

—Dr. Martin Luther King Jr.

CONTENTS

Introduction: **V**

ONE   A Precocious Child   **1**

TWO   The Tale of Two Marvins and a Pig   **13**

THREE   More Chicago Adventures   **25**

FOUR   Una's Wild Birthday   **39**

FIVE   Una's New Friends *Invent*   **48**

SIX   Una's Surprise   **61**

SEVEN   Hide & Seek   **72**

EIGHT   The Bleeding Bird   **86**

NINE   Relief   **96**

TEN   Dancing Toward the Light   **98**

ELEVEN   Never Lose Your Magic   **102**

TWELVE   Nothing Stays the Same   **109**

THIRTEEN   Discrimination Knocks on Una's Door   **120**

FOURTEEN   Standing Out and Standing Up   **133**

FIFTEEN   Something About Sasha   **144**

SIXTEEN   Coming to an Understanding   **151**

SEVENTEEN Friendship Triumphs 160

EIGHTEEN Taking the Rap 169

NINETEEN Searching for Ancestral Wisdom 177

TWENTY Social Reject 184

TWENTY-ONE The Healer 190

TWENTY-TWO Overcoming Interference 201

TWENTY-THREE Church Family 211

TWENTY-FOUR Aunt Candy's Invitation 217

TWENTY-FIVE South Carolina: The Good,
the Bad and the Ugly 226

TWENTY-SIX Mama Isa's Clan 239

TWENTY-SEVEN I Means We 247

TWENTY-EIGHT CHAG 261

TWENTY-NINE The Manifesto 274

THIRTY Dangerous Passions 288

THIRTY-ONE Hail to the No! 296

THIRTY-TWO Dating Games at the CHAG? 307

THIRTY-THREE When Push Comes to Shove 316

THIRTY-FOUR The Fight 323

THIRTY-FIVE More Questions Than Answers 335

THIRTY-SIX Trying to Carry On 344

THIRTY-SEVEN Thanksgiving 346

THIRTY-EIGHT I'll Fly Away 353

THIRTY-NINE Down the Road 357

Works Consulted 361

About the Author 363

CHAPTER ONE
A PRECOCIOUS CHILD

Una Zipley was named in memory of her Aunt Unabell on her dad's side, a rambunctious child who died at age three from leukemia. Her unusual name, Una, was that of the heroine of the first book in Edmund Spenser's *The Faerie Queene*, an epic poem written in the sixteenth century. But Una's family didn't discover this until years after her birth in 1985. They were also delighted to learn that the name stood for the embodiment of truth, purity, innocence, and common sense.

Nathaniel Hawthorn liked the name Una so much that he named one of his daughters Una, and many claim that it literally means the *personification of wisdom;* but again, Una's family didn't know all this when they named their lively little daughter.

As Una grew, she figured that plain Una was far too simple a name—because she could shoot at least five baskets a game for her elementary school basketball team (the Wildcats) and fix her bouffant curls on top of her own head whenever her BFF, Judy Light, and she went to tea parties with their dolls, Lucinda and Jackie. So she added the initial "F" to represent herself as *Una Francine Zipley*. The original "F" stood for buxom Francine, the lady dressed in a crimson sundress on the back of the noodle box. They were Francine West Noodles and were supposed to make you long-legged and lovable like the sexy red-haired lady on the box. Nobody but Judy ever called her Una Francine; however, teachers noticed the giant "F" when they asked her to sign her name, which she did in generous, swirly strokes. She wouldn't officially shorten her name until the end of first grade when the school discovered that her real name was just Una Zipley—without the glamorous Francine in the middle.

People referred to Una's dad as either Squirrel or Zippy due to his fast-moving pace. His real name was Samuel Zipley, and he was a busy lawyer. Her mom was a popular pediatrician named Dorothy (Doc) Zipley. She took care of a bunch of runny-nosed kids who whined and blew their noses in deafening blows like two steam engines leaving their stations at the same time.

Una's dad really didn't expect his wife to give birth to the overly stubborn, obnoxiously creative, and outspoken child Una turned out to be. There's no genetic test for those traits. Since neither Doc nor Squirrel considered that they had such an interesting genetic constitution, Una was definitely a surprise. She was born on the Fourth of July with red hair, porcelain skin like her parents', and an explosive smile. Her dad and mom beamed with pride the day they brought her home from the hospital.

When she was a baby, Una sometimes stayed with Squirrel while Doc took care of the clinic, because Squirrel said you could find any so-so Joe, Manfred, or Kip to handle litigation, but only one in a million could deal with a kid who needed a shot. Una was reared on books like *The OOOgly OOOOglebies* by Winifred Zigington and *The Job of the Purple Blob* by Dr. Russo Fuscha. She soon grew a talent for collecting fascinating facts, scribble-scrabbles that she felt could be helpful one day, and a notebook full of make-believe happenings.

Doc Zipley knew her little girl was different by the time she was two because she had more energy than a horde of young gerbils. One morning before her mom woke up, Una poured a thin layer of Lucky Charms on the beige silk sofa in the living room and then a quart of whole milk on top of it, with a few cherries sprinkled around for decoration. When she heard someone coming, she wiggled her index finger at the sofa and opened the front door. "*Go outside!*" she commanded.

The sofa didn't go anywhere, but Doc laughed at her toddler's determination.

When Squirrel found out, he laughed, too, but then Doc's face turned radish red with frustration. "We'll have to buy a new couch, I guess," she said.

When Una was three, Doc took her to Walmart to buy Halloween candy. The child accidentally opened a package of fake blood. It made bright red drip tracks down nearly every aisle. When she saw that her mother was upset, Una wiggled her nose and told the blood tracks to disappear. Nothing happened, but Doc was amazed at her little daughter's tenacity.

When they got home, Doc realized something was amiss with Una. "You're missing your left shoe, dear," she said.

"I only need *one*, Mom," Una said with confidence. "I like to hop." But Doc told her to look for it all the same.

Una pointed her index finger and yelled, "*Come back shoe!*"

Nothing happened, but again, her mom smiled at her determination.

When Una started third grade at John F. Kennedy Elementary on the corner of East Elm and Maple in Alexandria, Virginia, she walked two blocks from her house to school every day with her best friend and next-door neighbor, Judy Light.

Una and Judy loved to dig holes in Una's backyard. Then they filled them with moss, along with old pieces of their mothers' jewelry and feathers. Finally, they put clear plastic or glass on top and covered the edges with wildflowers and pine branches. Since it looked as though fairies might have lived there, they charged other kids a penny to look. (It was a nickel if someone got paid for losing a tooth.) They also dressed up in their mothers' best high heels and pastel negligees to parade around on the sidewalk. That lasted until Doc Zipley called Judy's mom, Emma Light, and suggested they lock their shoes up where their daughters couldn't *borrow* them.

But in fourth grade, things changed. Judy moved far across town where her parents would be closer to their work. They bought a catering business and a new home near Mount Vernon, Virginia, about twenty-five miles away from Una's house. It was a big blow for both Una and Judy. Their visits got further and further apart, until they had to be planned at least two weeks ahead; not at all like being able to walk next door to see your bestie.

Just a few days after that traumatic move, Doc was asked to be the matron of honor in her sister's wedding. Una's Aunt Candice (Candy) Melissa Jasper was marrying a strange fellow from Chicago, Illinois, named Bruce Plimpleton. The wedding was to be at a medium-size Baptist church in Alexandria. The entire bridal party would arrive by train and rented cars from Chicago, where Aunt Candy still lived four doors down from Una's Grandma and Grandpa Jasper.

On the wedding day, the bridesmaids dressed at Una's house. They were planning to drive in a long line of cars to the church. Aunt Candy and Doc were supposed to be the big stars of the whole shebang, but Una pouted over the fact that she wasn't asked to be in the ceremony at all.

Aunt Candy's afraid that if I were a flower girl I might need to suddenly pee or yawn or make dumb faces while she and Bruce try to say their vowels, she told herself.

She told Judy she'd heard that wedding vowels were the part of the ceremony where the preacher told the couple to say after him that the groom would obey the bride in richness and poorness, or forever hold his piece of cake in his pocket. But Judy said she didn't think it was that simple.

5

Doc's matron dress was a darker shade of lavender chiffon than the other maids' and she had a larger bunch of pink rosebuds and baby's breath to carry. She was also supposed to hold Aunt Candy's flowers while the groom put the ring on the bride's least fat finger, the one right next to her pinkie.

But Una felt increasingly uncomfortable about her mom's big-shot part in the wedding, and she couldn't see why there was so much commotion over a thing that lasted twenty minutes, tops. She knew that right after the pledge part, the groom would probably be poking his finger in the oyster dip and asking if anyone remembered to bring extra-strength stomach mints. He was known for struggling with gas.

She'd never worn dresses much, but Una figured that if she'd a been a flower girl, she would have worn one of those dresses with bunches of lace down the front and miles of ribbon all fixed up in small bows at every inch of lace. She would've had her hair done up with millions of ringlets and bows on top of her head.

I could've put on my shorts underneath my dress and tucked a little jar of hair spray and a stick of gum in the side pockets, she said to herself, judging that with the layers of that lacy junk blooming out, no one would've noticed that she had stuff in the pockets underneath. If she had gotten to be a maid or a flower girl, she told herself, she'd have insisted on getting her professional picture taken by one of those camera dudes who doesn't mess around only taking shots of animals.

They'd have been like Glamour Woman Shots of America, and she could've pasted them up on her bedroom wall and put them in the newspaper's "WHAT'S HAPPENING" section. Then she would have passed them out to Judy, the Wright twins, and her dad's friend, Ted Hadley, who always said she was darn tootin' gorgeous when she scrubbed her face good.

Grandma Jasper, Aunt Candy, and her maids were to dress for the wedding at two o'clock on Saturday. Aunt Candy got out of her limo with a little perky-faced girl right behind her. The little girl nearly tumbled out of her seat in a fancy dress that matched her stick-straight, vanilla pudding-colored hair. The dress ended in a ruffle just above her pudgy pink knees.

"Una, this is Bruce's niece, Marsha Plimpleton. She's going to be our flower girl because she's come all the way from Chicago and Bruce doesn't want her to be disappointed," Aunt Candy said. "Besides, she's almost a year older than you, age ten, and *very dignified.*"

"Dignified?" Una said with a pained question in her voice. "How can a kid her age be dignified?"

"That's enough about that," Aunt Candy announced. "Get Marsha some lemonade, please."

Just then, Doc came over with a glass of lemonade for Marsha and everyone began having glasses of pink lemonade, along with almond cookies and small finger sandwiches. But Una wasn't hungry or thirsty, so she crept around to the back of the house to find the hose. Aunt Candy always liked surprises, so Una thought she'd give her one. She carried the hose to the front of the house beside the side patio where the tables were set with ivy-leafed tablecloths. Then she watched Aunt Candy in her long white lace gown as she swept out of the patio door with her maids, who were talking excitedly as they filled up the lawn.

Una held her breath just a little before she squeezed the spray nozzle as hard as she could. First, she aimed it directly at Aunt Candy, soaking her white veil until it looked totally wilted against her wet face. Aunt Candy snatched off the veil and started bawling loudly. Una liked the way her rich brown hair, which usually flowed all over the place in nice waves, now zigzagged in flat loops up against her head, revealing too much forehead and not nearly enough soft spit curls. After Una soaked Aunt Candy's hair, the loops pointed up like dark torches aimed north of Aunt Candy's head, as if they wanted to go in a different direction from the waves that made her bangs.

Her face didn't look as much surprised as mad and sad, but Aunt Candy's hair looked extremely surprised. Then Una boldly turned the water toward Marsha, who squinted her eyes tight enough to see white spots for at least a couple of weeks.

"Well, I'll be darn!" was all she had to say, but she said it over and over like an odd echo, which reminded Una of those automatic scales that talk out loud when you pay a quarter to step up on them, saying, "I'll be darn if you don't weigh such-'n-such," and then they tell your weight like you'd better go on a diet fast.

Una also wet Candy's mom, Grandma Jasper, and each maid, giving each one a full drenching before going on to the next.

Grandma Jasper yelled, "Woo! Woo! Woo!"

That was a rather unexpectedly tame response, but the screams of the wedding party sounded like the ones in the scary movies of the living dead as they roamed, with a skinny actress passing out cold. Una felt like a dart-shooting champ while she held the hose and sprayed just where she wanted. She felt like a powerful wind, almost knocking people down with plain water.

She particularly liked the way hosing everyone made her head seem larger and her body appear stylishly longer, like Francine on the noodle box. That was, until a black umbrella came up in front of her face. Below it, Una spotted a gigantic pair of black boots that looked a lot like her dad's with someone's tiny feet in them.

Doc held the umbrella up to her chest and stood right in front of Una, making her shrink into a much smaller version of herself. At that moment she felt less and less like the girl on the noodle box and more like a helpless sparrow about to be crushed by a Doberman.

"Great-gram Jasper, please bring your wisdom to me at this moment before I do something I'll regret to this child!" Doc implored her dead ancestor.

Marsha stood a few feet away, looking like a pitiful wet kitten with large ears poking out of her straight, soaked strands of hair. Doc grabbed the hose and told Una in an uncharacteristically shrill voice to go in the house through the basement and to stay in the basement until she came. Una got stiff as an ironing board and didn't even know if she could walk, much less go down a flight of stairs into a dark basement. When Una did bad stuff, her mom usually just spanked her hands and talked to her in a calm voice, but what she did that day was really horrible—like something a black magic witch would do.

Doc's footsteps pounded loud and hard as she followed Una.

"Mom, maybe I can put everything back like it was," Una said. "At least let me try."

"Una Zipley, don't you dare do any more damage!" Doc ordered. "You'll enjoy no television or unnecessary phone calls after school for a week, and your job will be scrubbing the bathroom sink for the next eleven years or so, until you grow up and leave home!" she shouted.

"But Mom, let me try to . . ."

"Absolutely not!" Doc said resolutely. "You've been trying to do magic since you were a toddler and it's never worked, so now you'd better pray. And I won't even ask you to explain, because you couldn't say anything that would satisfy me at this moment!"

As it happened, the wedding was called off—rained out, you might say. Two weeks after the drenching, Aunt Candy changed her mind about getting married, because she won a dream vacation to Saint Thomas in the Virgin Islands and Bruce didn't want to go. He got sick a lot on airplanes and often got stomach cramps that caused a great deal of discomfort. So one afternoon after her daily mint leaf soak, Aunt Candy decided that she and Bruce didn't have enough in common.

Miraculously, Marsha and Una made friends and Una asked her to come again for a summer visit. Marsha said she'd a whole lot rather get splashed in the pool than hosed down at a wedding, but she didn't like her maid's dress anyhow because it cut her in the sleeves down under the arms. Una got her bubble gum out, gave Marsha some, and they sat under an oak tree that day and they each chewed a great big wad.

CHAPTER TWO
THE TALE OF TWO MARVINS AND A PIG

When Una was about to have her eleventh summer birthday, she, Doc, and Squirrel took a plane trip to Chicago to see Una's Grandpa and Grandma Jasper and her Aunt Candy. When they got out of their rented car, the first thing Una wanted to do was to get one of Chicago's famous foot-long hot dogs. She wanted to show Squirrel just how far mustard could be squiggled, so she convinced him to stop at Dougie's Hot Dog Stand on the way to the hotel. Then she accidentally spilled a glob of mustard on her new bubble-printed blouse.

"Whoops!" she yelled.

"Oh, well," her mom said, spotting the bright yellow stain. "All creative girls spill things on themselves from time to time. It's part of life and a mark of special distinction."

"Remember the little boy in your practice who had to go to a psychologist to get help for his problem?" Squirrel asked Doc. "His mother punished him every time he spilled milk or knocked over a glass of juice accidentally."

"Yes, I remember," Doc said. "Andy Long was his name. He developed a sickness of the emotions and needed a special doctor to help him get well. But his family couldn't afford the medical care, so they had to stop taking him for therapy after a few visits."

"Then what happened?"

"Andy's cousin Nora believed in miracles, and she prayed for his healing. After several months he began to get better. Last I heard, he was having fun and playing again, just as happily as Dracula on Halloween," Doc said.

"Was Andy's mom a bad person?" Una asked.

"Not really, but a woman who understands her own power and uses it to make the world better is probably a wise woman. Women who are not so wise often use their powers to hurt others. Of course, Andy's mom may not have known how to love herself, so maybe she wasn't bad or good, just sad and confused."

While Una and her parents were talking, she thought of how she'd like to be healed right away of the confusing growing pains she was having. After all, she was an *old soul* (one wiser than her years) at ten and nearly on top of her eleventh birthday.

Una's dad interrupted her thoughts. "I've decided to zoom up on an elevator to the top of the giant Sears Tower and take a few snapshots of the view from the top floor," he said. "Want to come along?"

"Okay," Una said. "I'll race you up the stairs."

"Oh, no," Squirrel said. "I don't want to take a chance on losing you, dear. You stick with me."

By the time they got back to the car Una was anxious to see how much Aunt Candy's dog, Marvin, had grown since the last time she'd seen him.

As soon as Una knocked on Aunt Candy's door, her dog, Marvelous Marvin, appeared. He nodded and drooled in an agreeable way, while padding ahead in a complete circle around Una as if he were inspecting her.

"M & M," Una said. "I'd like to go prowling, but unfortunately, we have no definite place to go."

"Ruff," Marvin said. "Ruff, ruff . . . ruff!"

"Oh, really?" she replied.

Then Una told Marvin if he didn't think Grandpa and Grandma Jasper and Aunt Candy would mind, they could just give Aunt Candy's old car an imaginary spin. She opened the door of the garage to Aunt Candy's antique Model-T and climbed in, holding the door for Marvin. She'd planned an imaginary trip down Oak Street, since she couldn't really drive, but by some miracle Aunt Candy had left her key in the starter. Una turned the key and tried pushing down on the longest pedal she could find, which happened to be the gas. The shift stick was already in reverse, so the car achieved one huge thrust backward, creating a sound like a giant burp. That thrust landed the pair just past the carport and halfway out into the street.

Una shouted with glee to her canine partner that they were on their way. Then she lifted the shift stick as high up in the air as she could and heroically pushed the gas pedal again with her right foot. She created a power surge that caused the old car to putt, cough, and squeal its way down the street. Fortunately, there were no stoplights within three blocks, but there were stop signs. Una ignored them, because it was all she could do to keep one heel on the gas pedal. Marvin noticed a fine-looking Dalmatian walking down the boulevard and thought he'd hop out to say hello.

Una realized she was coming to an intersection with its own stoplight, but she wasn't sure what to do. Two ladies in a white Cadillac were also coming to the light. Una squeezed the horn and took her foot off the gas, but she couldn't quite reach the long pedal located farther back on the floorboard, the brake.

The Cadillac came to the intersection just when Una's car was within inches of the light.

"Look, Monica," one of the ladies shouted loud enough to be heard around the block. "That poor child has gotten herself in a dilly of a spot! We've got to stop her!"

The concerned lady turned her wheels sharply in Una's direction until the front bumper of her car met with the front corner of Una's bumper. The white car came to a screeching halt as it gently bumped the Model-T. The older car let out a jolt and a bang!

The ladies got out and called the police. While Una was explaining her side of the story to the police, she realized that Marvelous Marvin had wondered off. She saw a park to her right with lots of play areas and picnic tables. A brightly painted sign said Grant Park, but she didn't see any children playing in it. She told the police she needed a breath of fresh air. They were on their walkie-talkies anyway, so they didn't really notice her.

"Young woman, hold on. You've just been on *some* adventure!" the lady who drove the Cadillac exclaimed. "What is your name and address?"

"My name is Una Zipley," she said. "I'm visiting my aunt and my grandparents from Virginia."

"Squirrel's daughter?" the smiling, dark-haired lady asked.

"Yes, ma'am," Una replied. "Who are you?"

"I'm your great-aunt, Samantha Zipley Myers, and this is your second cousin, Monica Myers Helms. You are our kin!"

"That's nice!" Una said.

"It is perhaps no coincidence that we should meet now," Aunt Samantha said, chuckling. "Well, since we know who you are, would you like us to give you a lift back to your parents in our car?"

"No, thanks," Una said. "Actually, I need to look for Aunt Candy's dog. His name is Marvelous Marvin, and he was in the car with me a few minutes ago. I can walk back to Aunt Candy's place when I find him. It's only a few blocks away. Then Mom, Dad, and I can ride back to pick up Aunt Candy's car."

"Well, if you're sure," Aunt Samantha said. "Here's my phone number on this card. Tell your father to give me a call when he gets a chance."

"Okay, thanks," Una said, wondering if she'd remember to do that, with so much going on and all. "Thanks for your help."

Aunt Samantha and Cousin Monica turned and walked away, stopping to consult with the police.

"Marvin!" Una cried, "Please come back here, Marvelous Marvin!"

She knew she would be in a load of trouble if she couldn't find him. She had not only messed up Aunt Candy's antique car, but she had lost her aunt's beloved dog.

"Here, M & M!" Una called. "Come to Cousin Una!"

Una noticed an elderly man on a bench drinking something out of a small brown paper bag. He looked up and let out a loud belch.

"Whad ya want?" he asked.

"Marvin!" Una continued calling. "Marvin, where are you?"

"I said, whad ya want?" the man on the bench repeated. "Are ya looking for my pig?"

"No, of course not," Una said. "I've lost someone named Marvin who happens to be a dog."

"My name's Marvin Delaney," the man said. "My wife thinks I'm a dog, but I'm not lost. My pig, Roberta, is the one who's lost. She just took off in this direction two days ago. I got so down in the dumps because of it that I'm resorting to a drink of liquor here in this paper bag."

"I'm Una Zipley, and I took a brief spin in my aunt's car with her dog," Una explained. "He jumped out, so I have to find him right away!"

"Aw, rats-ta-tarnation, it's only four o'clock now," Marvin (the man) said with an odorous belch. "You've got plenty of time to find your dog and my Roberta, too—before supper," he added, taking a long sip from his bottle.

"I'll do my best," Una replied.

"If ya find Roberta, bring her straight to me," Marvin Delaney ordered. Then he burped again. "The crazy city ordinance says I can't keep her in my apartment, but I'll be darned if those city hall geeks are gonna tell me I can't board my own pig when I'm closer to her than I am to my own mother-in-law. I board my mother-in-law, Madge, and my wife, Delores, so by-gosh I can have Roberta for company!"

When Una neared the swings, she spotted a hefty pig standing there watching a little boy who'd just climbed on a swing and had begun to arch up high in the air, screaming, "I'm Superman!" as he pitched a handful of rice from his pocket.

The rice landed like hard rain on the pig.

"Grunt, grunt, grunt," the pig uttered, obviously annoyed with the situation.

"That must be Roberta, that man's pig!" Una yelled to the boy as she pointed to Marvin Delaney. "I'll just herd the pink lady over to him."

She got behind Roberta to apply a big shove and then went around to the front and pulled the pig as gently as possible.

"That pig ate a firecracker!" the boy on the swing screamed. "Just an FYI."

"What?" Una asked.

"Yep, he's a walking explosive, too hot to trot!" the boy snickered.

"Who fed him that?" Una asked.

"I accidentally dropped one by the swing over there," the boy said, pointing to the patch of dirt where the firecracker was. "It ain't my fault he gobbled it up, because I done told him it was dangerous."

"What's going on?" a policeman asked, walking up behind Una and Roberta the pig. Two policemen positioned themselves behind them, followed by Aunt Samantha and

Cousin Monica. They had overheard part of Una's befuddled conversation with the boy.

"That boy told me this pig named Roberta ate a firecracker," Una said. "And that's especially bad because the pig belongs to that man way over there on the bench. He sent me to find it; I mean, the pig."

"Who is he?" one of the policemen asked.

"Marvin Delany," Una replied. "I think that's what he said his name was."

"Oh golly, you mean the pig is about to explode and the dog over there is getting drunk?" Aunt Samantha gasped, covering her mouth with a chuckle that sounded like bells.

When Una glanced over at Marvin Delany, she saw Marvelous Marvin vigorously licking drips from the elder Marvin's bottle full of spirits.

The policemen laughed, but as soon as Roberta heard all the noise, she trotted over and stared up at everyone as though she had witnessed a gang of warped thugs. She let out a huge and unbecoming belch. That sent the entire gathering into fits of laughter that ended only after Marvin Delaney discovered his pig was surrounded.

"Don't tamper with my Roberta!" he ordered. "She can get feisty and when she does, she's got a mind of her own!"

"Calm down, old man," one of the policemen said.

"Don't go making friends with that gal because she's got to go home with me," Marvin Delaney warned persistently. "Ain't trying to be disrespectful."

"How are we going to tell him that his pig might blow up at any moment?" Una whispered to the police.

"We just have to tell him," they said. "Mister, we're sorry, but your pig was reported as having consumed a large firecracker."

"That's quite okay," Marvin Delaney said. "Roberta's got a strong stomach. She ate a sizzler last time she followed me down here, but she won't explode unless she's shocked."

"Great," one of the policemen said sarcastically. "Don't you think your pig would be shocked by just being lost out here?"

Cousin Monica giggled again.

"Naw," Marvin Delaney said. "Her vet said she might dance around a little bit with gas after she ate that last cherry bomb, but she wouldn't go off unless she was shocked electrically."

Marvin Delaney explained that if just a regular shock were all it took, Roberta would have gone off a long time ago just looking at his mother-in-law, Madge, every morning when Madge put purple anti-wrinkle gook on her face.

"Madge puts that purple putty-gook on over the mustache above her lip and on all three chins because she says she wants to make them soft," he said.

Cousin Monica giggled again.

"Thank God, there goes Marvelous Marvin!" Una said.

The dog padded over and barked once in reply. After that, he went back and stood behind Marvin Delaney, barking three more times.

"Oh, I believe I done hit the bottle way too hard today," Marvin Delaney confessed, and then he let out an elephant-size belch.

"You're okay," Una said.

"Naw, I just barked, didn't I? I've been seeing lions, elephants, and other circus animals around my bed of an evening. Oh, Lord, if I can just make it home tonight in one piece to be with my dear wife, Delores, and even if I could see my sweet-as-a-pie mother-in-law, Madge, once more, I'll become a new man, Lord," he promised.

Then the unmistakable shadow of a dog crept into the old man's view.

"Lord, I won't bark, nor act like a dog no more," old Marvin promised, turning an apricot color as he wiped his hot brow with a tissue.

Marvelous Marvin, who had prowled all over the city streets looking for an attractive Dalmatian, was so moved by Marvin Delaney's words that he leapt up on his lap with the full force of his body weight and licked him passionately in the face. Roberta peered at the scene with an indignant air. Then she turned and walked off in the direction of Michigan Avenue.

One of the officers offered to take Una back to her Aunt Candy's apartment.

"Thanks," Una said. "I'll take you up on that. I've already put cousin Monica and Aunt Samantha through enough for one day, and this whole experience has taken longer than I thought."

"Good," the policeman said, "because we told your father we'd be bringing you."

Una waved goodbye again to Aunt Samantha and Cousin Monica. They were now chasing after Roberta.

But Una knew she had to get the smell of whiskey off of Marvelous Marvin before she could take him back to Aunt Candy, so she whispered the chant: "*Be gone evil smell, off the dog where you now dwell!*"

She'd learned the word *dwell* from her talking dictionary years before. She hoped the chant would magically replace the awful smell of whiskey with the sweet smell of lilacs, but it didn't work quite like she had hoped, so she asked the police officers to tell her parents and Aunt Candy that Marvelous Marvin wasn't at all drunk, just a little tipsy—as in, *high on life*.

CHAPTER THREE
MORE CHICAGO ADVENTURES

Una, Marvelous Marvin, and the antique car were finally returned safely to Aunt Candy's apartment later that evening. Squirrel found the damaged spot on the car, but it was nothing he couldn't repair with a slight touch-up job, so he and Doc scolded Una but spared the rod, so to speak. Una felt exhausted, as did her mom, dad, and grandparents, so pretty soon they all said goodbye to Aunt Candy and her marvelous pooch to spend the night at Grandpa and Grandma Jasper's house.

In the morning Una called her *almost* cousin by marriage, Marsha Plimpleton, who also lived in Chicago.

"Hey, girl!" Marsha said. "Glad you're here! Let's do something. Would you like my mom to pick you up and then maybe we can meet up with one of my friends?"

"Sure," Una replied, a little surprised to hear Marsha sounding so upbeat.

But when Marsha knocked on the door, Una barely recognized her as the same rosy, plump kid who had almost starred in Aunt Candy's wedding. Instead, she was as tan as a Fig Newton bar and had lost about twenty pounds.

"I want you to meet my friend Rowe Riley," Marsha said. "Her real name is Rosalind, but we just call her Rowe. She's a trip."

Rowe was waiting for them on the corner of Minnesota and Vine, not just because Marsha had called ahead, but because Rowe felt an adventure in the air. When she felt that way there was always something radical that was just about to happen, and if ever that something needed a little push, Rowe knew just how to give it one. The first thing Una noticed about Rowe was that she was what Squirrel would call *a character*, and she needed no introduction because her mammoth personality could be felt from miles away, even without her saying one word.

The next thing Una noticed was Rowe's sun-colored hair that hung in straight shafts of lemon-yellow light to her jaw. Thick, beige eyelashes fluttered just a little over her sleepy-looking sea-gray eyes. A sheepish smile began to brighten, the closer Una and Marsha got, but Rowe never changed her position: one arm propped at her waist with the opposite hip balanced on the edge of the lamppost.

"What's up, kid?" Marsha asked, hopping to the curb.

"Well, that'll be our call today," Rowe said. "I can think of a dozen things, but we'll see. Hey, I'll bet that's Una!"

"Hi," Una said, slightly out of breath. "Glad to meet you."

"I've got a little plan brewing in the back of my head, girls," Rowe announced. "Smells as sweet as a rose, too."

"Oh, no. What's that crooked brain of yours got cooking today?" Marsha asked.

"Well, it's a hot day," Rowe replied. "I thought we'd take a quick dip in the Michigan Avenue Pool, then hike down to Mount Comfort Funeral Parlor to check out the latest stiffs."

"Ugh. Mount Comfort sounds like Fort Relaxation," Una chuckled. "You mean, look at the dead people?"

"*When* did you get interested in visiting funeral parlors?" Marsha inquired, trying not to sound too judgmental. "I thought we discussed this awhile back and we decided—"

"Come on!" Rowe laughed. "I'm going to teach Una what *true big-city girls* do for fun!"

Una knew she had been away from Chicago for a long time, but she didn't think it had been that long. By the time the girls walked the two blocks to Michigan Avenue, Una had done enough thinking to realize she had a ton of stuff to learn about life in Chicago.

They took a fast splash in the pool, wiped the drips from behind their ears, and headed for the gate. From there Marsha and Una followed Rowe without complaint. After all, her strut shouted self-confidence.

"Una!" Rowe laughed. "We've arrived! Where have you been, girl, in a private haze or a public daze?"

"Both, I guess," she said, and asked if she needed shorts over her bathing suit to go into the funeral parlor.

"Heck, no," Rowe said. "Just follow me!"

Then she marched right into the funeral home's fancy vestibule, holding the door open for Marsha and Una while stretching out her other hand toward a lady greeter who was wearing a black Sunday dress and pearls around her neck.

"Hello, I'm Katherine Jenson," the mortician lady said. "May I help you young ladies?"

"No, thanks," Rowe said with death-defying confidence. *"We're just looking."*

Then she walked straight from the entrance hallway decorated with maroon velvet couches and crystal lamps to the guest parlors where the dead people were all dressed up and stretched out in their coffins.

Rowe wasn't the least bit self-conscious even though she, Marsha, and Una were all still dripping in their bathing suits with wet towels wrapped around their waists and flip-flops on their feet. In fact, her manner was so dramatically marked with purpose that anyone would have to respect her determination as she led the trio of voyeurs out of the vestibule and into the casket-filled parlors.

The three girls flip-flopped their way to a large, apple-red casket in the center of one chapel. Then Rowe leaned over each dead person, standing directly in front of their memorial services. An upright piano player played a sort of eerie, but catchy melody. Rowe swayed to the music while Una and Marsha gazed at the powdered faces of the deceased. Following a thorough examination of each corpse, Rowe trudged boldly ahead from chapel to chapel, with her partners in crime flip-flopping along behind her.

"In that ivory casket is Mrs. Bernice Putnam, of 122 Kilburn Street," Rowe announced. "Wednesday's obituaries told of her love for her husband, Maurice, and their grown son, Toby. I've got a clip from the newspaper in my towel bag, says Bernice was a member of Sweet Simmons Union for Former Undergarment Workers of America."

"How did she die?" Una asked.

"She had an infected bunion on her toe that, combined with sugar, took her down."

"I never heard of putting sugar on a bunion," Una said.

"That's sugar diabetes, you nut!" Marsha said.

Suddenly, Una felt like disappearing, but she reminded herself of how much she had to learn from these well-educated big-city girls.

"The guys in the gray caskets are Norton, Thornton, and Horton Singleton," Rowe said. "The paper talks about them being identical triplets who died together on the way to Vegas in a chartered plane. Their wives reported that they were actually penniless because every cent they had owned had been spent at the crap tables during an earlier visit to Vegas, so a local radio station raised money for their burial expenses."

Rowe later added the interesting tidbit that the triplets' clothes were donated by Convenient Bazaar Formal Duds, but their blue silk ties came compliments of Harrington Link, the downtown department store, where the triplets had shopped every Christmas when they were alive.

"Miss Riley, I would like to see you now in the front office please," Ms. Jenson whispered to Rowe in the chapel.

Marsha and Una felt a twist of panic as they looked down at their dripping suits. When they walked over to the French love seat, their flip-flops squeaked loudly. They didn't know whether it was best to stand or sit, since standing made them drip a series of pea-sized puddles, but sitting would get the love seat wet in the middle. Still, they decided to sit. A gust of air conditioning slapped their ankles, giving them a chill. Una was worried about the mortician calling her parents and telling them she'd done something outlandish.

Her teeth started chattering uncontrollably. She felt like she'd like to cry, but her face was transfixed in a pleasant gaze.

"You guys ready to go now?" Rowe asked, sporting a gleeful smile.

Marsha and Una kept still in astonishment like two frozen mannequins.

"Why do you look so happy, Rowe?" Una asked. "Our parents might be on the way at this very moment, thinking of some awful punishment for us."

"I know your mother said you and Una had to be home in an hour, Marsha, so snap out of it. We'd better get moving," she said, ignoring Una's comments.

Marsha and Una got up from the sofa, still looking at least partially frozen.

"What did that lady want?" Marsha asked.

"Oh, she told me she's having an old woman embalmed next Tuesday afternoon and wondered if I wanted to assist with makeup," Rowe said. "I've been begging her to let me try since last summer."

Una laughed and wiggled her nose in a way Marsha hadn't noticed before. Suddenly, a basket of fresh daisies appeared in her hands.

"Oh, you found those," Ms. Jenson said. "I was going to throw them out today, but I'm glad you retrieved them."

"Glad to do it, ma'am," Una said, breaking into a cryptic smile.

"What, you some kind of witch, Una?" Rowe asked, reading her mind for real.

"No, unfortunately, I'm not," Una said. "I've actually tried to do magic a number of times, but I've never been able to pull it off. This time I prayed and used the power of positive thinking. I guess the Devine loves flowers as much as I do."

By the time Marsha walked Una back to her grand-parents' house after the funeral parlor escapade, Squirrel and Doc Zipley had already left to find their rooms at the Conrad Collins Bed and Breakfast Inn. Marsha's mom, Joy Plimpleton, asked if Una could stay over for the night. Then Marsha asked if Rowe could stay over too. Ms. Plimpleton said that would be okay; Ms. Riley also agreed.

Doc told Joy that it would be a fine treat for Una to spend the night because, in fact, her birthday was the very next day on the Fourth of July. Marsha, Rowe, and Una burst into giggles the minute they reunited for their sleepover. They continued to giggle through a supper of pasta with chilled melon and limeade, and deep into the cool summer night from Marsha's king-size guest bed. The girls were even amused in the middle of the night by their six small feet protruding from the bottom of the floral coverlet. The clock had just struck 3:00 a.m. when Rowe woke Una up with a shove.

"Get Marsha up too!" she screamed. "You've got to show us some more of your witchy stuff before you leave town!" she said, directing Una to poke Marsha, who slept soundly to her left.

"What witchy stuff?" Una asked, ready to go back to sleep. "I told you I'm not a witch."

"Can't you *levitate* something?"

"Nope," Una said. "Let's nod off now."

"Have you tried?" Rowe nagged.

"Nope," Una said.

"Then how do you know if you can or can't?" Rowe asked, wide awake and propping herself up on one elbow.

"Oh, God," Una said. She asked Marsha if she had any candles.

"The three candelabras with long candles in the living room," Marsha mumbled, half asleep.

"Get them!" Rowe ordered. "And get some of those long matches."

"Okay, already."

"First, levitate something, Una," she demanded. "Put your hands under a chair, but don't actually touch it. Then we'll help you levitate it up in the air on the count of three."

The girls all stood up and rubbed their eyes. Una and Marsha obediently circled the lightest chair in the room, a sturdy but thin ladder-back with a wicker seat. Una knew that extreme pressure was mounting on her to lift the chair up with pure magic, but she'd never successfully done something like that before.

"I'll try my best," she said.

Then she nervously directed Rowe and Marsha to make a circle of hands around the chair and rock a little back and forth while they put a whisper of wind on it.

"What should we say?" Rowe asked. "Isn't there something we can chant while we do it?"

"We can say: *Rise up chair, rise now, by gravity unbound!*"

Una had read that in her *Witches' Tricks that Totally Work* book.

"Look!" cried Rowe. "It's almost moving!"

"It's about to rise!" Marsha screamed. "I can feel it!"

"Okay, now drop it," Rowe said.

"What do you mean, drop it? It never went anywhere," Una said.

"Well, let's try something else. I lit one candle," Rowe said, desperate to see some magic. "Now you conjure some fire to light the others," she ordered, looking fiercely at Una.

"What if I don't?" Una asked with a scowl.

"If you don't, that's fine, too," Marsha said, staring back hard at Rowe.

"Yeah," Rowe agreed. "I just thought you would want to give it a try. After all, I've heard that magician junk dries up if you don't use it."

"But she doesn't have to," Marsha insisted.

"No. You don't have to," Rowe agreed, looking at Una with a pleading look.

"Oh, all right," Una said. "I'll try, but you both have to close your eyes and repeat seven times after me: *Grow bright, sweet sight, until you create the firelight!*"

Twice Una circled one of the candles, then sat in front of the candelabras that Marsha had borrowed from the living room. Concentrating with all her might on the light, she thought about heat, then fire. She even wiggled her nose, but when nothing happened, she found a lighter in Marsha's drawer and quickly lit all of the candles.

Buzzzzz! A loud, haywire-sounding noise shot out of nowhere. Then a pounding buzz, buzz, buzz. All the candles flickered frantically.

"Help!" Marsha cried. "Mom, help!"

She was screaming as she ran to hide under the bed. Rowe and Una clapped their hands over their ears and joined in the screaming. Their shrill, horrible cries alerted the Plimpleton's neighbor, Mrs. Dentson, to come running over in her fluffy gray slippers and drooping silk nightgown. She said when she heard the screaming, she felt like reeling and falling to the floor, she was so surprised and frightened by the commotion; however, she bravely resisted the urge and held on to the kitchen sink with all her might. Then she mentioned something about calling the fire department, because she thought she'd heard the alarm going off.

"No need, Mrs. Dentson," Joy explained calmly. "There's absolutely NO fire. Every candle in the house is apparently lit and there may be a little bit of smoke, but no fire."

"I've already called the police, the rescue squad, and the fire department just in case," Mrs. Dentson said, patting her sponge rollers. "I had a tuna casserole catch on fire just the other day, and I always call when there is any question. Even if it was just a faulty smoke alarm, it couldn't hurt for the fire department to investigate."

Sure enough, a siren could be heard in the distance. Una still had on her Mickey Mouse t-shirt and hadn't awakened enough to realize why the clock alarm was set for 8:00 a.m. It was playing an incessant round of "Ain't No Mountain High Enough," by Marvin Gaye. She had not had a moment to think about her birthday or her promise to call her mom.

While Joy scurried to put on a robe, Marsha yawned a gigantic yawn and Una stretched her neck out the window looking for any signs of the fire truck. Six fire trucks and two emergency service vans came in response to Mrs. Dentson's fears of a fire, one she'd said, ". . . might engulf the entire city in crimson flames by noon," adding, "Chicago already had one great fire!"

After the emergency services arrived, the neighbors farther down the street became concerned, too. A lady named Mrs. Portnappy rang the doorbell just before the firemen came in. She brought two garden pails full of water, rushing in to deposit them in the middle of Joy's living room floor. Then she asked Rowe if there was anything she needed.

"No thanks," Rowe said, looking pale and bewildered.

"Can I offer you some breakfast?" Joy asked the girls.

"Well, what have you got?" Mrs. Portnappy snapped nervously, thinking the question was posed to her.

Then Mr. and Mrs. Heath, distant neighbors, came down for a look-see. They said they had been wondering what all the *to do* was about. They asked Joy if she'd mind if they took pictures with their new Polaroid camera. Joy said that was okay, except that there was no fire. But they said they wanted close-ups of the engines anyway, a shot of Joy coming out, and an action shot of Mrs. Portnappy hustling to help.

They felt that this sort of thing would be talked about for years to come. The Montclair High School bus was on its way to summer camp activities when the driver, Mrs. Shirington, noticed the fire engines. She parked the bus and unloaded fourteen of her strongest students to see if they could help.

"Hello, I'm Amy Shirington," she told Marsha at the door. "My boys have come to be of assistance!"

"But there's really no fire," Marsha said. "Thanks, but we don't need help."

"Wherever there are sparks, there just may be fire, so let my boys come in and shoot a little here and there from our extinguisher," Mrs. Shirington said. "Every bus is equipped with one, and this will at least put your mind at ease."

"But we . . ." Marsha started to say something when her voice drifted off.

Without pausing, Mrs. Shirington burst through the door with all fourteen students. "Come on boys, go at it!" she commanded.

The boys from Montclair High poured water all over the Plimpleton's entire condo. They used pots and pans, and any vessel they could find when the extinguisher went dry. After they had completed their mission and the firemen had completed theirs, Joy offered them all some powdered sugar donuts which they happily gobbled up, spilling a little sugar here and there on their way out. The firemen and rescue team said they might want some coffee, so Joy brewed five pots of her best java blend. She also served scrambled eggs and toast buffet-style to them and any other neighbors who straggled in.

After the living room, kitchen and bedrooms had been thoroughly soaked with power hoses, extinguishers, garden pails, and pots and pans full of water, Una finally prepared to say goodbye to everyone, because Doc Zipley was parked outside waiting. Joy sent a jar of leftover melon balls to Mrs. Dentson as a peace offering, since she had complained that this event had made her twenty minutes late to her massage appointment across town. She also wrapped a few leftover donuts in foil for Doc and Squirrel.

"I have one thing to do before I go," Una said. "Actually, two things. First, I wanted to say I'm very sorry, Ms. Plimpleton, that my spell may have led to your condo getting soaked, and I'd like to try to fix it, if you don't mind. And second, it wasn't really a spell at all."

"What do you mean?" Marsha and Rowe asked in unison, their eyebrows slanted with concern.

"I mean I lit the candles with a lighter because the magic didn't work, and I didn't want to disappoint you."

"Hah!" Rowe chuckled. "I never believed it."

"Well, I did," Marsha said, looking bewildered.

"I want to try to undo the damage," Una said, launching into a mystical chant: *"Wet rugs, you've got to go! Bring back dry carpet so this won't be such a blow!"*

"Oh, gee!" Marsha said, observing that the carpet was still wet and still smelled foul.

"Sorry. Guess that didn't work either," Una said. "Thanks for a lovely time, Mrs. Plimpleton and everyone."

Then everyone said, "Happy Birthday, anyway!"

But when Una explained what happened to Squirrel and Doc, they insisted that she pay for all the damages to the Plimpleton's carpets with her allowance—over time.

"Hope you've learned your lesson, Una, about the damage that pretending to do magic can bring," Doc scolded. "But since it's your birthday, the only spankings you'll get are birthday spankings."

Una felt relieved, but she didn't know if she was through with magic forever. She loved God and wanted Him to direct her life, but magic was cool too.

CHAPTER FOUR
UNA'S WILD BIRTHDAY

oc and Squirrel took Una back to Aunt Candy's place, where they met up with the rest of the family to celebrate Una's eleventh birthday. When the doorbell rang, Una ran to get it. It was a short, full-figured lady holding a tiny dog with a cerulean bow fastened in its head fur.

"It's a lady with a dog!" she yelled.

"Let her in," Grandma Jasper said. "She must be a friend of Candy's."

"Hello," the lady said. "I'm Paulette Bun, and this is my Chihuahua, Olivia. We're Candy's best friends and she invited us to drop in anytime."

"Well, I'm sorry, but she's on the phone in her room with the door closed right now," Una said authoritatively.

"I see," Paulette said. "And who are you?"

Before Una had a chance to explain who she was and that her family was getting ready to go to Wrigley Field for the Fourth of July fireworks and to celebrate her birthday,

Olivia came dashing in the door, barking enough for eight dogs her size. She hid somewhere under the sofa in the den. Grandma Jasper ran after her. Doc and Paulette followed.

"Come out, you wicked little dog!" Grandma Jasper yelled. "We wouldn't want you to do anything unladylike under Candy's couch. Come out right this minute!"

Una had never heard her grandma's voice sound so harsh.

"Oh, you don't have to be strict with her," Paulette said. "Just talk to her calmly and gently; flatter her a bit and she'll fly to the moon for you."

"All right, come on out now, you enchanting little dog," Doc coaxed.

"Come out right now, or I may personally fly you to the moon!" Grandpa Jasper yelled, emerging from behind his newspaper. "In fact, a swat with this paper might encourage you!"

Nearly twenty minutes passed as everyone tried to convince Olivia to come out from under the sofa. They stared at Olivia's incisors, which appeared to be the size of otter tusks, threatening an enormous bite if anyone dared pull her tiny legs toward the light beyond the underside of the sofa. Marvelous Marvin had gone out on the patio for a nap.

"Come out!" Una screamed, again forgetting that the dog was a guest in Candy's house and fearing that Candy was already going to be mad that Una had damaged her antique car. She boldly leaned her head under the couch. Her red hair hung in tight curls to her shoulders, proving to be too tempting a target for Olivia to resist. She snatched a mouthful of locks tight between her canine incisors and jerked with all her might.

"Ouch!" Una screamed. "Ouch! Ouch! Ouch!"

"I have an idea," Grandma Jasper said. "Let's all lift the couch up as high as we can while Paulette grabs the dog."

On the count of three, everyone except Paulette lifted the dotted Swiss sofa into the air. Paulette knelt on both hands and knees so she could grab Olivia. Then she felt her skirt pull just a tad behind her. The snug black skirt she was wearing could not quite accommodate the size of her hips when they were spread in that upper-thrusted position. A rip began to tear loudly at the seam that connected the entire left side of her linen skirt to the entire right side. Fortunately, although she'd forgotten to wear a slip, Paulette had on pink cotton Spanx. The effect of the rip and the Spanx got to Una.

"Hah!" she laughed, sending Doc and Grandma Jasper into extreme giggles.

"Oh, sorry," they said.

"What was that?" Paulette asked.

"Dear, your skirt had a . . . well . . . it was—" Grandma Jasper tried to explain, but she couldn't. Her considerate nature wouldn't allow her to cause the woman any embarrassment.

"You might say your skirt has experienced a *chasm* of sorts; you know, a split," Doc said. "Actually, it's a chasm of major proportions, depending on how you look at it. I'll just run and get the sewing box."

Several minutes later she came back holding what she thought was a tube of cloth glue. "This is all Candy has in her sewing box, a few buttons and some of this stuff," she said, "so you'll have to lie down on the floor and let us apply the stuff."

After the glue was applied, Paulette rose gradually back to her tubby knees. As she got to her feet, it was discovered that the back of her tight skirt had stuck to her Spanx and her hose. A great divide between the left and right parts of her outfit had once again become undeniable. As she tried to fix the problem, Paulette widened the distance between her legs as far as she could and walked slowly toward the door like a broad, bowlegged mamma duck.

"Oh, no!" Doc screamed. "Does anyone wear glasses?

"Contact lenses," Grandpa Jasper said.

"Do you have them on?" Doc asked.

"Yes."

"Then can you look here a minute? I don't have my glasses on, but I believe that was cement glue that I put on Paulette. Candy must have accidentally put it in her sewing box."

"What!" Paulette hollered, heading quickly toward the door. "Am I cemented to my Spanx? Help, I'm stuck permanently to my undergarments!" she screamed, waddling out the door. "I'll return later for Olivia, when I get out of the hospital!"

Squirrel was standing on the front porch. Paulette bumped into him, and he caught her solidly by the shoulders.

"May I help you, ma'am?" he asked.

"Sir, I've endured all the embarrassment I could possibly imagine tonight, so what's a little more? My seat is cement glued to my bloomers, which are also cemented to what remains of my skirt, and my little dog is still roaming hysterically around in there somewhere," Paulette said, huffing and puffing.

"Ma'am, how did this happen?" Squirrel asked.

"Before I answer that, who are you, sir?" Paulette asked. "I don't really know any of you people."

"I'm Squirrel Zipley, Una's dad," he mumbled. "Una is the redhead. Ma'am, I'm afraid I'm going to have to lie you flat down on a stretcher since your situation does not lend itself easily to bending."

When the rescue squad finally came, Doc told Paulette that she was a physician and directed her to stand erect while she and Squirrel knocked her back on to the stretcher.

"Try to put your legs together; not so impossibly far apart, dear," Grandma Jasper suggested. "That will help you get more strength in your limbs."

"I can't. I'm afraid!" Paulette cried. "I may stick together if I do and then I'll be thrust into a constant, stiff salute pose like a girl soldier frozen at attention. And I'll never again be able to slide around the floor at my Arthur Murray lessons, much less find a husband!"

"Ma'am, if a man really loves you, he'll love you for better or for worse. You just happen to be at the opposite end of better right now," Squirrel reasoned. "Try to remain calm. Think of how bad it might have been," he said, without careful consideration of what he was saying.

"Will that lady ever have a future?" Una asked, feeling bad right after she said it.

Grandpa Jasper tried to conceal a chuckle. "Hush, child!" he said.

"Please go inside now while Miss, ah . . . while this lady backs up on the stretcher," Squirrel instructed his family. "Knocking her on the stretcher has not worked, so Doc and I need to concentrate on solving this predicament another way."

"Squirrel, the lady is going to have to fall back on the stretcher because that small rescue squad can't pick her up," Grandpa Jasper insisted. "She's too heavy and besides, she might stick to one of the men."

"I suppose you have a point," Squirrel said. "Young lady, you are going to have to relax so Doc Zipley and I can knock you back and secure you on the stretcher," he told Paulette, who was dripping with sweat and had turned as white as talcum powder.

"You're in a complex and sticky situation, no pun intended," Grandpa Jasper said.

Just then Aunt Candy came out of her room and tried to assess the situation. She asked Paulette if she had ever accepted the Divine and would let a minister hit her temple forcefully so she could fall back in total grace and trust.

"No, I haven't had the pleasure," Paulette said sarcastically.

"I didn't mean to pry at all," Aunt Candy said. "I just thought it would have been good practice."

The rescue squad was speaking rapid Spanish while nodding and smiling at Paulette to direct the back of her body toward the stretcher.

"I can't do it!" Paulette cried. "I *won't* do it!"

"Do it for that little dog in there," Aunt Candy coaxed. "She needs you, Paulette. You're the only one she feels close to. I'm fairly confident of that."

Marvelous Marvin had just risen from his lengthy nap and had scented out the foreign dog under the couch. One bark from the larger animal was frightening enough to command Olivia's hard-won respect. She came scurrying out from under the sofa like white lightning, barking up a storm. Just as she did, Una was able to snatch her and stick her in the downstairs bathroom. Olivia appeared so startled by the capture that she must have forgotten to sink her incisors into the flesh of Una's arm. Of course, Una was no slouch at defending herself either. She would probably have slapped the dog right in her prissy nose, had Olivia dared to bite.

"Marvin, you really are marvelous!" Una shouted. "Without your courageous growl and bark, we would never have been able to catch Olivia."

Outside, a tall, dark-haired man was striding up the walk. He must have seen the ambulance, with the stretcher being held at a very sharp angle.

"That's my other former manicurist and facial expert!" Aunt Candy shouted over the sound of the firecrackers that had begun to go off, illuminating the silvery sky with a thousand blinking diamond stipples. "His name is

Lawrence Mochly Jr. He and Paulette work together at L & M's Super Nails and Facials."

"Wonderful!" Doc exclaimed. "Perhaps he has some nail polish remover in his case there. Candy, you're plum out."

"What's happening?" the man asked. "I'm Lawrence. What's wrong with Paulette?"

"To make a long story short, her skirt tore in the house and in an attempt to mend it, someone accidentally applied cement glue to a large portion of her backside," Aunt Candy explained.

"I'm sorry; I'm Dr. Dorothy Zipley," Doc announced. "Is there any chance you might have some nail polish remover in your case, sir? That might work."

"Yes, I think I do," Lawrence said. "In fact, I believe my kit has at least four bottles of polish remover and twenty different kinds of nail glosses!"

When Lawrence handed Doc his kit, she opened the bottles of polish remover one by one and poured the yellow liquid on cloths from the kit. Then she applied dabs of the remover to Paulette's rump, gradually separating her Spanx from her skirt.

"Ah, that feels better, even though it's still wet and smelly," Paulette sighed, obviously relieved.

"Dr. Zipley, you've saved me from becoming one of those *stuck-up* gals," Paulette said with a mischievous grin.

"You're quite welcome," Doc said, not responding to the joke.

But the rescue squad didn't understand this instant miracle. They continued to order Paulette to fall back on the stretcher, so they could escort her to the hospital for a complete checkup.

"Oh!" Paulette yelled. "My skirt just fell off!"

The rescue squad felt even more compelled to duty when Paulette lost her skirt, leaving her wearing merely an extra-large pair of pink Spanx, red high heels, and a thin white sleeveless blouse. The ambulance attendants rushed to cover her with a sheet, wrapping it around her twice. Then Paulette willingly crawled on the stretcher, collapsing all her various muscles, which had by now been overcome with exhaustion. When the ambulance drivers fastened their seat belts and prepared to leave, Una ran out holding a large cerulean tote.

"Please don't forget this important little girl!" she cried.

The ambulance drivers smiled innocently at the furiously barking dog, setting her gently down on the floorboard. Everyone waived goodbye to Paulette. Then they all looked up at the sky, blazing with the last of the rainbow sparklers dancing before the silver trimmed clouds.

"Oh!" Aunt Candy gasped. "We forgot to sing "Happy Birthday" to Una!"

First, Squirrel reminded them of the spankings. Then everyone sang "Happy Birthday" and Una cut her applesauce cake, homemade by Grandma Jasper. When she blew out the candles, Una kept her wish a secret.

CHAPTER FIVE

UNA'S NEW FRIENDS *INVENT*

"Come here, gal!" Sylvia Leonard cried. She was Doc's nurse at the pediatric clinic and Una's friend. She insisted on meeting the Zipley family at the airport in D.C. when they returned from Chicago. Then she drove them home to Alexandria.

"Come right here, Sistuh, and let me give you a hug!" Sylvia said to Una as the family walked in the door while Squirrel retrieved their suitcases from the trunk. "How was your birthday, gal?"

Una said it was fine. Then she ran up and hugged most of the air right out of Sylvia. She asked her what in the world she was up to other than wiping little kids' noses and holding them down when they got shots.

"I got some bad news," Sylvia said with a dramatic change in her expression. "My brother David got the cancer, and he has a daughter about your age, Una."

"We're so sorry," Doc and Una said, hugging Sylvia sympathetically.

"Yeah, me too," Sylvia said. "Jazz Jones is my niece's name. She's twelve, but she still needs some lookin' after. Her mother died, and David is just not up to watching her after his chemotherapy and all. He'll be in rehab for a while."

"I'm so very sorry," Doc reiterated, "but Una will be here for the rest of the summer. Jazz can come over anytime and go to the pool with her or go bowling; whatever they'd like to do. Just bring her to work with you in the mornings."

"Well, that would be right nice of you folks," Sylvia said. "How about letting me bring her on Monday? Sound agreeable, Sistuh?"

"Sure," Una said. "Can't wait to meet her."

"I reckon she'll be tickled to meet you too," Sylvia said.

"What is David's prognosis?" Doc asked.

"Not good at all. He'd been sick for long time, only he didn't know it. And to beat all, he's only forty-five."

Then Squirrel invited Sylvia to stay for supper.

"I'm the chef tonight," he bragged. "How about some broiled trout almondine and pasta salad?"

"That appears to be an offer I can't refuse," Sylvia said, "'long as we can whip up a pound cake for after the main course."

"Call your hubby to join us," Doc said.

"No use," Sylvia replied. "Most of the romance done gone by the wayside long time ago; Saturday night is poker night for Mathew Leonard now."

"Well, good," Squirrel said. "We'll have you all to ourselves."

Then Sylvia wanted to know more about the Chicago trip and Una's birthday. Una told her about the fake Chicago fire, and by the time she finished the stories about Marvelous Marvin and Olivia the dog, everyone was howling.

"Mercy, chile, if you say one more thing now to make me laugh, I'm going to break my funny bone and I need that particular bone!" Sylvia teased.

"Dear, please pass the pound cake," Squirrel said with a goofy smile after supper.

Everyone laughed at his quirky expression until their eyes watered up and Sylvia said she believed she was going to have to run to the bathroom and rearrange herself.

"Nothin' so crazy ever happens here, Una," she said with a pretend brood on her face, "'least nothin' so funny but I needed a good laugh. Yeah, that'll do me for a couple of weeks."

Sylvia didn't leave that night until she'd had her supper and two pieces of pound cake with strawberries and whipped cream on top. She bet Una she couldn't eat three, but she lost that bet. Then she tried to teach Una how to play chess, only that didn't last long, because just as Una was figuring on moving her rook, she looked over and Sylvia was sawing major logs.

"I won!" Una yelled, prompting Sylvia to jump as high as Mark Twain's bullfrog.

Monday morning, Jazz came over to swim. Una was amazed at her beauty. She had smooth mocha skin with deep blue eyes, high cheekbones, and shiny black braids coiled on the top of her head. She wore thin gold bracelets and had painted her long nails pale white. She said they were alabaster. Her eyelashes were jet-black, as though they'd been painted with mascara, but you could tell they were natural, like her hair.

She appeared to be the most elegant, poised, and sophisticated girl Una had ever met. And Jazz's heart seemed beautiful as well. Una didn't really know her yet, but she felt that if she was any kin to Sylvia, she had to be a wonderful person.

"My mom's skin was olive," Jazz said, realizing that Una was staring, probably evaluating her looks.

"I didn't mean to stare."

"It's okay. Mom was French-Canadian, but she looked sort of like a Gypsy with blue eyes, so I guess that's how I got my blue eyes. And Dad is African American with a lot of other stuff mixed in."

"What happened to your mom?" Una said, feeling a little embarrassed to be asking.

"She died in a car accident when I was three," Jazz explained. "It's been just my dad and me ever since, and Aunt Sylvia and Uncle Mat."

"It must be fun having Sylvia as an aunt!" Una said.

"It is. Uncle Mat is fun too. I don't know what I would do without them."

Jazz seemed smart and wise, a lot like Sylvia. She laughed like ten frat brothers at an initiation party when Una unleashed her collection of jokes, even though Jazz had already heard some stolen directly from Sylvia. Then Jazz told Una some things she didn't know about becoming a woman.

"You've got to start with a little perfume and lipstick," Jazz explained, pulling her cologne bottle and her glistening peach lip gloss out of a lavender zipper bag. "Of course, we'll have to give you a manicure and put polish on those rough nails, once you quit biting 'um."

It didn't take long for Jazz to find out that Una knew all about hair spray, but her red curls were always as electrified as a field of windy weeds, despite whole cans of the sticky stuff.

"We've got to chemically straighten your hair," Jazz announced in a serious tone. "And what about a gold rinse on it to bring out the nice highlights?"

Una agreed, and by Thursday she had hair as straight as a board with satin nails, an odor of moonlight and opals, and a recklessly peach mouth. Una's bra size had even increased a little over the summer, and she was feeling a buzz of possibilities and impulses that probably should have been illegal for a girl her age.

She and Jazz lounged at the poolside several days a week reading *Teen Throb* magazines and swerving their hips rhythmically when they got up for a dip or a drink.

"Have you noticed that *dime* in the navy trunks and shades?" Jazz asked.

"He's sort of cute," Una said.

"Cut your eyes at him," Jazz ordered.

"How?"

"Like this," she said, lowering her lids, then batting her glamorous jet lashes.

Una's lashes were painted lightly with sable mascara that she'd borrowed out of her mom's top drawer. Her eyes were green, not exotic like Jazz's, but pretty enough. She tried to cut them at the cute blond guy, but all she managed to do was roll her eyeballs and blink. He must have thought she was either mentally unbalanced or had a gnat in her eye.

She decided to take a dip in the pool, thinking that maybe if she went underwater, he'd forget about her.

Una stood on the edge gripping her toes on the curve of the cement, because the water was cold, and she wasn't feeling very brave.

"Need a push?" asked the cute guy, pushing her from behind as hard as he could.

Una hit the water like a torpedo. The impact of the splash stung her face. She went under until she had no more breath. Then she swam to the surface near the diving board at the opposite end of the pool from where she'd entered. When she pulled herself up on the edge, the blond boy was waiting for her.

"You're hot, whoever you are," he said. "I'm Patrick Cox, and who are you?"

"Una Zipley," Una replied, still breathing in gasps.

"Whaz up?" Patrick asked, not waiting for an answer before diving in.

"I'm not impressed," Una said with clinched teeth. "Why did you push me?"

"Not impressed with what?" he asked, ignoring the question.

"Your dive," Una said. "I've seen better. Let's see how long you can stay under."

She stared at him as if he were a slug.

"Not long," he confessed unexpectedly. "How about you?"

"Watch!" Una said, diving down to the bottom for as long as she could hold her breath. When she finally popped up, she swam around the pool, showing off.

"You stayed under water longer than any girl I've ever seen," Patrick said. "And where did you pick up that bangin' butterfly stroke?"

"Nothin' special," Una said dismissively.

"Do you mind telling me how old you are?" Patrick asked.

"Do you mind mindin' your own affairs?"

"Affairs?" he said with a fake smirk. "Ma'am, I don't believe we know each other that well, but I'll try my best."

"Let's go," Una told Jazz. "The pool is infiltrated with lowlifes today."

She said it plenty loud enough for Patrick and his friends to hear, and she didn't look back when she walked off with her lime-green beach towel and magazines. In fact, her stride had never been so rhythmical before.

Jazz and Una rode their bikes home from the pool, stopping for ice cream on the way. Una got French vanilla and raspberry swirl and Jazz got a double scoop of coffee.

"You know you like that guy," Jazz said. "And he represents the right look, too. Sure enough, I suspect he's got plenty of bling."

"So?" Una said, peering down at her graying Value Mart sneakers and her bright orange thrift shop cover-up.

"What do I represent?" Una asked.

"The punk creature from the orange lagoon?" Jazz asked, laughing.

"Gee, thanks," Una said.

Sylvia met the girls at the door. They screeched their bikes to a roaring stop, just to show off.

"Ya'll have fun?" she asked.

"Well, if meeting a weird guy who represents the right sneakers but pushes you into the pool against your will is fun, then I'd say we did," Una said.

"Represents *what*?" Sylvia asked, grinning her cryptic grin.

"Aunt Sylvia, you don't know about representing *the best* because all you think about is family, getting me through school and stuff," Jazz said. "And you don't know about judging boys our age because Uncle Mat is as close to a square as anyone can get, so you guys are just in your own little world!"

"Got it," Sylvia chuckled. "So what I *represent* is not designer dresses, but a lot of old thinkin' that don't amount to hill of beans?"

"Well, not to be nasty, but sort of," Jazz agreed.

"We happen to have a guest just in from Africa who has been my friend for a long time," Sylvia said. "She's in the kitchen havin' coffee. Maybe she can shed some light on a few things."

When Jazz and Una followed Sylvia into the kitchen, they saw a tall, shapely African American woman wearing a turquoise scarf with a black dress, beige sandals, and peacock feather earrings. She smelled fresh and lovely, but Una couldn't put a name to the perfume.

"You smell my aroma?" the woman asked. "It's sandal-wood and rose."

"Dr. Anna, this is my friend Una Zipley and my niece, Jazz Jones," Sylvia said. "Girls, this is Dr. Anna Ozzina, my old friend from grade school. She became a child psychologist before she moved to Africa for a while."

"Nice to meet you, Dr. Ozzina," the girls said.

"Dr. Anna is fine," she said. "I can already see that you are wondering if I came here just to see Sylvia. My husband James is getting his doctoral degree in entomology at Georgetown University and seeing her again is a dream come true."

"What's it like?" Jazz asked. "What's Africa like?"

"My husband spent many years in The Republic of Zambia near the Zambezi River in southern Africa," Dr. Anna said. "I met him there when I was on a brief tour of mission with my church while I was living in Ghana in a town called Ada Foah where the Volta River meets the Atlantic Ocean. The people are very poor, but strong; the land and the river are resplendent with ancient beauty."

Dr. Anna explained that her husband also helped build mud huts and repair sewer lines in the neighboring country of Mozambique, lines first installed by the Portuguese years before. There had been in a civil war and for thirty years guerrilla warriors had destroyed roads, bridges, and entire villages.

"I heard there were elephants there," Jazz said, her eyes widening like an owl's.

"Oh, yes, and many other wild animals!" Dr. Anna said.

"Dr. Anna," Sylvia said, "I hate to interrupt, but you are a psychologist. Speak to these girls about the meaning of American social practices. My lovely niece here thinks it's important for young people to *represent* the most expensive name brands in order to be popular and happy."

"What is most valued is what people should represent," she said. "I value being myself, so that means I don't represent, I *invent*."

"Kickin'!" Una said.

"I invent myself," Dr. Anna continued. "Sometimes that means wearing peacock earrings and sometimes it means wearing dime-store jewelry and a burlap skirt from a yard sale that I bought for a dollar. Whatever clothes I wear, it's me, and should reflect my originality."

"I told Una and Jazz the *real gems* are on the inside of a person," Sylvia added.

"That's true," Una said. "Like I think Betsy Olander's Italian-made shoes are the bomb. She's that conceited girl in my math class at school; but the day after I wear my old leather work boots, I notice that two or three of the popular girls wear theirs, too. Then Betsy will ask me where I got them."

Dr. Anna smiled, but she didn't say anything more because Doc was driving up the driveway, waving like she had some good news. When she got out of the car, she almost skipped up the walk.

"You must be Dr. Ozzina," she said, extending her hand.

"Dr. Anna is fine. How excellent to meet you, Dr. Zipley."

"Dorothy is fine, or just plain Doc."

"I tried to take Sylvia to Africa with me, but she refused to leave Mathew. She said he couldn't make a cup of soup without her."

"Hah," Doc laughed. "I'd venture to say, that's the truth! How long are you here?"

"My husband and I are here in the States for at least five or six years this time," Dr. Anna explained.

"Then I have a proposition for you," Doc said, with a slightly strained yet excited look on her face. "I need a child psychologist here in my pediatric office. The patient load is just more than I had foreseen, and many of the cases have a psychiatric component. What do you say?"

"Well, it would give me a chance to see more of Sylvia, wouldn't it?" Dr. Anna said.

"She's my nurse, so you'll see her often."

"Why not, then?" Dr. Anna replied. "I'd be proud to do business with you."

"I sure am relieved that you ladies are here," Doc said, "because I just found out I'm going to have a baby this coming March, and I'll have to stay off my feet a little more often."

"*What?*" Una asked, not believing what her ears had just taken in.

"I'll be twelve next summer, and you're aging fast, Mom!" she cried. "Besides that, I need as much of your time as I can get to help me deal with all the crap in my life! I'll be a teenager soon!"

Jazz dropped her beach ball and looked over at Una, who was throwing her towel on the ground. Una suddenly felt clammy and seasick, like a jellyfish had stung her big toe.

It was good that Dr. Anna's husband, James Ozzina, offered to take everyone to supper at Maxim's Rendezvous in Vienna. The restaurant was elegant and had a scenic view of a meadow full of wildflowers. The view was so breathtaking, in fact, that it made Sylvia's pulse quicken, or so she whispered to Mat, and he laughed and said her pulse hadn't quickened in 'long 'bout twenty years. She gave him a wicked side glance.

In the car on the way over, Una interrogated her mom, demanding to know what in the world she was thinking of by getting pregnant when she was already over forty. But when they got to the restaurant Jazz immediately changed the subject.

"Dr. Anna, please tell me more about Africa," she begged. "I want to go there one day myself, like Nettie in *The Color Purple*."

"James can tell you much more than I because he was a missionary in Zambia for nearly ten years," Dr. Anna said. "I was only in Ghana for five years."

James was a tall, slightly stocky man who looked as though he might have been a pro football player at one time. He wore a full beard and wiry moustache that curled up beside his lips like a hook. His skin was so shiny and dark that it almost turned silver in the afternoon sun.

James' eyes shone with pride. "Well, probably what's most important for you to remember is that Africa is the lush place that cradled the earliest civilizations that arose out of the fertile crescent, fed by the Nile River and the Tigris and Euphrates," he said.

"Home of the dark and lovely queens and kings, the lush flora and fauna, and exotic animals," Sylvia added.

"And Africa still is a lush place," James said. "White men and greedy players have not yet destroyed the continent, but many of its people are hurting. Colonialism and wars have harmed African cultures. Technology has helped in some instances, but colonialism has stolen resources and land from the indigenous people."

"Colonialism has divided the people," Dr. Anna added. "White bounty hunters have tried to buy loyalty and ensnare African tribal leaders in their nets of greed."

"Lordy, I'm just glad I'm a poor ole insurance salesman and disc jockey here in America," Mat said.

Sylvia poked him hard in the ribs.

"Mistuh, you're an ole jackrabbit," she said. "You own two successful garages and a ceramic store on top of your insurance job and your disc jockeying job, yet I hardly see a greenback from you 'cept on Valentine's Day when you take me down to Tula's for filet mignon and champagne!"

"Now she's got you, Mat," Squirrel said. "Doc Zipley and I even tried to get you to grow us some pumpkins in your garden last year and you said you thought it would be too much fussing for a mediocre crop, but now we see the real reason why."

"You've been too busy for worrying about gardening," Doc said.

"Uncle Mat, we don't want to hear about your jobs or the pumpkins," Jazz said.

"Because we should discuss Mom's surprise pregnancy," Una cut in.

"Sistuh, it was no surprise to the Good Lord, just to you!" Sylvia said, grinning.

Una shot an evil grimace Sylvia's way and jammed her elbows up on top of the table.

"Una, you know how much you love calendar babies," Squirrel said. "Well, now we'll have our own little angel baby."

"I don't want a squirmy infant in the family!" Una shouted. "Babies are annoying. They also cry a lot and stink!"

"Yeah, but they do grow up, and then they can be kind of fun to have around," Squirrel said.

"Maybe ya'll will get another girl just like Una," Jazz said.

Una's eyes flashed greener than usual. She didn't know what Jazz meant by the comment, and she didn't want her to get involved.

"Just mind your own business, Miss Jazz!" Sylvia said.

"*Prophecy* is a lesser gift according to the Bible," Squirrel said. "I know you wish you had more of that, but the imagination is also a Promethean gift, and you have a ton of that, Una. I hope the new baby has lots of it too."

"How do you feel about being creative and intuitive, Una?" Dr. Anna asked.

"How did you know, I mean, about my being intuitive?"

"Sylvia and I talk fairly often. You've impressed her."

"Well, in answer to your question, I don't feel too great about it 'cause I still can't get out of washing the dishes and very few of my magic tricks have ever worked."

"Have you tried using your *radiance*?" Dr. Anna asked, "not to get out of doing the dishes, but for other things?"

Dr. Anna explained that in the American South there have long been *Gullah* women who used their radiance to heal. "The *Gullah/Geechee* people came to the southern states during slavery times from West Africa," she said. "Sylvia knows. She comes from a Gullah family."

"Dr. Anna, you may have to explain to the girls what you mean by *radiance*," Doc suggested.

"Radiance is light," Dr. Anna said. "Light that dances like a prism reflecting the sun."

"Ah, yes," Sylvia said. "The happy heart is a place of such light that comes from God. And this power heals mind, body, and spirit. I sense that Doc will give birth to a girl who will bounce beams of light back and forth with her big sister."

"Like a basketball?" Una asked, suddenly feeling herself perk up.

...

On a windy March day (four months from Una's twelfth birthday) Virginia Elizabeth (Bitsy) Zipley was born beneath a full moon, wailing like a baby wolf, or maybe it was Doc who was raising Cain the most. Anyway, Sylvia and Una heard a bunch of loud noises coming out of the hospital ward marked "PRIVATE, SURGICAL STAFF/ MATERNITY WARD."

Squirrel was in there too, and the whole fifth floor of Northern Virginia Regional Hospital could hear that something major had just happened behind closed doors; it was something big enough to evoke the highest decibels a woman could muster, and it was broadcast all the way to someplace in Wisconsin. Several tired-looking adults walked by and stared at Una and Sylvia as if all the noise was their fault.

"A lot of racket going on in there," Sylvia said, "but it's all good."

Most of the other adults in the waiting room ignored the noise. They sat down and flipped through magazines on the coffee table. Una and Sylvia played several rounds of Slapjack.

"Let's face it," Una said. "Our day has been shot."

"But just think about what your mom has been through. Try to be nice."

Just then Dr. Anna poked her head out of the door.

"I've got somebody for you all to meet," she said, her face all bright like something cuddly, fuzzy, and delicious had been happening behind those closed doors.

"What?" Una asked, hoping they'd thought of giving her a new puppy or a kitten.

"Una," Dr. Anna coaxed, "this is a good thing; the best, in fact."

"Another girl!" Squirrel screamed, bursting out of the operating room door. "And she's a beauty, just like Una!"

Squirrel grabbed the little pink parcel out of Anna's arms, kissed it in the face and then handed it to Una, quick as a wink. She cautiously flipped back the blanket to witness the thing she feared. It had, at last, come into the world despite her protests.

"No doubt, she will continue to show her little puny self in upsetting ways in the future," Una whispered to herself.

Bitsy had strawberry curls a few shades lighter than Una's, but dark eyes like Squirrel's.

Una was distraught. "Dad, she's just caused you to break out in a drenching sweat, caused Sylvia and me to worry and be bored out of our minds, and on top of all that, you gave her a pixy name like *Bitsy?*"

"Now, Una," Squirrel said, like this was going to be one of his pulpit sermons, "a few years ago you looked forward to having a baby sister. You were going to teach her how to play basketball."

He needn't have said that because Una had already changed her mind. She'd decided that she didn't want to share her athletic skills with a little monster who might brag or even, God forbid, get better than she was at the sport, grow up to join the WNBA, and then try to make her older sister look like warmed-over snot.

"Dad, let's go eat," Una suggested. "And as far as teaching it basketball is concerned, I've decided against it, so let's don't even go there."

"Una, Bitsy is your sister, your only sibling, and you *will* learn to love her," Squirrel said. Then he tried again to hand her the drooling little package.

Una looked at Sylvia sitting on the other side of the waiting room, hoping for comfort, but Sylvia didn't smile or try to soothe her. She just stood there looking concerned, as though the young girl she had come to know and love might have automatically turned into a mean villain who could eat babies. But what she, Squirrel, and Dr. Anna didn't understand was that Una was as cool as hundreds of nice, green cucumber sandwiches stacked one on top of another, but she didn't *choose* this loud, troublesome new kid and she wouldn't accept her without a fight. As far as Una was concerned, Bitsy was already beastly and red-faced, demanding as a greedy queen, yet only minutes old.

Una turned her back on her dad and left the hospital room like the first woman officer out of the Citadel, ready for combat. She marched down one corridor, only to confront another longer corridor filled with chatty doctors and overly serious nurses, tots blowing bubble gum bubbles, and even two fat preachers in white collars walking fast enough to escape death. Her stomach was beginning to rock and roll, only not in a musical way. She tried to find the stairs and make a dash.

Then she spotted a tall man in a moss-green sweater. He had the largest, purple-veined hands she'd ever seen and was walking briskly toward the elevator. She tugged gently on his sweater and was greeted by a prominent smile. When she looked closer, Una could see that the man's enormous hands were gentle-looking.

"How can I assist you today, young lady?" he asked.

"I'm not sure," Una replied. "I'm lost and I'm trying to find the stairs."

"You're not lost, just exploring in a place you're not familiar with," the man said. "Where is your family?"

"I'm an orphan," Una lied. "The orphanage had to get rid of me because I was too much trouble, so I'm trying to get to the airport to catch a plane somewhere else."

"Do you have cab fare?" he asked.

"No, sir," Una said. "Could I borrow some? I'll try to pay you back, of course."

"Not at all," the man said. "Just pass along a smile for me and adopt a few friends along the way."

"Okay," Una muttered.

The man handed Una a twenty-dollar bill. "Good luck, young woman," he said.

"Thank you so much," she said. Then she stepped on another elevator and looked out into the hall as the doors closed. She'd find a pay phone at the airport and call Marsha in Chicago.

"Una, is that really you?" Marsha asked.

"Yes, I'm coming back to the Windy City for a few days. Mom just had the baby, and it was terrible."

"What do you mean, *terrible?*"

"I can't go into it over the phone, but if your mom would wire me the money to come for a brief visit, I'll pay her back as soon as possible."

"What was the trouble?" Marsha asked, sounding distressed.

"It's not like that," Una said. "I'll explain later."

"Mom's not here, but I can borrow one of her charge cards," Marsha said. "I'm sure she won't mind. I'll send you the money right away."

Una called Marsha back as promised and by two o'clock she boarded Flight 98 to Detroit and Chicago. She flew right above the hellish hospital where Bitsy was probably screaming for attention this very minute, as though someone had abused her. But the hospital looked much smaller from the air. Its negative happenings and emergencies seemed to vanish with cloud cover. At last, the white puffs of heaven surrounded Una. She put her headrest back for a nice nap.

But she awoke on a giant roller-coaster ride, or so it seemed, except that she was still in her belted seat on the plane. The lady sitting next to Una grabbed her hand and then she heard a voice that sounded like a mean god over the microphone, "Attention, please," the voice said. Then there was a long period of total silence.

"I am the pilot," the voice said, "and I believe we have a Miss Una Zipley on board. She is wanted by the state of Virginia, the local police there, and by her parents."

The passengers sitting near Una seemed to sense that she was the infamous Miss Zipley. They all turned to stare at her as though she were completely naked or wanted in several states for murder.

CHAPTER SEVEN
HIDE & SEEK

J oy Plimpleton sat in the study finishing her tea and looking lost in her thoughts. She resembled someone who'd accidentally swallowed a worm and wondered whether they ought to keep it down or cough it back up. Una didn't want to stick around to find out what Joy's choice would be, so she grabbed her a sweater and headed out of the Plimpleton's kitchen door with Marsha.

Rowe answered the door when Una and Marsha got to her house. She suggested that they spend a little time walking around at Grant Park. "I can even bring a couple of skateboards if you want," Rowe said. "I can borrow my brothers.'"

"I'm in," Una said.

"Me too, let's do it," Marsha said.

"So, what happened that you came back here to Chicago?" Rowe asked.

Una had anticipated the question, so she detailed her reasons with all the flair of an ingenue and plenty of unnecessary drama thrown in for good measure. She may even have added a few juicy fictional tidbits.

"The shock-value of this problem is huge," Rowe said, with her usual sense of authority. "We're going to have to hide you someplace and we need to think fast."

"I don't think we've got time for that now, Rowe," Marsha said.

"What do you mean?" Una turned and snapped at Marsha. "Aren't you still *with us* on this?"

"Actually, yes, but that has nothing to do with it."

"Oh, I get it," Rowe said. "Look over there, Una."

"Oh, no," Una murmured, feeling her hands get suddenly damp, while her face felt as cold and numb as a freezer pop. Two policemen were fast approaching them.

"I have a feeling they're not looking for a lost dog or pig," Marsha said.

"This time I bet they're after a lost girl," Rowe added, staring at Una.

"Yeah, I know. And that misplaced person is probably me," Una said, slouching down low as if slumping her shoulders could make her disappear.

"You could try to disappear, *for real*," Rowe said.

"Not this time," Una said. "They've already seen me. But maybe trying is not such a bad idea."

The police were marching toward the girls faster and faster with each step. Una felt increasingly paralyzed.

"Hello there, officers," she said, managing a fake charming tone, with Rowe and Marsha hovering behind her like two ghostly shadows. "Nice afternoon."

"Well, that all depends on who you are and what kind of trouble you're in," one of the policemen said. "I'm Officer John Kitt, Chicago Police Department."

Una already knew that was his name because of the silver tag on his shirt. Below his belt a black club hung on one side and a big, black pistol on the other.

"We were just looking for a lost pig," Una said lamely, lacking a better excuse for being in a Chicago park on a Saturday afternoon while her parents were back in Virginia searching for her.

"Is that so?" Officer Kitt asked. "You're an interesting sort of girl," he said, eyeing Una as though she was a strange beetle under a microscope.

"Oh?" she said, not really wanting him to clarify that statement.

"Yeah," the officer said with a mean grin. "You got a lot of *chutzpah*, Miss Zipley; that is your name, isn't it?"

Then the other officer laughed and moved around a little as though he was letting off steam.

"Let's see, I happen to have information here that says you belong back in Virginia," Officer Kitt said, smirking. "Whad 'ya do, catch a plane under an assumed name?"

"No, sir, I didn't *assume* anything," Una replied as respectfully as she could. "I just needed a little vacation. You know how it is."

"How old are you?" Officer Kitt asked.

"A lady never mentions her age," Una said, feeling her knees shake.

"And does a lady go off without telling her parents to a city across the country where she can be kidnapped, raped, or used by any pimp off the street while the so-called lady's parents are at home going ape with concern over where their lovely daughter is?" Officer Kitt asked.

He was beginning to make Una feel lousy, but he shouldn't have said that word, *concern*. As soon as he did, in her mind she could see Sylvia's face looking at her as if she were a potential baby eater. She could also feel disappointment oozing from her dad's eyes like hot demon-fog.

"Una Zipley!" a high voice echoed from behind the bushes. "What in the world have you done?"

Suddenly, Aunt Candy came into view. At first Una thought she was seeing things, like the apparitions of summer come to haunt her in her guilty, confused state.

"Una!" Aunt Candy snapped at her. "Let's go! I'm going to escort you to the plane; you are going home NOW!"

"Oh, hi," was all Una could think to say.

"See, officers, I knew she'd cooperate with me," Aunt Candy said.

"We'll accompany you and Miss Zipley to make sure she gets to the airport safe and sound," Officer Kitt said.

"Ruff!" said Marvelous Marvin, tromping out of a bush. "Ruff! Ruff! Ruff!"

"Marvelous Marvin!" Una screamed, hugging the shaggy dog.

Marvelous Marvin must have sensed that Una was frightened about something. After all, they communicated on a different level. He walked up to each person gathered around Una, sniffing each one thoroughly. Just as he was sniffing the policeman standing near Officer Kitt, Marsha's mother walked briskly up the sidewalk toward them.

"Una, I've talked to Doc Zipley and Squirrel on the phone," Joy announced in a shrill tone. "You need to go with your Aunt Candy immediately to catch the next flight back to D.C. Marsha, you and Rowe come with me!" she said.

Marvelous Marvin had sniffed all he needed to. Now he was getting truly upset. Una looked him in the eye and told him with *mind speech* to topple the guys with the clubs first. That would give her time to run while he detained the rest of the crowd. He seemed ready to follow her command when a white car pulled up to the curb near the park entrance. Out jumped Olivia, the dog-from-hell, with Paulette. Arriving simultaneously were Grandpa and Grandma Jasper. As soon as Marvelous Marvin saw Olivia, he was ready to kill someone. He looked at Una first, however, out of respect. She told him to wait.

But he'd waited as long as he could. Una thought he was going to maim Olivia, but he must have figured it would be best to take care of business first. He leapt up on Officer Kitt, toppling him to the grass. Then, as he toppled the other policeman, Olivia decided to take a nibble out of Officer Kitt's hairy chin. While she was at it, Olivia decided to also take a sample of choice tenders from Officer Kitt's left leg. The more the officer flailed and fought against the tiny energetic Chihuahua, the more determined she was to have her just desserts. Una was about to scream when she saw Marvin Delaney and Roberta the pig getting out of a green truck. Marvin was waving with both hands yelling, "Hey there, little gal!"

Roberta ran toward Marvelous Marvin. He returned her friendly approach by licking her in the snout. After that, she was off, as if driven by some animal command, to distract and disarm everyone she possibly could. She circled around the entire crowd in a running prance. She was mesmerizing and wild.

"Halt it there, gal!" Old Marvin screamed. "What the devil has gotten you in such a tailspin, Roberta?"

But the pig could not be stopped. She was young and full of life. Most importantly, she was on a mission. As soon as that thought sank in, Una realized that all the animals sensed her fear and were trying to help. She began to feel warm in her face and legs again. She felt that she could run at least a mile and a half, nonstop. Maybe she could run two, or even three miles! She waved to everyone, then turned toward the lake and ran with a kind of wind behind her and through her that she had never known before.

Una ran past three delicatessens, a library, a city school, a Star's Coffee Shop, and a Brent's Bookstore in about seven minutes. Then she ran past five galleries, a pawnshop, a copy shop, and a dry cleaner. Finally, she saw Mount Comfort Funeral Parlor where she, Marsha, and Rowe had once tromped through several funeral services in their bathing suits and flip-flops.

Her heart sounded like a bongo drum. Sweat rivers pooled around her face and chest. While she had nearly flown three blocks back, she was now dragging every muscle in her body. Slowly, she crept into the dimly lit vestibule of the funeral home. Miraculously, there was no one posted near the guest book to greet her or to ask if they could help, so she crept on through two wake rooms, being careful not to breathe too hard or brush up against the flower arrangements. Then she saw a door marked, "EMBALMING ROOM. EMPLOYEES ONLY." She tiptoed down the steps and slipped into a side room. It was a small cubicle of a room that smelled like heavy chemicals and perfume, blended in an unholy union.

Then Una spotted her immediate salvation—a gray wig and a tin of stage makeup. Behind them on newspaper-lined shelves to the ceiling were hats of various shapes and sizes and pairs of white ladies' gloves. On a rack near the shelves hung several suits for men and women, with silk dresses and jackets of every description. Some costumes were made from materials with exotic colors and others were just solid browns or black. She stepped into a matronly black silk dress with a white lace collar.

But where are all the shoes? she wondered. Then she figured that since the casket covered the corpses' feet, they naturally wouldn't need shoes. God would know. But he had gone barefoot or wore skimpy sandals when he was walking around Israel as a carpenter, so why would he care? After putting on the gray wig, Una applied lots of violet lipstick and rouge. Last of all, she chose the longest pair of white gloves she could find.

She didn't mind if the gloves made people think she was a princess. Not now. Except when she took a quick glance in the mirror, she realized that she looked more like a plain kid with a wig and lipstick on. She dug around the tin for an eye pencil and drew a spidery web of lines under her eyes, and across the youthful contours of her face.

I look bad *now*, Una thought. *Sickly. I appear to have been an old lady with a serious blood disease, or maybe I died of a broken heart. Whoever I was, I had definitely died ill and exhausted.*

Una had no slip under her outfit, but she figured in her condition no one would mind. She crept back up the stairs and found a real dead lady in one of the caskets. She happened to look a tad like Una, so she carefully climbed into the casket and landed as gently as possible right on top of the dead corpse. The body was hard as a rock and twice as cold, so it was sort of uncomfortable, but Una snatched the pillow from behind her head and leaned back on that. Now she could settle in for a lengthy nap. The organ was piping in some soft, melodious music.

Hmm, she thought. The music sounded curiously like "Winchester Cathedral," a song she'd heard on one of Squirrel's '70s tapes. That song also reminded her of Sylvia for some reason. Maybe she'd had it on one afternoon while they played cards.

For some reason she felt imaginary creepy-crawlers inching closer to her face. They *had* to be imaginary. *How could real bugs get in here?* she puzzled.

Her thoughts reeled back and forth from the creepy-crawlers to the matter of the missing kid (herself), but her eyes were closed to look peaceful, just like an old woman chillin', which dead ladies always are, no matter how boisterous and fidgety they were when they were alive.

"Whoahhhheeeee!" Una screamed, sitting up in her casket with a jolt.

A huge, crusty spider had jumped on her nose! She'd slapped herself in the face, trying to remove it. Then she heard a loud *thump*.

She looked over near the chairs lined up in six neat rows in the chapel. There on the floor was a fat, bald man with a fringe of wispy hair around his ears. He had apparently fallen out of his folding chair and was now lying on his large stomach on the floor. His bulb of a head was turned slightly toward Una. His eyeballs seemed to be bulging slightly out of their sockets. He wasn't focusing on anything, just staring out like a zombie.

"I must have killed him," Una told herself, trembling like a nervous gopher. But she lay back down promptly when she heard someone else entering her parlor.

"Oh, mercy!" cried a lady's voice. "Mr. Hegelmeyer has collapsed!"

"I'll get help!" Una heard another voice yell.

It sounded like the voice of a girl, and it seemed to be coming from behind Una's casket.

"You've probably got some smelling salts down in the basement," the voice said.

It sounded like Rowe Riley, but how could it have been?
Oh Lord, where is she? Una wondered.

"She was my old kindergarten teacher," the voice said. "Did you hear me?" the voice inquired.

"What?" Una asked, looking up into Rowe's smiling face.

"Do you mind, I'm supposed to be dead!"

"The lady you're on top of is Mrs. Hegelmeyer, my old Kindergarten teacher," Rowe said. "Can't a girl pay her respects?"

"Is *that* why you're here?" Una asked.

"Not exactly," Rowe said. "About half the town is looking for you. It's merely a coincidence that you happen to be napping on top of my old teacher," she said.

"Did you know she was here?" Una asked.

"I didn't even know she was dead until I came into the funeral parlor and saw that Parlor C had a Mrs. Fanny Hegelmeyer."

Rowe said she wasn't sure it was Una at first, but she knew that if she lowered her fake spider onto the face and it screamed, it would probably be Una. If it was quiet, then maybe Mrs. Hegelmeyer had gotten a facelift.

Then Una took her gloves off and asked Rowe for a hand getting out of the casket. "I think I gave Mr. Hegelmeyer a heart attack!"

Mr. Hegelmeyer was now moaning. "I'm sorry, Fanny. I shouldn't have had the affair. It was just a fling, nothing serious. Forgive me, dearest."

A gray-haired lady in a navy dress with pearls around her neck had come in to see what the commotion was about. It wasn't anyone Rowe recognized. She looked down at Mr. Hegelmeyer and then over at Una, who was now sitting straight up in the casket. Rowe was standing beside her just next to the casket.

"Oh, Mary, Mother of God!" the woman screamed, immediately collapsing next to Mr. Hegelmeyer, with one leg stretched over his chest.

"The Old Rugged Cross" began playing softly in the background as two elderly men entered the parlor.

"Geesh!" one of the old men exclaimed. "What have we got here?"

"I'm sorry," Una announced in the highest, eeriest voice she could muster. "Mr. Hegelmeyer, my husband, was a cheater. You see, even in the very parlor where I was laid out to rest, he couldn't resist playing around with another woman. There she is, hovering over his chest at this moment when he should be paying respects to his departed wife!"

Both old men jumped up slightly in the air.

"You don't say!" cried one of them.

"But Fanny," the other one said, "don't you recall the summer we saw each other on Jim's poker nights?"

"No, all I recall is that I told him I would haunt him to his grave for what he did to me!" Una screamed, jumping out of the coffin. She was swinging her arms up and down like she imagined a proper ghost would do and prancing madly around the room like a true haunted spirit.

One of the men fell back into a chair, but the other one pointed directly at her.

"Fanny, you don't have on your petticoat," he said in a matter-of-fact voice, "or your shoes."

"You were always such a critical person," Una said.

"And who's that lying there in your casket?" he asked.

Rowe grabbed the real Fanny Hegelmeyer's dress and put it up over her face.

"It's no one important," she said. "I guess you weren't aware that this funeral home is in the red and they've been forced to double up bodies."

"No, I didn't realize that," the man said.

"The ones on the bottom had no families, anyway," Rowe explained. "But they were all Christians, so their spirits have already gone up to heaven."

"She's telling the truth!" Una yelled. "Anyway, it's really none of your business who that woman beneath me was because I'm the spirit of Mrs. Hegelmeyer come back to haunt you and all those who disturbed me in my life!"

"I can see that for a fact," the old man said, "and Fanny, you're just as spry a gal now as you were thirty years ago!"

The old man had a weird twinkle in his eye. He began dancing around the room like someone had slipped him a Mickey of Malibu. His eyes were dancing, too, in their sockets. Una suddenly wished for her dad. She even wished for her mom and the little brat. She especially wished for Sylvia, and she could imagine the comfort of her arms when she held Una and told her everything would be okay.

"Run!" Rowe ordered, in a shriek loud enough to break up three other funeral services and send the attendants scrambling into Parlor C to find out what the problem was. "The Old Rugged Cross" that had been playing on the computerized organ now switched to "Go Tell It on the Mountain." A reporter from the *Chicago Tribune* inched his way through the mourners, displaying a press pass, but the old man continued to chase Una around the room.

"Oh, no!" Rowe cried. "Someone must have squealed already that Mr. Hegelmeyer passed out in the parlor with a woman who was his former lover, and that Mrs. Hegelmeyer's spirit had risen up from her casket to haunt him!"

"Kind of a catchy lead!" Una said, succumbing to a few seconds of humor. "How 'bout '*Miss Una Zipley Finds Herself in a Humongous Pickle!*'" a voice said, coming from the door behind Una.

"Sylvia!" Una screamed, "Oh, diamonds and rubies! It's Sylvia!"

"Come here to me, *leetle mischeebus* gal!" Sylvia said.

Una rushed into her arms and held on tight. She had never been so glad to see any human being in her life. If someone had offered her the choice between a tin of real diamonds or seeing Sylvia at that exact moment, she'd have chosen to see her friend.

"Where's Dad?" Una asked, "and Mom, and the brat?"

"They're all waiting outside in the limo we rented at the airport," Sylvia said.

"But how did you know where to find me?"

"Well, honey, we had a hunch," Sylvia said, looking at Rowe.

"Poor Mrs. Hegelmeyer," Rowe said. "From the looks of it, she is going to be front-page headlines tomorrow."

After Una got home, Aunt Candy and Joy Plimpleton both sent copies of the *Chicago Tribune* so everyone could see the Fanny Hegelmeyer/Una Zipley headlines; but by the time the mail arrived, Una was busy in the nursery, rocking Bitsy. Sylvia and Dr. Anna were grinning at her like she had a halo.

"There's no halo," Una said with a giggle.

"We know," Dr. Anna said.

"We're looking at those two little horns on the top of your head," Sylvia said, grinning.

Sunday afternoon was a hazy, humid day. It was early June, but it felt like July. The Zipley's supper was almost always at five on Sundays and almost always a hot meal like fried chicken with mashed potatoes. Bitsy liked mashed potatoes better than bananas or almost anything else. However, this Sunday was so hot that she would drink only little squirts of vanilla Coke. No one felt like cooking, so the family had coconut coolies for supper.

Cherries dominated this sweet ambrosia, which was arranged on a lettuce leaf with a hint of mint and a corn muffin on the side. After enjoying this treat, the family was content.

"If there is a heaven, it is not without ambrosia," Squirrel announced.

He always said that, and Una believed him. Sylvia often said that heaven had its fine details. For Una, that would also have had to include licorice jellybeans. Doc said jellybeans were not mentioned anywhere in the Bible, but Sylvia reminded her that the word *reward* was mentioned, so the category of reward would've included licorice jellybeans.

Just as Una and Squirrel were getting into a discussion about the theological merits of licorice jellybeans, the doorbell rang.

"Wonder who that could be?" Doc asked. "Hope it's not a sick child."

Una's dad opened the door. Sylvia's niece, Jazz Jones, was standing there with tears running down her face so hard and so fast that they had formed dots all over her blue gingham dress.

"Are you all right, dear?" Squirrel asked.

"No!" she sobbed.

"Come in, Jazz," Una's mom said.

"Hi," was all Una could think of to say. She wanted to say a lot more, of course, but something about Jazz's swollen eyes felt scary.

"What's wrong?" Doc asked. "Come in and sit down. Tell us what has happened."

Una wondered how her mom could be so sure that something terrible had happened. Maybe nothing really bad had happened. Maybe what was wrong was that nothing sweet and real had happened in a very long time, like eating coconut coolies with your family on a hot Sunday evening. Maybe Jazz was smart enough to need and want something uniquely good to happen.

"Dad's dead!" Jazz cried, breathing in a sob so deep it seemed to invade the contours of her small chest. Una could envision the crevice near her lungs, the small burnt red muscle pounding, a hole filling up her throat and a tiny, bleeding bird fluttering behind her eyes.

When Jazz sobbed, a dark whisper of breath oozed in around her chest, but the rain from her eyes did nothing to dissolve the gray beneath them. The charcoal mist was becoming thicker, like sludge. Molten mud began seeping from the small red muscle of her heart.

"Help her!" Una screamed. "Her heart is broken! Help her!"

Doc grabbed Una and then grabbed Jazz. She folded both girls into her arms like two dying birds, holding each of their heads on either side of her chest. Una listened to the steady beat of her mom's heart until it became close enough to provide cover for her own.

Squirrel knelt on the floor beside them. He was holding Bitsy in one arm, but he gently rested his head on Una's shoulder and stretched his free arm around Jazz. Bitsy closed her tiny eyes and slept while everyone else cried softly, like four weeping willows.

Jazz's maternal grandmother, Nannie Clayton, had dropped her off. Sylvia was still at the hospital where Jazz's dad, David Jones, had died an hour earlier. Everyone wanted to be with Sylvia now, too, while she suffered the passing of her brother.

Jazz, Doc, and Una huddled into the back seat of Squirrel's car as he drove to Dove Memorial Hospital. Una took Bitsy to Mrs. Fossy, the next-door neighbor and babysitter. Squirrel drove slowly, as though they were already in a funeral procession. There was a respectful air about his turns. He guided the wheel slowly and deliberately, easing onto Bellview Boulevard off the highway, headed toward the hospital.

"EMERGENCY ENTRANCE," flashed red over the side doors. Una thought of the day Bitsy was born. She'd felt then that her baby sister had been an unnecessary emergency brought about by her mom and dad, making Una an unwilling participant. The whole experience had made her angry. But since then, Una had discovered that Bitsy was just an innocent, weird little kid—like she had been. Bitsy had come to like squash with apple butter and a bunch of other nutty stuff to eat, just like Una. She even seemed to like Una's comic books, and she listened when her big sister sang songs to her.

Bitsy liked Una to hold her fat little legs and pat her feet together as if she were dancing a jig. They played patty-cake, too, and Bitsy could almost roll her baby hands all by herself. Una knew she was going to be funny and smart, and active. Yet, not long ago, Bitsy had been Una's emergency.

I'm so ashamed that my secret birthday wish last year was to be the center of attention forever, Una confessed to herself.

But when Jazz's dad passed, her heart broke, and there was nothing Una could say or do to make Jazz feel less pain. In the past, all of Una's emergencies had been lost socks or rotten bananas; they were about mean kids at school who stuck their tongues out or called her an igno-ramus-nerd-ball. Sirens had gone off in her head when she had to do laps at basketball practice or write a hundred sentences for Mrs. Gerheart, the math teacher, saying, "I will not speak in class unless I am called upon."

Una didn't know then that sirens weren't really for lost pigs or dogs that had a rendezvous in the park, or for girls who sprayed wedding parties or lit too many candles. Some sirens announced that people you loved and needed were leaving you forever.

Squirrel pulled up at the door to the hospital lobby. Doc got out of the car first, then Jazz and Una got out and stood gazing up at the tall glass doors with green awnings. The emblem of a serpent zigzagged down the bricks above the doors. If Jazz felt as small as Una did at that moment, she felt about as small as those mute, miniature dolls with ponytails and glass eyes that never change expression. Those dolls never cried, but always looked like they were just about to. Jazz had no mom or dad anymore. Her mother had already died and now she had lost her dad to cancer. Una wondered who Jazz would live with.

Squirrel knocked softly on the door of Room 509, and there sat Sylvia on the side of an empty bed. Her face was swollen as large as an overripe pumpkin. Tears filled the corners of her eyes and all the creases underneath them. Una and Jazz had never seen her that way before.

"They took David away from me," she said. "Took him about forty minutes ago."

Jazz hugged Sylvia tightly around the neck and Sylvia put her hand on Jazz's plaits, but Sylvia's eyes looked glazed and her hug was not tight like Jazz's. Una seemed to be patting a rag doll or a mop instead of a real person. The Sylvia that Una and Jazz knew had somehow slipped away.

The person they saw sitting on the hospital bed was a whisper of that woman. The laughter and Gullah energy that had made her eyes flash with passion were gone. Una grabbed her mom's arm, tugging it as gently, but firmly as she could. She wanted to get out of there. Wherever God had taken Sylvia's brother, he'd probably taken Sylvia's spirit too. She could never take care of Jazz in this condition.

...

Jazz stayed with Una's family for the next several weeks. Her grandmother wasn't feeling well, but she was able to pick Jazz up for summer school every morning and drop her off after school in the evenings. After supper, Una often read, and Jazz did her homework. They talked a lot about Sylvia. Jazz called every day to ask her Uncle Mat how she was doing. Una and Jazz both worried about her and prayed for the day when she would come back to herself and to them.

Jazz soon developed recurring nightmares about her dad. She often woke up crying for him. Twice a week before his death, Jazz's Uncle Mat had taken her to the hospital to see him. He'd lain there, his skin blue, with tubes of blood running into his hands and oxygen lines in his nose, making him look like a bionic man. Toward the end, he no longer knew Jazz or Sylvia, but kept calling for *Doll Baby*, the nickname Sylvia said he had adopted for Jazz's mother when the couple was young. The memory of her dad so weak and unable to care for himself preoccupied Jazz's mind. Sylvia also grew ever more despondent.

Jazz asked her Uncle Mat if he thought a *haint* had attacked Sylvia. Every time Una, Doc, and Jazz visited they saw the same troubled look in her eyes. She never cried during the day, but Mat said that at night all the grief mounted up like an army battalion and struck her while she slept. Dr. Anna visited as often as she could, trying to help, but Sylvia refused to be comforted.

Finally, one Saturday morning about a month after David's death, a ray of hope appeared. Doc said Sylvia was feeling a little better. She agreed to come to work at the clinic the following Saturday. Doc, Una, and Jazz went to fetch her at her home while Squirrel watched Bitsy. Doc didn't want Sylvia to drive because she had taken herbs for her depression, and she told everyone that the *boodaddy* had visited her frequently to conduct his *mojo*.

When Jazz knocked at her door, no one answered so she peeked in the window. No one was in the kitchen with Sylvia; yet there she was, talking loudly and laughing at someone or something.

"David, you haven't changed a lick!" she exclaimed. "You always were a scoundrel when it came to Pop. Poor ole Pop never had a chance at poker, long as you were at the table, you sneaky dog!"

Then Sylvia laughed some more and poured her cornbread batter out into a dozen lined tins. Jazz's eyes got wet and then became small, dark oceans instead of seeing-holes. Sylvia was obviously living in another world now; not the real one, but a world she preferred. The world she lived in still had David, her cherished brother, and her dad, Kelvin (Pop) Jones, who'd died years before of cancer. He had been a tailor; people said he'd made the suits of all the bankers and doctors in town.

Sylvia had told Jazz about her granddad, but then she was talking *about* him; now she was talking *to* him and *to* David, believing that they were talking back.

"Sylvia!" Doc yelled, pounding on the kitchen door. "Aren't you coming to work today?"

At last, the door opened slowly to a crack. "No," she said. "I just can't. I thought I'd feel better, but it may take some time. I'm sorry you came all the way over here to get me."

"But Aunt Sylvia," Jazz pleaded, "don't you think you'd feel better if you were near us where we could talk and joke around like we used to?"

"No, thanks," Sylvia said, still looking blurry-eyed. "And thanks, Doc, for keeping Jazz in the afternoons. She's a good girl most of the time."

"We love having her," Doc said. "She's a great friend to Una."

"Sylvia's just on a kind of vacation," Squirrel assured Jazz and Una, "visiting some old home places in her mind, but she'll be back."

Jazz kept a tissue in her pocket and used it to wipe her eyes whenever she thought of Sylvia's make-believe talks. She wished for her dad to be back, too, but not this way.

One day Doc, Squirrel, Bitsy, Jazz, and Una had just come home from a picnic when Jazz got her tissues out and ran to Una's bedroom in tears. That's when Una got an idea. She tapped lightly on the bedroom door.

"Yes," Jazz answered, like a little chicken peeping.

"Jazz, would you like me to ask my friends Marsha and Rowe to come to Alexandria to see us?" Una asked. "If anyone in the world can do magic, it's those two characters when they get with me! We'll think of something to snap Sylvia out of her blues!"

Jazz slowly opened the door. Her eyes brightened immediately. "Yes, thanks," she said.

When Marsha answered the phone in Chicago, Una suddenly felt a substance like butterscotch in her throat, but it wasn't that. This was something thick and lumpy, but not sweet. In fact, it was a lump of sadness caught smack in the middle of her throat and all she could do was squeak, "Hi, I—"

Marsha kept asking, "Una, is that you? Are you okay?"

Finally, Marsha put her mom on the phone. Joy Plimpleton demanded to know where Una was. Una couldn't blame Joy after Una's last surprise visit that everyone called a *fiasco*.

"I'm in Alexandria," Una said, at last able to get her voice box to work. "Do you think Marsha could come here for a few days? School will be out a little longer and we really need her," she pleaded.

"Are you still upset about Bitsy?" she asked.

"Oh, no!" Una said. "It's far worse. It's my friend Jazz and her Aunt Sylvia. Jazz is Sylvia's niece (as I just said) and Sylvia is Mom's nurse. She's my good friend too. Her brother died recently and . . ."

"Sounds like it's complicated."

"Very," Una replied.

"I think I'm getting the picture," Joy said. "May I speak to your mother?"

"Yes, let me get her." Una ran into Doc's office looking for her.

Doc was examining a little girl's parrot. The child looked up when Una walked in and said that the bird had been injured and she could not rest or get better until her bird was fixed.

"Mom, could you please talk to Joy on my phone?" Una asked. "She wants to talk to you from Chicago."

"Sure," Doc said.

Una hadn't had time to tell her mom about her plans to ask Marsha and Rowe to come for a brief visit, but she must have figured out the direction of Una's brainstorm, because when she returned from taking the call, she said it would be fine for the girls to come.

"How about the day after tomorrow?" Doc asked. "We can all drive up to the airport to get them."

"Sweet!" Una exclaimed.

Just then the little girl's parrot echoed, "Sweet!"

Una and her mom laughed so hard that they didn't notice the patient's bird-patient flying around the room saying, "Sweet, sweet, sweet."

CHAPTER NINE
RELIEF

Soon after Jazz left and Doc's patients finally left, Patrick Cox rang the doorbell.

"I just thought I'd come by to say hi," he said.

"Hi, yourself," Una said in a cheerful tone of voice. "I haven't seen you lately. What have you been up to?"

"Not much," he said. "That's why I stopped by. Swim club is dead these days, I'm getting tired of tennis, and football practice won't begin for another few weeks."

"Oh, I get it," Una said. "You called me because you had absolutely nothing better to do."

"No, Shorty," Patrick said. "Actually, I think you're a pretty cool girl. You still friends with Jazz?" he asked.

"Of course!" Una said. "But she's been down lately. Her dad died recently, and it's been tough."

"Oh, I'm very sorry," Patrick said. "That's awful. Is there anything I can do? Does she like flowers?"

"Heck, no," Una said, remembering the barrage of flowers in the funeral parlor.

"Well, what about us all going someplace, like bowling?" he asked. "Or roller skating? This weekend we could all go skating at Munsey Skate Center. My dad will take us, and we could order pizza."

"That'd be perfect!" Una said. "Oh, my other friends, Marsha and Rowe, will be here from out of town. Could they go too?"

"I don't see why not," Patrick said, bending down slightly to give Una an unexpected kiss on the cheek.

"Who was the visitor?" Doc asked.

"Who?" Una asked, still in a daze over the kiss.

"The nice-looking blond visitor?"

"Oh, that was just Patrick," Una said. "He's nobody."

"He seems to be a very attractive and polite nobody," Doc said.

"He's just a boy I met at the pool. He was wondering if he and his dad could take us roller skating."

"Sure," Doc said. "I'll have your dad look him up, but I'm sure it will probably be fine."

Una went to sleep that night dreaming of Patrick.

CHAPTER TEN
DANCING TOWARD THE LIGHT

The Zipley family, Jazz, and a few other people attended the house church that Dr. Anna and James started in their living room. It was for all races, all faiths, and for anyone who believed in God. The new church gathered on Saturday mornings, so when Rowe and Marsha arrived on the 9:00 a.m. flight from Chicago, they also attended the church. Jazz and Una prayed for Sylvia's spirit to return and for her gloom to be replaced by a new radiance.

Sylvia had once told Una that life was like a dance. "We get joy from the rhythm we make together," she said.

Una wished Sylvia and Mat could have been there with her and the others as they sang hymns. But when Jazz and Una visited Sylvia, they could tell that she wasn't getting any better. Her eyes still looked like they had witnessed someone's grisly murder; they were filled with rage and pain.

"I should be able to generate my own joy, even without Sylvia and even if she and Jazz never come back from their blues," Una said, trying to comfort herself.

She thought this on the one hand, while the on the other hand, she felt something very different. Maybe the real reason she'd asked Rowe and Marsha to come for a visit was not just to comfort Jazz or Sylvia, but to cheer herself up. Maybe death, darkness, and despair were contagious things, even more toxic than the Black Plague. Maybe that kind of darkness could spread from one heart to another as fast as the real Chicago fire. Maybe it chose its own victims, hitting them like a bomb while they were eating their tapioca or trying to work in the garden. And maybe the destruction decided just whose gizzard it would nestle in, and how deep.

Certainly, these wounds were more devastating than a young girl like Una might ever understand or hope to melt, ignore, laugh away, or heal. Even a trinity of light-bearing girls like Marsha, Rowe and Una could not—

"Una," Dr. Anna's voice spoke to her from behind a cloud of her dad's pipe smoke. "There has always been a bright light about you, child, but it is shadowed now by a deep, lavender haze. I dream of you."

Then Una felt Marsha touch her arm.

"Ouch," Marsha said. "Una, you're ice cold!"

"What about Jazz and Sylvia?" she asked. "They're the ones who've had the serious blues."

"Their cheeks are scarlet," Dr. Anna said, "but yours are like white marble. Look in the mirror."

Doc's eyes were the only reflections Una needed. When she looked at her mom, she could clearly see her fear.

"I am a scientist and a woman with some wisdom," Doc said, "but this problem goes beyond my ability to reason away or to comprehend."

"I think we'd better try the *circle dance*," Dr. Anna said. Then she asked James to put on the CD of Miles Davis' music. Jazzy sounds began to flutter and float about the blue-painted room. Smoky, floating sounds brought the feel of smiling moons to the pockets behind Una's tired eyes. She felt foam and shells, driftweed and other sea trinkets at her feet.

Marsha held her left hand. Jazz held her right. Rowe held one of Doc's hands and Squirrel held the other. A circle was forming. Dr. Anna and James began to sway, forming an undulating pattern with their bodies and moving to the rhythm. The circle swayed and moved like a chain of light. Dr. Anna whispered something.

"All right," James said.

"Yes," Jazz said.

Then Una could hear Sylvia entering the room and saying something, but she couldn't make out the words.

"All right," Dr. Anna said. She chanted something in another language. "Lift your arms like a bird toward the light and let your spirit fly."

Una heard Sylvia's voice again, whispering something. She looked around the room, but Sylvia wasn't there and had not joined the circle.

"Her spirit is with us," Dr. Anna said. "Her countenance will return one day."

"Fly with us," James said.

"You're the *dove*, Una," Rowe said. "Fly above the clouds."

"Swing and sway, and dance!" Dr. Anna shouted.

"Put the devils to shame!" James yelled. "Circle dance with us and fly, girl!"

Una closed her eyes. The circle had become a dancing flame in her heart. Each tightly clasped hand in the circle was a gate. Then, the song changed. The tempo picked up to a faster, more exotic beat. She could hear the sound of a drum. The gates flew open, arms everywhere moving like snakes toward the sun.

Then the circle broke free and the whole church danced wildly, and some of its members flew. Una was one of them. Her spirit began at that moment to know things that her reasoning mind couldn't fathom. She had always supposed there were places beyond this hemisphere, but she had never dreamed that a circle dance could take you there. She never supposed that a touch and a chant could evoke the passage rites of an ancient people, create light in the darkness, and teach mortals to fly. But now she was flying past air itself, into the source of *Being*, where the world is calm. There were no guns there. No drugs. No nukes. No terrorists. No illnesses. There was only light.

After church, Patrick came by Una's place to get her and her friends for roller skating. His dad, Howard Cox, waited patiently in the van. On the way to the skate center, Una introduced everyone. She could tell they all thought Patrick was nice-looking. The boy had practiced his small talk, but as soon as the girls got in, he realized he needn't have done that—because four girls are hard to shut up. They talked and giggled nonstop the whole way there.

Finally, Rowe zeroed in on Patrick, asking him about his interests and activities.

"Do you play football? Basketball? Chess? Badminton?"

The answers were: yes, no, no, and no.

"She's trying to get you to loosen up," Una said. "Can't you say anything but 'yes' or 'no'?"

"I don't know," Patrick said. "It's kind of hard to get a word in edgewise with you babes."

"Babes?"

They all laughed until their stomachs ached.

"Wait a minute," Patrick interrupted. "I thought part of my job was to cheer you girls up, but I see there's no need to do that!"

"Cheer them up?" Mr. Cox chuckled. "Wish I was that cheerful, EVER."

"That's right, Dad," Patrick said. "I can't recall you ever being *that* cheerful since I've known you. And I guess I've known you all my life."

"My wife and I were planning a vacation to Ireland this fall," Mr. Cox said, "but if I could just borrow you girls for a few days, I think we could skip the vacation altogether, and it would save me a load of cash!"

"No, you're still going, Dad," Patrick said. "So Bill and I can have the house to ourselves."

Patrick explained that Bill was his older brother.

"I see," Mr. Cox said. "And you're saying this in front of the young ladies?"

"How old is Bill?" Jazz asked, "And not to be nosy, but is he as fine as you?"

Patrick smiled, but everyone else giggled, including Mr. Cox. "Yes," Mr. Cox said, "Bill is a very fine young man, if I do say so myself."

"Hah, hah," Jazz replied.

"Who is ready for some pizza with extra cheese and anchovies?" Mr. Cox asked, changing the subject as he pulled into the skate center parking lot.

"Meeeeee!" everyone yelled.

"Six root beer floats and two large anchovy pizzas with extra cheese, please, Connie," Mr. Cox told the waitress. "And a birthday cake with twelve candles for Miss Zipley. Her mom told us she will turn the big one-two punch (12 years old) in a few weeks."

"Wow! Thanks, Mr. Cox!" Una exclaimed. "Much appreciated."

"I never knew how much preteen girls ate!" Mr. Cox said after the pizzas had magically disappeared and the root beers were on their last couple of slurps. "Your mom actually donated the cake, thank goodness."

After two hours of Patrick showing off his Zen skating and roller rink dance moves, and Una falling and bumping her helmet on the side of the rink, everyone was ready to call it a day.

Marsha, Rowe, and Jazz had a pajama party that night with Una. They played eleven rounds of gin rummy, ate burgers, finished the birthday cake, and shopped at the mall before the Chicago girls boarded a plane to go home. It was a *normal girls'* end of summer mini-vacation for them all and a nice break blessing for Una and Jazz, who had not had a normal day since Jazz's dad's death. Una had called her best friend, Judy, to see if she could join them, but Judy's family was in Arizona for the week.

"Happy Birthday! Bye!" Marsha and Rowe yelled to Una and Jazz when they left. "Bring Jazz to Chicago next time!"

Una and Jazz nodded and waved back. They held hands on the way to the car.

"Thanks, Una, for the last couple of days," Jazz said. "I really needed some fun."

"Me, too," Una said. "I'm glad we're friends."

...

The following week, Patrick called to say he and his dad were going on a fishing trip to the Rappahannock River for the last few days before school started. He and Una talked for about a half hour. She was sure she'd hear from him again when he returned, and she really looked forward to it. He was honest, attractive, polite, and fun to be with. Besides all that, he laughed at her jokes.

She was also looking forward to seeing Sylvia again, which happened the very next Monday morning when Sylvia came to work with a blueberry pie (Una's favorite) and a smile as big as the state of Indiana on her face.

"I missed you, Sistuh," she said. "This pie is for you, gal. Birthday gift."

"Can I have a piece too?" Doc asked, sneaking into the kitchen to greet Sylvia when she saw her car pull up in the driveway.

"Be extra good and we'll see," Sylvia said with a chuckle.

Doc hugged her friend and Una joined in. "Group hug," they said.

"We're so glad to see you, Sylvia!" Doc said. "You look great!"

"Yeah, you look fantastic," Una said. "I feel like a new woman, just seeing you like this."

"Ditto," said Sylvia. "I heard that Dr. Anna laid the prayers on for me pretty heavy."

"She did," Una confessed. "We all did."

"You didn't mind, did you?" Doc asked.

"Heavens, no!" Sylvia said. "That's why I'm feeling so much better. You never can have too much prayer!"

"Speakin' of that *new woman* thing, I got my monthly since I saw you last," Una said.

"All right, now," Sylvia said. "How was it?"

"No fun. I got bad cramps."

"Oh, Lordy," Sylvia sympathized. "I used to have 'um too. I know what you're dealing with, girl. Try chamomile tea."

"I'll live."

Both Una and Doc felt like a great weight had been lifted from their shoulders when they realized the old Sylvia had returned. Una discovered that there was truth in the saying: *You don't know what you've got until you lose it.*

•••

That evening, Judy Light called.

"Hey, girl," Una said. "How was your trip to Arizona?'

"It was good," Judy said. "But the part I need to talk to you about is, well, I'd rather not talk about it on the phone. Can I come over?"

"Sounds serious," Una said. "Sure, come on over. We've already eaten."

Judy banged on the Una's front door about forty minutes later.

"What's up?" Una asked. "Do you want to go to my room?"

"Yes," Judy said. She looked downtrodden.

106

"I'll just come straight out with it," she said. "Mom and Dad want to move to Arizona to be closer to Mom's relatives there. Well, they're my relatives too."

"Where in Arizona?"

"Chinle. Mom is Navajo, so she wants to go back to the reservation there."

"That's exciting," Una said, trying to be upbeat but looking the opposite.

"Anyway, we really haven't been able to see as much of each other as we did when we lived next door," Judy said. "But I . . ."

Una wiped a tear from the corner of her eye with the back of her hand. "I know," she said. "It stinks for us, but the world is a smaller place than ever before. I can fly out sometime soon."

"And my mom said I could fly in to see you," Judy said, adding, "But if you come to AZ, make sure to ask your folks."

She looked half serious.

"You nutcase!" Una laughed. "You know that after the mess I made in Chicago, I won't make the same mistake again."

"And don't ever stop trying to be a magical girl, either a witch or a fairy, girlfriend."

"I may just settle for being a fairy like Flora in Cinderella," Una said.

Then both girls laughed and hugged each other.

"When are you leaving?" Una asked.

"Soon," Judy said. "Mom and Dad had it all arranged before they told me. It was sneaky, but they like to avoid confrontation."

"Did you see where you're going to live?'

"Yes," Judy said. "It's a very roomy house near Canyon de Chelly. It's surrounded by lots of pine trees and a park. You'll like it."

"I'm sure I will, but more importantly, sounds like you will."

"Don't forget me," Judy said. "I promised myself not to cry but I know I'll never have another friend like you."

"You'll give me an excuse to write more, and I'll call a lot," Una said, continuing to wipe her eyes. "You know I'll never forget you and I'll pray for you every night."

Judy turned to go. "Say bye to your folks and Bitsy for me?"

"I will," Una said.

"And never lose your sense of humor!"

"I won't."

"And your imagination!"

"And my magic? I won't."

"Yeah, never lose your magic! Oh, and here's a present for your birthday. Open it later."

"Gee, thanks!" Una said, hugging Judy.

Immediately after Judy left, Una opened the gift. It was a beautiful white Bible. That made Una cry, because Judy was her Jewish friend, and she loved her.

CHAPTER TWELVE
NOTHING STAYS THE SAME

When Judy left for Arizona, Una savored her friendships with Jazz, Sylvia, and Dr. Anna even more. Still, she and Judy kept in touch by phone and mail. Una planned a trip to Arizona for her fourteenth birthday, but the universe had other plans.

Squirrel was working in his garden one morning in early July when he felt chest pains. He didn't pay much attention to them at first, but later that afternoon, he asked Una to call the rescue squad. Ironically, Doc was tied up in a meeting at the hospital.

Una asked Sylvia to watch Bitsy so she could ride in the ambulance with her dad.

"Of course, I will," Sylvia said, pulling Una closer, until their cheeks touched. "And I'll be prayin'."

Doc met Squirrel and Una at the hospital. Una kissed her dad on the forehead and squeezed his hand before the attendant strolled him into his cubicle in the emergency ward. Una had to stay in the waiting room, but within thirty minutes Mat, Dr. Anna, and James joined her. She was glad to see them, but seeing them made her more worried, because she knew that their coming signaled something serious.

In about two hours, Doc came out of Squirrel's room in the ER by herself. She had been the only one allowed to go in. Her face looked flushed, and her eyes were swept with tears. Still, she brightened and managed a calm smile.

Una ran to her side. "How's Dad doing?" she asked.

"Sit down, dear," Doc said. "Please sit down."

Una glanced at Anna's face. She knew something.

"No!" Una screamed. "Tell me what's going on! I don't want to sit down!"

James and Dr. Anna ran to Una and held her between them.

"It's all right, Una," Dr. Anna said.

"Your dad died a few minutes ago, my darling girl," Doc said. "I'm so sorry."

Una looked up, panicked. She broke away from James and Dr. Anna and ran with all her might down the hall and out the side door of the hospital. She kept running past the river and the tennis courts, past the picnic tables and the park. She didn't stop until she couldn't breathe anymore. Then she fell to the ground and writhed in pain, like she'd been bitten by a snake or a rabid dog.

The policeman who found her gently picked her up, took her to his car, and returned her promptly to the ER where Doc and the others were waiting.

"Are you okay?" Doc asked.

"I think so," Una said, wiping tears with both hands.

"Mat will take you home while I settle some things here."

Mat had notified Sylvia about Squirrel's death and she'd called Jazz.

"Would you like to have Jazz come over for the night?" Sylvia asked as soon as Una got home. "She'd like to come."

"Yes, please," Una said, feeling empty, like a rag doll.

Jazz came right away. She held Una close to her all night; she remembered that not long ago she, too, had been a helpless, bleeding bird and Una had been there for her. Jazz called Judy and held up the phone to Una's ear.

"Here, talk to your friend," she said. "The number was in your address book."

Una rested her head in Jazz's lap while she told Judy what had happened.

···

The summer of Squirrel's death, Una turned fourteen. It would be another momentous year in her life, because Aunt Candy had earned her doctorate at Northwestern University and decided to move to Blacksburg, Virginia, to teach at Virginia Tech. Doc had been depressed with grief since Squirrel's death. She wanted a change of scenery, so she asked Una how she felt about moving to Roanoke, Virginia. It was in the majestic Blue Ridge Mountains where Doc could be much closer to her sister.

Aunt Candy had seen Bitsy only a few times and she was already three years old. Una understood all this, but she was anxious about leaving Sylvia, Jazz, and Dr. Anna, who had been her steadfast support. Still, she wouldn't try to stop her mom from doing what she needed to do.

Doc had a dinner party the night she announced that she and her girls would soon be moving to Southwestern Virginia. Una expected tears, but there weren't any, just lively discussion.

"Come with us, Sylvia," Doc suggested toward the end of the meal. "You too, Dr. Anna. I need you both, and I promise to make it worth your while."

Mat and James chucked. "And what about us?" they asked.

"And me?" Jazz asked. "What about me?"

"You come too, Jazz," Doc said. "Una will love it. All of you come, *please*."

"Yeah, please," Una begged, looking longingly at Sylvia.

"Please, Aunt Sylvia?" Jazz begged. "Please let me go with Una to Roanoke."

Una laughed to see who wore the pants in the family.

"I know what you're thinking," Mat said, chuckling. "And she does. Sylvia wears the pants."

"Please, Uncle Mat!"

"Naw; now you done asked Aunt Sylvia. Too late to ask me."

"How 'bout if we spend some time and think about it?"

"Sounds good!" Jazz said, nearly trembling with excitement—as if she'd won a nice lotto prize.

"We will think about it as well," Dr. Anna said. "Won't we, James?"

"Sure," James said. "We'll pray about it too."

But the day Doc, Una, and Bitsy were ready to leave, they packed their bags into their Nissan hatchback by themselves. Most of their belongings were already halfway to Roanoke on a moving van.

Traveling down the highway, Una felt like she'd not only lost her dad but her two best friends. Judy had moved to Arizona, a full two-day drive from Roanoke, and Jazz was still in Alexandria, five hours away. Marsha and Rowe were good friends too, but they were in Chicago, nearly eleven hours away by car. Patrick was still a dream of what might have been. She had texted her goodbyes. And there were Sylvia and Dr. Anna, both beloved mentors and friends, but their families had not decided to move yet. So it was just the three Zipley females, headed to an unknown town, into an unknown future, *alone*.

After Bitsy fell asleep in her car seat, Una put her head on the headrest and nodded off too, but she soon awoke to Doc's voice.

"In this area, four universities are tucked into the shadows of the exquisite Blue Ridge Mountains," Doc said, sounding like a paid tour guide. "You'll appreciate the beauty."

Una noticed that despite all the highbrow academics in the area, a bunch of lazy cows could be heard mooing in the wide-open, wheat-colored countryside. Upon closer inspection, they looked like they were gathering for an open-air prayer meeting. It made Una giggle.

In what seemed like a short drive from the fields and mountains, Doc pulled up in the driveway of a white mansion with Ionic columns.

"Whose house is this?" Una asked, thinking that whoever lived in it must be loaded.

"Yours," Doc said. "Come on in and I'll give you and Bitsy the grand tour. But let me get Bitsy's potty seat out first!"

It was a good thing she did, because Bitsy didn't give a hoot about the elegance of the house; she immediately clamored for her potty.

The grand tour included fourteen rooms, a pool, and a hot tub on the back deck.

"I'm hoping to establish my clinic here in the back," Doc said. "What do you think? A little overwhelming?"

Una looked more than overwhelmed; she seemed baffled, like a kid who was just told she'd have to live in a museum the rest of her life.

"But Mom, the clinic will only take up five rooms in the back."

"That's right," Doc said with a coaxing smile. "There's a ramp that leads to it off the deck, but it also has its own entrance."

Una noticed fragrant boxwood hedges lining the front walk and giant elms and cedars spaced around the yard. She viewed the house as a huge, open hole that she, her mom, and Bitsy had fallen into. The slot happened to be open for occupancy and they fit, though it was far too large, so they fell right in.

"It's nice, Mom, but why such a big, splashy spread when it's just the three of us, and with Bitsy it's really just two-and-a-half?"

"That's just the way it is," Doc replied.

"I'm not sure I buy that, Mom," Una said. "And where are the black people? Are there *any* black or brown people in this neighborhood? Any Asian people?"

"Well, we just got here, darling," Doc said, looking around as if a black person might pop out of the hedge. "I'm sure there must be."

But as the weeks went on, Una never did see a black or a brown person living anywhere near her new neighborhood, nor a person of any description who didn't look exactly as she did—white. Everyone looked like their great-grandparents were plantation owners who had fought for the South in the Civil War. The only exception were African American and Hispanic housekeepers and nannies, and the men who came to clean chimneys or debug homes. Many of them rode the local buses in the mornings and left before sunset, because the buses didn't run into South Roanoke after 6:00 p.m.

About a month after the move, Sylvia and Dr. Anna both called to say they hoped to visit in the summer, but they had decided against moving to Roanoke right away. That naturally meant that Jazz would be stuck in Alexandria with Sylvia and Mat.

Una had prepared herself for the bad news, so she didn't cry, except on the inside. But what her mom couldn't see was a different story. Una knew that after Squirrel's death, her mom had cried enough for several lifetimes. Fortunately, not long after that difficult call, Doc hired a physician's assistant named Polithia Davis.

She was a wiry, athletic-looking woman in her early forties with mahogany skin and a black-eyed, Gypsy smile. Her small, worn hands moved in the air like she was tossing homemade pizza whenever she talked, and she always spoke with an air of authority like she knew what she was talking about. She also had a rocking sense of humor, a breezy personality, and a deep understanding of what it meant to be an outsider.

That was important to Una, because she prided herself more and more on being *an outsider;* someone who didn't feel the need to fit in as much as to be herself, even if that meant standing out to an embarrassing extent. And while she had once wanted to be the center of attention, that had changed since she'd turned fourteen.

Like Sylvia, Polithia was *Gullah.* She was originally from South Carolina. Like Una, she could sometimes feel things before they happened. One of her best talents was talking to her dead ancestors. At least, Una thought so. But when Doc overheard Polithia mention it, she asked Polithia not to talk about it around Una.

"She's impressionable at her age," Doc said.

"I understand," Polithia replied.

But Una sensed that when it came to communication and emotions, Polithia wasn't the type to follow precise rules. At least she hoped she would be the kind of soulmate that Sylvia was to her, not that anyone could ever replace Sylvia.

Doc usually saw her last patient at 7:00 p.m., but Polithia often popped in to see Una when she left the clinic about 6:35 or so. They chatted about everything from boys to biographies to the newest recipe for beef jerky. Sometimes, if Bitsy was still in playschool or at the sitter's house, they'd go down to the cul-de-sac and shoot a few baskets. Like Sylvia, Polithia and her husband, Paul, didn't have any kids, so there was more time for new relationships.

Polithia lived in Northwest Roanoke, about thirteen minutes from Una's house, twelve in light traffic. Doc, Bitsy, and Una drove her home one day when her car was in the shop. She and Paul had a nice one-bedroom, one-bath, single-story bungalow. What Una liked most about it was its gunpowder-blue color. Polithia reminded Una that the color blue brought good luck. She and Paul needed it, because the city wanted to take their house so it could extend the interstate near Hotel Roanoke.

Polithia figured they would eventually take another large tract of African American land between the fancy hotel in Gainsboro and the city of Salem, a small city eight miles west of Roanoke. Years before, city officials had taken Polithia's grandma's home in Historic Gainsboro. She was relocated against her will to a house across town that she couldn't afford to heat, a place without a front porch. Her grandma had prized that front porch. It was like a second living room where all the neighbors could gather to chat. But the worse part was that she was never compensated properly when the city called *eminent domain* on the property. This happened to many African American citizens in Virginia over the years.

"I can explain DNA easier than I can explicate the cruel mysteries of racism," Doc said when Una questioned her about how and why such things were allowed to happen.

Polithia said the way she saw it, powerful people who deliberately acted racist formed a sick-spirited club in a town.

"I can't live in a community like this!" Una insisted.

But Doc told Una to hold on because real change took time.

"Well, I don't have time to waste," Una said. "I want to do something about it *now*."

"Una, we had racism in Alexandria too," Doc said. "It goes way back in our history and it's all over the country; not just here."

"Let's get a few things straight," Una said. "I'm fourteen now, so I'm more aware of the corruption going on. The fact that it's *everywhere* is all the more reason to fight!"

Una reminded Doc that when Squirrel was in third grade, he and some friends of his parents marched with Dr. Martin Luther King in the 1963 March on Washington.

"Dad said he stood just a few yards from King as he made his "I Have a Dream" speech. He felt then that he was a part of history, a courageous history that would change America forever, and it made him proud to be an American."

"But Dr. King was murdered," Doc said. "Sometimes change can be risky."

Una told her mom that people like her must change things if they're ever gonna change. "I want to either make this city become the kind of place where I want to live, or I want to leave it!" she said. "If I must become *a warrior* to do that, then I will."

Doc patted Una on the head, but Una slapped her hand away.

"No offense, Mom," Una said, "but I'm not a kid anymore and I'm not in the mood to be patted."

CHAPTER THIRTEEN
DISCRIMINATION KNOCKS ON UNA'S DOOR

The village where Polithia and Paul lived on the outskirts of the historic community of Gainsboro in Northwest Roanoke was a hub of African American Southern culture in the '30s, '40s and beyond. People came from far and wide to see Dizzy Gillespie grace the stage at the Moroccan Club, blowing his jazz trumpet deep into the smoky night. Greats like Louis Armstrong and Ella Fitzgerald appeared at the Dumas Hotel, now in sore need of repair since it was taken over by the city and tossed from one agency to another over the last several decades.

According to the *Star Tribune*, the African American family that originally owned the Dumas was never properly reimbursed when the city took it over.

"Paul and I know the Lawson family that owned the old hotel, and it's true. It's typical of how the folks in power treat black citizens around here," Polithia said. "Those in power simply steal black land. They never call it that, but that's what it is."

She explained to Una that when the city demolished black homes, stores, businesses, and parking areas to widen streets and highways close to Hotel Roanoke, the community lost its identity. This happened both during and after urban renewal in the 1960s and '70s.

Where Gainsboro once stood out as the sparkling musical and artistic Renaissance of the South, large parts of it deteriorated (see "Family Notes"). Barren gray lots dotted the land in between the few houses and businesses that survived. The city even tried to take the iconic Gainsboro Library. It would have bulldozed it to the ground if black activists hadn't inspired hundreds of the city's kids to write letters to save it. Thanks to dedicated activists, Gainsboro eventually received historic designation as one of the oldest areas in the Roanoke Valley. That stopped some of the destruction, but not all.

"Paul and I still go to bed worried every night that the city will see fit any day now to send us our relocation orders," Polithia said. "We think about what happened to the African American who owned *Star Tribune* office. One day the publisher came in about 9:00 a.m. to find the bulldozers already digging up dirt where her newspaper office had been down on Henry Street. They said it was a result of *eminent domain*."

Polithia said Ms. Whitt, the owner and publisher of the paper, told the diggers she had gotten no notice concerning the demolition, but got no reply and no apologies from the city. Una learned that years later, the *Star Tribune* published a story about the misuse of funds by the local housing authority. The authority allegedly took federal block grant money to buy up many of the most expensive properties in town, including the top three floors of the Toler Bank and Trust building. It was prime real estate. The bank property could be used to create luxury condos. The money from the uptown properties would line the pockets of the city administrators and influencers but would not help black people or poor people much at all.

...

One night a few days before school started in late August, Una got a call from Jazz.

"Una, I miss you," Jazz said.

"Miss you, too, girlfriend," Una said. "But aren't you excited about starting your sophomore year?"

"In answer to your question, the answer is no," Jazz said. "I'm not into thinking about school or anything else right now. I miss Dad and nothing's copacetic since you left. I was so sure Aunt Sylvia and Uncle Mat would let us move to be closer to you."

"Well, maybe there's a way," Una said.

"Explain?"

"For one thing, our new house is huge," Una said. "We have two guest rooms, four baths, a giant kitchen, a den, a pool, a hot tub, and more. Mom's office is on the back of the house."

"Go on," Jazz said, smiling to herself.

"So what if we could convince Mom, Sylvia, and Mat to let you come for the school year and see how it works out?"

"I guess I could take the bus home for holidays unless they wanted to come down."

"There's no harm in giving it a shot," Una said. "Let me talk to Mom first and I'll call you back."

"Sounds good. Thanks, Una."

"No need to thank me. You might just save me from dying of boredom."

As soon as she got off the phone, Una fixed Doc a cup of Earl Gray with extra sugar and lemon. "Mom, I have something important to discuss with you."

"Go ahead," Doc said. "I'm tired, I'm but never too tired to listen when you need me. Besides, I just got Bitsy down for the night, so I'm all yours."

"It's about Jazz," Una said. "She just called."

"Oh, this already sounds ominous."

"Sort of. She misses her dad, and I was hoping she could come to live with us just for the school year."

"Has she asked Sylvia and Mat?"

"She will, but I wanted to clear it with you first."

"That was thoughtful."

"You don't think it's a good idea; I can tell."

"It's not that," Doc said. "It's just that living with someone and staying close friends are two different propositions. What if you two don't get along as well when she has to live by our rules, or what if you both like the same boy, or . . ."

"Mom, that's always a possibility, but there's just as great a chance that we will get along. Please, Mom, give us a chance."

"I'll talk to Sylvia about it. But whatever we decide, Jazz will have to move fast. School starts on Monday."

...

Jazz came down on the bus that Sunday with only two suitcases and a beach bag full of treasures. Polithia visited that afternoon as well. Doc had asked her if she would mind keeping an eye out for Bitsy while Jazz unpacked. Besides, she'd made Polithia some lemon tarts, one of her specialties.

Polithia asked if she might bring her niece Sandra Davis to meet Una and Jazz.

"Of course!" Doc said. "That's a super idea. I'm sure they'll be congenial."

After Jazz finished most of her unpacking, she, Una, and Sandra chatted about school, boys, books, and a little about themselves.

"What do your mom and dad do for a living, Sandra?" Jazz asked. "Sorry if I'm being too nosy."

"Mom died when I was little," Sandra said. "But Dad is a cardiologist."

"My mom died when I was small too," Jazz said. "It stinks; but how exactly are you related to Polithia?"

"My dad is Uncle Paul's brother; you know, Polithia's husband is Paul."

"Oh, I've got it now."

"Sometimes I feel guilty that our home is not threatened like Uncle Paul's and Aunt Polithia's," Sandra said. "We live in the suburbs about twenty miles out of the city where a lot of newer homes are located. I go to a private school and I'm one of the few black students there, but I've just about gotten used to it. In fact, we're the only black family in our neighborhood."

Sandra said she had to get used to kids asking her how her family could afford for her to go to private school.

"That's a shit bomb," Una said. "And I get the guilty thing. I don't understand what gives me the right to live in a mansion when people who work just as hard as Mom often have to struggle."

Jazz didn't respond to Una's comment. She asked Sandra how she dealt with kids who asked her weird questions at her school and wondered if they kept Sandra out of the nasty cliques.

"Of course, they do. It's annoying and sometimes worse. I just have to try to stay calm and think of creative ways to respond, I mean besides calling someone a stank-eyed so-and-so . . ."

Then Sandra said that her Uncle Paul did construction work and created building designs.

"I'd like to meet your Uncle Paul and your dad, Sandra," Una said.

"Ditto," Jazz said.

...

Two weeks later, the girls got their chance to meet both Paul Davis and his brother, Dr. Martin Davis. Paul and Polithia asked Doc to bring everyone to Burger King to talk about some ideas that had been swirling around in their heads. Una, Jazz, and Sandra all had Big Kings and onion rings while they talked about basketball. Jazz mentioned trying out for cheerleading and Una said she wanted to try for the freshman girls' basketball team. Sandra said she'd hold out for soccer.

Doc listened to three different conversations while she fed Bitsy little bits of bread and meat with applesauce she'd packed. Finally, she asked if anything special was on Paul's mind.

"Maybe," he said. "I've been doing a lot of thinking."

"Go on."

"Well, I know that you and Una have been concerned about the housing problem for a lot of folks around here."

Una nodded her head violently while she slurped her Coke. "I am!" she said. "Do you think you have a solution?"

"Well, not exactly; not a solution for everyone, but perhaps a way to make a start," Paul said. "I figure, if some folks like you, Doc Zipley, could—"

"Spell it out, Paul," Polithia said.

"Well, if some folks with money and influence like you, Doc, could invest in duplexes and assist us in renting them out with an option for renters to buy, it might help stop the city from land grabbing like they've been doing; that is, if others like you got the hang of the idea."

"I see," Doc said, looking serious, like she was about to do a risky operation on someone.

Then she asked if the duplexes would be in Northwest.

"Yes," Polithia said. "Northwest and Gainsboro, but we'll start with Gainsboro, because I know that people, like my grandma, Hatie Dunbar, want to return to Historic Gainsboro where they grew up. Grandma Hatie still remembers it the way it was."

"It takes a ton of money to build sturdy new structures, you know," Doc said.

"Yes. Very few buildings were maintained or renovated in Gainsboro and Northwest after urban renewal; it will take plenty of money to bring the area back," Paul said. "But Polithia, Martin, and I are willing to work with you."

"You really need my backing?" Doc said.

"Yes," Paul replied, lowering his head into his hands like it ached. "You're a respected white doctor with connections in South Roanoke. People in positions of power in this town will listen to you."

"But your brother is also a very respected doctor," Doc said. "I can't believe it's that hard to secure a loan if you're . . ."

Black, Sandra thought, but she didn't say it out loud and no one else did either.

Polithia told Doc not to feel any pressure.

This kind of talk made Sandra nervous and queasy.

Una is cool, and I like her mom, she thought, *but hearing who has true power in this city and who doesn't makes me want to puke. My dad is a doctor just like Una's mom, so why should she need to help us build up the black section of the city?*

Doc Zipley's words broke Sandra's concentration. "Of course, I'll help, in any way I can," she said.

"I don't want your help!" Sandra said under her breath. "I know your heart is in the right place and so is Una's, but this is just another shit bomb."

Sandra considered telling Una how she felt, but she didn't think Una would get it, and that could destroy their chances of friendship. It could even get Sandra's dad mad at Sandra.

"I believe that if we work by using small steps to rebuild Gainsboro, we can encourage others to take another look at Northwest," Dr. Davis said.

Jazz looked at Sandra and back at Una. She guessed what Sandra was probably thinking, just like she knew how impossible it would be for Una to understand.

If you're not black, you don't know what racial discrimination really feels like, Jazz thought to herself. *Our people were the first kings and queens of the world, but now we have to wait on some wealthy white lady's financial help to save a community that belonged to us in the first place.*

"I'm glad you shared your thoughts with me, Paul," Doc said. "How about all of you coming for supper next Wednesday?"

Paul and Polithia accepted for the group. Sandra tried her best to muster a smile.

The following Wednesday, it rained so much that it looked like the trees in the yard would float away. Sandra was hoping the meal would be canceled, but it wasn't. She and Dr. Davis arrived first at 7:00 p.m. sharp. Polithia and Paul came a few minutes later.

When Una answered the door, Sandra started to introduce her dad.

"This is my brother, Dr. Martin Davis," Paul interrupted.

Dr. Davis smiled broadly and reached out his hand to shake Una's.

Sandra cringed, goosebumps zipping down her back.

"Nice to meet you," Una said. "I'll get Mom, Bitsy, and Jazz."

"Let's have some brandy in the den before we eat, shall we?" Doc asked, emerging from the dining room to walk her guests through the foyer, past the venerable antique grandfather clock.

"Love to have a taste of the spirits," Polithia said.

Sandra was hoping for some brandy too, but Doc poured lemonade for her and the girls. Doc Zipley and Dr. Davis seemed to have a lot in common. In fact, both were single parents, both had graduated from the University of Virginia Medical School, and both loved classical music. Still, it was obvious to Sandra and Jazz that Doc wasn't seeing the elephant in the room: *racism,* the very thing she was supposedly going to fight.

"Paul, I did some research this weekend," Doc said. "I found a small piece of land in Gainsboro for sale at a reasonable price, and a reputable builder."

Paul and Polithia scooted their chairs in closer and Paul wiped his mouth carefully with his napkin. Sandra wanted to crawl under the table.

"So soon?" Polithia asked, looking at Doc in near disbelief.

"I have some extra money from my husband's estate, and I need to consult with my financial advisor, but I'd like to be a part of this project and I think the money will work out."

"Exactly what do you have in mind?" Dr. Davis asked.

"As you know, Paul and Polithia suggested we build duplexes. I'd like to start with one duplex—two apartments—to be located on Grace Street near Valley Baptist Church in Gainsboro."

Polithia let out a sigh of relief.

No! Sandra thought, but she stayed quiet.

"I'd like to propose that Paul and Polithia take one of the apartments at reduced rent, and I will ask my bank to provide a low-interest loan when you're ready to purchase the property. I'm on the board of Freedom Atlantic."

"That's very generous of you," Paul said.

"And I was hoping Mrs. Dunbar would consider renting the other side; then if she would like to buy her apartment, I'm sure we could arrange something."

"Two baths, a laundry room, and a porch?" Polithia asked.

"Exactly," Doc said. "And a nice yard with a fence."

Dr. Davis and Paul asked what they could do to help.

"I was hoping that you, Paul, would help draw up the plans and approach the city with me. Martin, could you find some contacts in the community who might support more building in the area?"

"I'll do more than that!" Dr. Davis said. "I'll put up half of the cash."

"That's great," Polithia said. "I'll work on some landscaping and the girls can help me."

"I can attend city council on a regular basis and let them know that we want to get a few things straight; we'll fight any further stealing of property in the Gainsboro and Northwest neighborhoods," Una said.

"That's good," Dr. Davis said. "Neighborhoods need to make their own decisions about their plans. Government grants are fine, but that doesn't mean city administrators need to direct and control everything without the input of the community."

"I'd like to help with that, too," Jazz said, "by attending council meetings."

"What about you, Sandra?" Una asked.

"I'll *think* about it," Sandra said, attracting a grimace from her dad. She knew she'd have to keep her feelings to herself or risk a major confrontation.

Polithia and Paul said the Bureau of Historic Resources would probably assist them since Gainsboro was the oldest area of the city.

"And Habitat Homes for Humanity will probably help," Una added. "We just need to get people to apply."

"Sounds like a plan," Polithia said, hugging both Doc and Una.

Sandra wondered if Doc or Una noticed how stiff her shoulders were, or how stoic her gaze.

"Soon we'll be ready for a community meeting to discuss further details," Doc announced.

She asked Polithia to write a couple of editorials to submit to the *Star Tribune*. Dr. Davis said the *Roanoke Gazette* owed him a favor for supporting them over the years, so he would speak to their editorial department.

I'll just have to think of a way to tell Una how I really feel; a way that won't mess up the plans that are already in motion and get me in trouble with my family, Sandra thought to herself.

When she looked up, Jazz caught her eye with a look of acknowledgment. Sandra smiled at her; it was her first sincere smile of the night.

CHAPTER FOURTEEN
STANDING OUT AND STANDING UP

Jazz and Una both had adjustments to make at their new school, Warren G. Harding High. Jazz was starting her tenth-grade year and Una was a freshman. Both girls were excited about the new computers in their classes but there were also more challenges than ever before. There were academic and social challenges. More homework. But on the lighter side, Una began to see herself as a fan of Mariah Carey-inspired Y2K style and music. She refused to identify totally with that or any other group because she didn't believe in glorifying any one artist. Una was no longer as cool with *standing out* as she once was, but she realized that the choices she was making required her to stand out if she planned to stand up for what she believed. She was getting used to it, but relaxing to Mariah's music helped to soothe her.

Jazz favored Whitney Houston's music and sequined chic, but she considered her own style *eclectic*. Jazz stood out primarily because of her piercing blue eyes and high cheekbones; in short, she was knockout gorgeous. But she was intelligent, too, and that never hurt a girl's social status.

Una stood out physically because she was tall and lanky for a girl. Her skin was as pale as tapioca with small brown freckles, and her hair had just been dyed Kool-Aid lime green before green was cool. Her eyes were a mud-colored mix of hazel and brown until she discovered aquamarine contacts. Then they became bluish green. Jazz had encouraged her to keep her nails long, so she had them professionally done and painted with yellow sunflowers and eggplant purple dots, the school colors of Harding High.

Una, like Jazz, was smart, but in more outspoken way. When she raised her hand to give an answer in class, people usually laughed because she *over answered*. For example, if the subject was the Colonial Period in America and the question was about the main objective put forth in one of Jonathan Edwards' sermons, she answered with a treatise on how the Great Awakening led to African American Protestantism. She had to. She got easily bored.

Una soon found out that people with serious, loud opinions don't win a lot of popularity contests. She never expected that, but it made her even more grateful for Jazz.

Fortunately (or unfortunately), the first book Una checked out of the library was about witches. She was still obsessively intrigued. When Jazz asked her about it, Una said she identified only with positive role models like Glinda, the Good Witch of the South, featured on yearly reruns of Frank Baum's *The Wizard of Oz*. But she also saw value in Macbeth's witches, who were cloaked in the wisdom of darkness and tragic clairvoyance. She tried to pull any inspiration she could find to embody the characteristics of a light being: a good medicine woman, as the Native Americans might say.

Still, she was as human as anyone, so sometimes she didn't feel or emit much light at all. There were plenty of days when she said she felt that she'd lost her personal magic, her occasional gift of clairvoyance, and her cool; in short, her whole bag of tricks. Anger was all that was left, like a ten-day-old dried-up crust of bread found behind the refrigerator. But Jazz was usually there for her on those days, despite their differences and occasional disagreements.

Take the day someone wrote: "FYI, SHE'S A LOSER" on Una's locker at school in red magic marker. Her new friend, Kiki Rogers, told her to skip class if necessary to rub it off, then permanently forget it happened. But she must have forgotten that it's easy to erase tough words from your locker but much harder to erase them from your mind. Then there was the day someone dumped Una's clothes in the toilet during gym. She had to walk miles home to change out of her gym suit into dry clothes. Stuff like that nearly convinced her to start dabbling in black magic, but she fought the urge.

"Just say *barf or bitch*, or something, and go on," Jazz suggested.

Eventually, Una found the ignorant turd who wrote on her locker. It was the same one who dumped her clothes.

135

The girl liked a guy in her science class and got mad because he always wanted to share labs with Una.

"Some people are just trivial," Jazz said.

Then there was the day some jerk hit a kid with learning differences in the head with a rock and broke his glasses. It happened just outside the gym. Una got riled and gave him the *diluted evil eye*. According to Una's *The Power of Witchery* book, the undiluted evil eye can kill someone. Anyway, the dude twitched for a week and didn't hit anyone else for a while.

Sylvia and Mat came down in October to bring the rest of Jazz's things. They were delighted that Jazz seemed to feel at home in her new surroundings, but hoped she'd realize that the real world was very different from most of what she was currently experiencing. Doc had a luncheon party before they left so Sylvia and Mat could visit with Sandra, Martin, Polithia, and Paul.

The entire coterie of adults seemed to click, especially around the subject of the revitalization of Gainsboro, and Sylvia promised to bring Dr. Anna and James on the next visit.

"I told you that you would like it down here," Doc said. "And the jobs in the medical field are in great demand in Roanoke right now."

"We like the people so far," Mat said. "That's for sure."

"I agree," Sylvia said. "We miss you, sure enough. We'll keep praying about it. You know I love my job at the hospital, but again, we'll pray on it."

During the next few weeks Polithia, Paul, Sandra and her dad came to the Zipley's house quite a few times to talk about plans for the new duplex on Grace Street. They wanted the builders to be ready to pour the cement before winter set in. A group of African American ministers met with them at the Gainsboro Library to talk about revitalizing the neighborhood. The *Star Tribune* sent a reporter to cover the meeting. Paul was interviewed, along with several ministers from Northwest. Someone from the Southern Conference on Black Leadership (SCBL) was there too.

Suddenly, it seemed like the whole community was getting on the same page, at least until Una found out that *The Gazette* wasn't too cool with publishing any specifics about the new duplex. But Una and Sandra did hit its front page for protesting with signs and chants at a city council meeting. They also appeared on WKDX News with signs pointing to the lack of affordable housing. That's when they discovered there were kids in their own schools who hated them for standing up for the right to fair housing.

Sandra said these kids started using the *N-word* under their breath in the halls and someone wrote SUPER FREAK on her locker. That's not a compliment at Tilbury Academy. Martin Davis set up a meeting with Sandra's principal. Doc, Polithia, and Paul asked if they were needed, but Dr. Davis declined the help.

"I think I can manage, but thanks," he said.

Someone wrote GO TO HELL WHITE TRASH on Una's locker. Of course, she took a photo of it and sent it to her closest school friends with a note seeking support.

"Leave it right on your locker, Una, as a mark of distinction," Jazz said. "Let the school worry about scrubbing it off. They need to see that they have a problem."

Sure enough, Principal Harris called Una into his office the next day to ask her what it was all about.

"How would I know?" she said.

"Surely, you must have some idea why they wrote that."

"Why does anyone do any evil thing?" Una replied.

When she explained about standing up in city council, Mr. Harris, a black man, seemed to have no sympathy for her.

"A girl your age shouldn't be involved in *adult issues* like housing," he said.

"But my mother and our good friends are committed to civil rights like fair housing, so why wouldn't I be?"

Mr. Harris shrugged his shoulders. "Try to stay out of trouble, Una," was his most profound advice.

Boy, he sure didn't know who he was dealing with. Una was the *Queen of Trouble* and always had been. When she told Doc, Polithia and Paul and Dr. Davis about her conversation with Mr. Harris, the next day before school, they accompanied her to visit him. They sat in his office for twenty minutes. Finally, his secretary informed them that the school system's media advisor, Mr. Snipes, would have to sit in on the meeting and an appointment would have to be made at least two weeks in advance.

Dr. Davis personally contacted Mr. Snipes at the city's school administration office. "Mr. Snipes, if you want to make a bigger issue of this than it is, I have some friends in the media who will be glad to accompany us."

After that, Mr. Snipes agreed to set up the meeting the next day at 8:00 a.m. Polithia, Doc, Paul, and Dr. Davis were all there with Una. Paul addressed Mr. Harris first. The whole time he was talking, Mr. Harris kept a sly and somewhat ironic smile on his face, almost like he was about to burst out laughing when everyone left the room. Then he addressed Dr. Davis with eagle eyes.

"I meant nothing by what I said to this young lady," he said. "It's just that these kids are already thinking about adult activities way before their time."

Dr. Davis was about to speak when Doc Zipley cut in. "Sir, with all due respect, you have no right to compare my daughter's activism in this town with teens interested in inappropriate adult activities," she said. "You owe us all an apology."

"That's right, Mr. Harris," Polithia said. "How dare you suggest . . . !"

"Okay, okay, calm down folks," Mr. Snipes directed.

He was a tall, thin white man with a grayish complexion and a silver goatee.

"This is getting way out of hand; in fact, this meeting is over!" he said. Mr. Harris rose to shake everyone's hands, but none were offered.

"Let's be decent about this," Mr. Snipes said.

"You let us know when you folks decide to treat us with some respect and decency," Dr. Davis said, "and then we'll be back."

With that, Una and her supporters left Mr. Harris' office and prayed they would never have to return. The following week, Dr. Margaret Hanover, superintendent of the city's schools, called Doc. She asked her to bring Una in to meet with her. Doc and Una decided not to prepare too much, just to hear her out and respond sincerely off the cuff. They arrived promptly at 4:00 p.m. the following Friday. On the way over, Doc asked Una if she felt like she was in trouble.

"Kind of," Una said. "At least I make good grades and my courses are mostly advanced."

"Yep, you can't be faulted for that," Doc said.

They were ushered into Dr. Denise Hanover's plush office and asked to be seated on the beige silk couch. Una had on a skirt, so she tried to remember to keep her legs closed.

"Would you ladies like bottled water?" Dr. Hanover inquired.

"It depends; how long are we going to be in here?" Una asked.

"No, thank you," Doc said, shooting Una the nasty eye.

"Then I'll get right to the point," Dr. Hanover said, wearing a confident grin like it was a Dior necklace. "Una has created some commotion in her school."

"Please be specific, ma'am," Una said, beating her mom to the punch.

"Well, dear, let's start with your hair," Dr. Hanover said. "Even though our school system does not dictate the color of our students' hair, green hair does attract some rather negative attention, and I'm not sure if that was your intent."

"Anything further?" Doc asked, looking half mad and half bored.

"Yes," Dr. Hanover said, looking down at the floor as if she'd spotted a roach. "Mr. Snipes reported to me that in your meeting with Mr. Harris you displayed a *belligerent* attitude, one that, frankly, showed a lack of restraint."

"What?" Doc and Una gasped. Una didn't know exactly what *belligerent* meant, but she sensed it wasn't a compliment.

"Yes, you and your entourage of defenders were aggressive, without restraint and this made Mr. Harris feel most uncomfortable."

"Dr. Hanover," Doc said, "Mr. Harris is a grown man who is not only an executive and a professional in your school system, but a very outspoken one. I don't think he needs your defense; indeed, he seems quite capable of attacking anyone he pleases—whether or not the attack is warranted."

"And that's what he did to me," Una added. "He made me feel ashamed of being an activist. From the time I was five, my parents have taught me that an activist is a kind of hero, but he obviously doesn't see it that way."

"Shouldn't my daughter be praised for her efforts to stand up for fair housing and social justice," Doc said, "instead of warned to avoid trouble? Besides, she wasn't the vandal. Shouldn't the vandal who wrote all over her locker be found and penalized?"

Dr. Hanover managed a mean grin and summoned Mr. Snipes. "Please escort these people out of my office," she said.

"Wait!" Doc said. "Dr. Hanover, what are you hiding here?"

"I'm sure I have no idea what you're referring to!" Dr. Hanover barked. "You need to leave immediately. I have an important meeting in a few minutes."

"No, ma'am," Doc said. "We're not leaving until we're done here, and this may be the most important meeting you'll have all week."

Mr. Snipes grabbed Una's arm and shoved her toward the door.

"I seem to recall an article in the paper last fall announcing that you, Dr. Hanover, wrote a check for a million dollars to city council. Why would you do such a thing?" Doc asked.

"If you ladies don't leave now, I'm afraid we will have to call security," Mr. Snipes said.

"All right," Doc replied, "but if my daughter receives any more harassment, we will be back, Dr. Hanover, and I assure you we will bring others with us!"

When they got to the car Doc sprouted some tears. She said they were from anger and frustration. "How dare she!" Doc exclaimed. Then she took several deep breaths. "Shall we go get some ice cream and try to calm down a little?"

"I'm game," Una said, feeling vindicated. "Thanks for taking up for me, Mom. You were magnificent!"

"I'm very proud of you, Una," Doc said, dabbing her eyes with a tissue from her purse.

"Standing up for things you believe in can cause trouble. I've warned you about that before. That's why I've always tried to stay away from controversial issues. I'm not as brave as you are, Una, but I am very proud."

"You're plenty brave, Mom," Una said, grabbing her for a hug as Doc paid for their ice cream. "You wouldn't be a doctor if you weren't brave. You're competitive as hell in a profession where men still dominate."

Doc didn't say anything else, just smiled a tear-swept smile and licked her pistachio cone.

CHAPTER FIFTEEN
SOMETHING ABOUT SASHA

On a Saturday morning Jazz and Una had planned to get their nails painted solid black at Marie Maiden's Nails & Company, but Una's friend Kiki said that if Una's green hair was shocking to Dr. Hanover and Mr. Harris, maybe she'd better postpone the nails. So Una decided to go to the library to work on her term paper about Colonial America. Jazz said she'd stay home and listen to music while getting her math problems done.

Una asked Kiki to go to the library with her since they were in the same history class, but Kiki said she and a girl named Sasha Carter had already made plans. Una had never heard of Sasha and neither had Jazz. Kiki said they'd met at a pep rally the first week of school.

"Una, want to go play some pinball with Sasha and me?" Kiki asked. "My mother can take us."

"What about my friends Jazz Jones and Sandra Davis?"

"Bring them too!"

"Sounds good." Una cleared it with Doc, Jazz, and Sandra; then told Kiki they could go after they finished some of their homework. Kiki's mom was going to drive, but when it was time to pick up the girls she wasn't feeling well, so Sasha's mom drove. First, she picked up Kiki in Southeast, then Kiki told Mrs. Carter how to get to Una's house in South Roanoke. When they pulled up in front of her place, Sasha's eyeballs just about erupted.

"She lives in a mansion that looks like the damn White House!" Sasha exclaimed. "It has an outside pool and a yard the size of a football field!"

Una, Jazz, and Sandra jumped in the back seat with Kiki. Sasha kept quiet in the front and didn't extend her hand to anyone.

"Hello, I'm Sandra Davis," Sandra said, waiting for a response.

"Hi, I'm Kiki."

"Nice to meet you," Sandra said.

Jazz and Una said nothing until Kiki finally introduced them to Sasha.

Still, Sasha kept her mouth shut.

"Sasha, what's wrong with you, girl?" Mrs. Carter said. "Hi, I'm Annie Carter, Sasha's mother. Cat must've snatched her tongue today."

"Hello, ma'am," Sandra said in her princess tone. "Nice of you to pick us up, Mrs. Carter."

"And who is this *Miss Green* back there again?" Mrs. Carter asked. "I missed your name, Sugar."

Sasha chuckled.

"Oh, you mean me?" Una asked. "I'm Una Zipley. I'd try to shake your hand, ma'am, but you're driving."

Then Mrs. Carter told her she liked the green tint on her hair.

"Mom, you're embarrassing the girl," Sasha said.

Mrs. Carter didn't reply, but she gently eased up to the curb in front of the House of Pinball and barked out orders, telling Sasha and the girls to be ready to go before suppertime.

"I will, Mom!" Sasha shouted. "Don't put the hassle on me!"

"All right, then, watch your mouth," Mrs. Carter yelled, driving off into the traffic, her tires squealing.

Sasha acted like a queen leading her ladies-in-waiting into the House of Pinball. Her well-toned ebony arms flowed into smooth, tapered fingers with sharp, white nails; her arms looked like matching works of art. Una was grateful that due to her normally outspoken personality, she possessed a little extra *zing* in the presence of this black goddess. Still, even she was in awe of this powerful girl. They played Space Adventure, Hotrod 2, Drop Dunks, and Temple Quest for over an hour. Then Sasha headed over to the snack bar and everyone followed.

"You gettin' anything?" Una asked Jazz and Sandra. She was feeling slightly sweaty from the excitement of the games.

"Too close to dinner," Sandra said.

"Maybe it is," Jazz agreed.

"Forget about damn dinner!" Sasha said. "I'm getting some fries. Anyone else in?"

"I'll take a Pepsi," Una said. "Want one, Jazz?"

"Then put down some bills!" Sasha ordered, grinning at Una and Jazz like they were circus animals.

Kiki got a drink too, and she was daring enough to break out with a small fries.

"Kiki, you nice and petite; you run track?" Sasha asked.

"Sasha, you know I ran last year 'till my grades went down," Kiki said. "Why you asking me that? I told you Dad put the halt on me 'till I could pull my grades up."

"Crap," Sasha said. "Maybe it's good my daddy in the service so he ain't around to tell me what to do."

"My dad and I are actually pretty tight," Kiki said. "We do a lot of stuff together when we get the time."

"That reminds me, what'd you say he does?" Sasha asked.

"Maintenance for the county schools," Kiki said, "and my mom works at a hair salon."

"Is your mom home when you get there after school?" Sandra asked.

"Nobody's home when my brother and I get there, but we like it that way."

"Kiki, you in this city council stuff with Una, Jazz, and Sandra?" Sasha asked. "I saw them on TV but ain't seen you."

"Nope," Kiki said. "Too busy."

"What about you, Sasha?" Sandra asked. "Would you like to get in on some action with us?"

From her tone, Una couldn't tell if Sandra was being sarcastic.

"Not the kind of action you talking 'bout," Sasha said. "Ain't got time for that mess."

"Where do you live, Sasha?" Sandra asked.

"On Magnolia Boulevard over in Northwest," Sasha said. "Why are you concerned with that?"

"Because Northwest and Gainsboro are the parts of town where the city has been land grabbing for over fifty years, and if we don't stand up to them now, there will only be more destruction of African American property."

"Nope," Sasha said. "Nobody gonna stop the power brokers around here, especially no teenagers like us!"

"What about the Gainsboro Library?" Jazz asked. "Una said that a bunch of kids wrote letters to stop it from being bulldozed and it worked. The city backed off."

"Not interested!" Sasha said, too quickly to hear the rest of Jazz's speech about the city. "I just want to be left alone to live my life as I see fit."

"You planning to go to college?" Kiki asked.

"Unlikely," Sasha said. "Not in the budget."

"Not in mine either, but there's always the Pell and other grants and loans," Kiki said. "If you don't do that, then what will you do?"

"I'll find somethin'. Why ya'll care so much about what happens to Northwest?" Sasha asked, changing the subject again. She looked at Una, Jazz, and Sandra like they were a couple of dumb suckers. "Ya'll sittin' on money, college, and big jobs someday, so I don't get it."

Sandra shrugged her shoulders like she didn't think Sasha would understand her spiel. Jazz kept silent.

"Seriously, I wish you would help," Una said.

Sasha stared at Una like she was losing it for real. "You dopin', girl?" she asked.

"Well, you're a black goddess and I'm a green-haired wannabe light witch, so what if we hung out more? And besides, what's wrong with trying to help create better housing for people?"

"Look, I only know Kiki; I don't really know you, Miss Witchy; don't really know you or the black princesses."

"I'm no princess," Jazz said. "You don't know me at all, girl."

"Just think about it, Sasha," Kiki said.

"*You* think about it," Sasha said. "Okay, almost time for my mom to be here. Let's wait outside."

"I thought you told Kiki you wanted to meet us," Una said in her defense.

"Meetin' and hangin' regular is two different animals," Sasha said as if she were about to spit on the ground.

Una had been effectively silenced.

...

By mid-January, Una had become a ferocious point guard for the freshman girls' basketball team, the Lady Titans. She was a three-point shooter who could shoot several feet from the line with a fast release. Jazz was jubilant to have made the cheerleading squad. She enthusiastically cheered Una on, shaking her purple and yellow pom-poms until she almost wore them out the first week. Sasha also made the cheerleading team, adding her own dash of pizzazz, and Kiki proudly played clarinet in the marching band.

Sandra was sometimes envious of the busy camaraderie that her new friends had, but she was more often content to watch the games with her dad, Polithia and Paul and Doc and Bitsy, from the bleachers on Wednesday nights. Occasionally, Mrs. Rogers and Mrs. Carter joined Doc and the others in the stands. Mrs. Carter knew how to whistle with two fingers, and she frequently did, to express her support for the team. If someone were whispering something in her ear when she decided to whistle, it was just too bad, because it was understood that whistling was one of Mrs. Carter's special talents.

"GO, GREEN WARRIOR!" she yelled.

Una glanced over her shoulder out of polite acknowledgment, even if it made her miss a dribble.

CHAPTER SIXTEEN

COMING TO AN UNDERSTANDING

February, March, and April were hard months for Una. She was sent to detention hall twelve times for talking and laughing during study hall and home economics. She couldn't help it. Kiki sat right behind her in study hall and Sasha sat next to her in home ec. In other words, it was all too tempting to tell an occasional joke or two, or discuss a new song, an annoying guy, a cute guy, etc. Finally, in May, Doc got a call from the D Hall secretary and Una was put on warning at home; kind of a probation that dictated that if Una didn't straighten out there would be hell to pay. *Hell* meaning no TV, no computer time, and very few calls for a month. Miraculously, there were no incidences of bad behavior in May.

After school let out in June, the weather quickly got as hot as poppin' cookin' grease and Grace Street sizzled with activity. Jazz was allowed to stay on for the summer.

She, Sandra, and Una worked on fliers addressing the need for more affordable housing in Gainsboro. They passed them out all over town and at the city council when they weren't concentrating on landscaping for the new duplex. It did Polithia's heart good to see the girls working together, almost like sisters. While they were working, they shared some of what was going on in their social scene with Polithia.

Polithia told Paul, "I guess they think of me kind of as a big sister, even though I'm more than twice their age. But I enjoy playing mentor to them. They're all good kids, and I hope they stay that way."

Una told Polithia about Sasha and her mom, Mrs. Carter. "Sasha let it be known that she was dating a boy named Roy Hunt, a member of the *Bloods* who was kicked out of school," Una said. "Her mom must have scented it out."

It appeared to Una that Mrs. Carter was probably setting up play dates to distract Sasha, because she'd offered to drive all the girls to bowling, the movies, and an outdoor concert. Sasha still seemed shy about bonding with Una, Sandra, and Jazz, but she had so much fun drinking mocktails at the summer concert downtown that she seemed almost tipsy.

The next Saturday, Una invited Sasha and Kiki to her house for a pool party. It had rained most of the week and continued to rain the morning of the party, but it passed by 2:00 p.m. When the guests arrived, the skies looked as sunny as a day at Cocoa Beach. Doc put up turquoise beach umbrellas and threw *Teen* magazines and purple-striped towels on the lounge chairs.

She told Una she had a surprise for her. Una thought it might be ice cream, but that wasn't even close. Polithia knew about the surprise, but she'd been asked to keep it mum, so *mum* was the word for as long as possible. But Una was itching to know and Polithia was itching to tell.

Doc finally gave in to pressure. "It's at the airport," she said.

"What?" Una screamed. "Tell me!"

"It's your old best friend, Judy Light!" she announced in a flood of words.

"Your sweet mom flew her in from Arizona for the weekend," Polithia said, waving her arm in the air like a wand, "so Judy can meet your new friends."

Una ran to hug Doc, burying her head in her mom's shoulder.

"I wanted to get Judy down there before you forgot what she looked like," Doc said, patting her daughter on the back.

"Una, you watch for the door," Polithia said, "while I run to pick up Judy."

"Thanks, I owe you one," Doc said.

"Come on now, Doc," Polithia replied, winking at her.

But just before Polithia left for the airport, Sasha was asking where the snacks were. Doc pulled out chips and onion dip, a large dish of plump red strawberries, and a few cartons of Pepsi. She put everything on a tray with purple-striped napkins and plates. Then she set a cooler of ice on the patio near the refreshments.

"Thanks, Dr. Zipley," Sandra said. "That looks delicious."

But Sasha ignored Doc and everyone else; grabbing a handful of chips from the kitchen, she headed straight to the pool like she had radar in her feet.

Polithia smiled and shook her head. "That gal is somethin' else!" she said.

Una suggested that Kiki go to her room upstairs to change into her swimsuit. In a few minutes she came down in her new rust-colored bikini. Everyone said it set off her tan, her tawny hair, and green eyes. She let her hair fall straight down her back, even though she usually tied it up at the public pool.

Sasha wore a hot-pink one-piece with matching sandals and silver hoop earrings. Her hair was in tight box braids to her shoulders. But Sandra just wore red shorts with a white tank top. Her hair was in crocheted braids pulled up into a bun in the back, set off by a red ribbon.

"Princess, change into your suit!" Sasha demanded, staring at Sandra.

"Can't," Sandra said. "I'm on my period."

"You ain't on no period," Sasha said. "Your skin's too clear."

"I am so!"

"Bull."

Kiki told Sasha she was being rude. "Chill out, Sasha."

Then Una came out to the pool in her black bikini. Her hair was barely long enough to put into pigtails on either side of her head, but she managed to do it and put a tortoiseshell headband on to keep the bangs out of her face.

"You can still stick your feet in the water, Sandra," Una said. "It feels pretty nice in this heat."

Sandra said she might later. Then she asked where her Aunt Polithia was. Una said she'd gone to get a surprise from her mom at the airport.

"Must be a big one. You know what it is?"

"I just found out," Una said. "My best friend from child-hood is flying in from Arizona. I want you guys to meet her."

"Sweet," Sandra said.

Kiki asked Una what her friend was like.

"Her name is Judy," Una said. "She can be really funny sometimes and sometimes she's as serious as a rock, but she's usually a lot of fun."

"Is she *a brain* like you?" Sasha asked, as if that were the farthest thing from a compliment.

"She's smarter than me," Una said. "But what do you think *you* are, *stupid*?"

"Shut your mouth!" Sasha said.

"Seriously, you know you're as much of a brain as any-one. Mrs. Carter told me you made the honor roll all the way through middle school. You just don't like the label."

Kiki agreed and asked Sasha what was so lame anyway about being smart. Sasha ignored them and continued walking toward the pool. She glided over to the edge with her signature stride, slowly dipped her toes in first and then slipped gradually in the rest of the way.

Una jumped in, splashing Sasha in the face with a two-handed splash. "Try to catch me!" she yelled.

Kiki and Jazz jumped in, too, and they all splashed each other hard. Una tried to catch one of Sasha's braids that had fallen over her shoulder, with no luck.

"Sandra, stick your legs and feet in, at least!" Sasha yelled.

...

"I think I hear the doorbell," Sandra said. "I'll get it."

Una jumped out and toweled off, hoping it was Judy, and it was. Polithia and Sandra brought her out to the pool, chatting away. Una ran to embrace Judy with a bear hug.

"And this must be Bitsy!" Judy exclaimed, pointing to the three-year-old walking out with Doc, holding tightly to her hand.

"She's a little shy right now," Doc said. "She just woke up from a nap."

The tiny girl had a peach-colored ponytail and was wearing a bikini with purple polka dots and had a lavender ribbon in her hair. She smiled at Judy like she remembered her, and Judy knelt to give her a gentle hug.

"I've missed seeing you, little stuff," she said. "And whoa! Your big sissy has gotten even taller, and I'm still short."

Una hugged Judy again.

"Watch out, you're about to topple me!"

"Everyone, this is my friend, Judy Light," Una said. Then she told Judy everyone's name and pointed them out, one by one.

Judy wasn't actually short. She was almost as leggy as Una and sharp-looking. Her cheekbones were high and tan with a hint of pink blush and her dark eyes were lined in black eyeliner.

"Bring your swimsuit?" Una asked.

"Right here under my dress," Judy said, pulling a floral printed dress over her head, revealing a silver bikini that matched her sandals.

"Let's play Marco Polo!" Sasha screamed.

With that, everyone except Doc, Bitsy, and Sandra jumped in the pool. Doc took Bitsy back to the kitchen to get more snacks. Sasha agreed to be Marco. She counted to ten with her eyes closed, then everyone in the pool yelled, "Polo!"

As many arms sliced into the water and splashed, it looked like half the water got tossed out of the pool. Finally, blindfolded Sasha caught Kiki. Now the others flailed around trying to avoid Kiki, since she was the new Marco; that is, until Sasha got bored.

As Sandra sat on the side of the pool, Sasha jumped out and pushed her in. Only Kiki and Una noticed. Neither would have worried about it, except that Sandra panicked.

"I can't swim!" she yelled.

Sandra hadn't admitted this to anyone. Kiki was far across the pool from her, but Una was about six feet away. She jumped out and dove back in as close to Sandra as she could. She pulled Sandra's head out of the water and dog paddled to the edge, tugging Sandra along while trying to keep her own head above water. By the time they were safely to the edge, Sandra was gurgling water.

Polithia jumped out of the water, and everyone screamed for Doc, who was still in the kitchen with Bitsy. Polithia slapped Sandra's back several times until she spit up. Doc ran out and gave her CPR. Finally, Sandra spit up, took a gasp of air, and began breathing normally again.

"You did this, Sasha!" Una yelled, angry as a mad bull-dog. "We need to talk NOW in my room!"

Sasha followed Una like a scared little girl, though Una knew she was neither scared nor a little girl. After Una closed the door, Sasha timidly apologized.

"I know that sucked," she said. "I'll go home now. I'm sure you want me to leave."

"No," Una said. "You're the life of the party. I don't want you to leave. I just want to know why you pushed Sandra."

"She's a *princess!*" Sasha said, tears appearing in her eyes like tiny falling stars.

"So?" Una said. "You're a *goddess!*"

"A goddess who will be working my ass off my whole life just to keep my pretty little head above water!"

"I see, so you're jealous."

"Don't shove my face in the poop; I already said what I did was rotten."

"Okay, I understand."

"No, you don't!" Sasha said. "Someone like you will never understand. Look where you live in this palace on a side of town that people like me hardly ever see!"

"Okay, I understand that *I don't* understand. So, do you hate me?"

"I don't know," Sasha said, wiping her eyes with her hand.

Una gave her a tissue and did something she hadn't expected to do. She put her arms around Sasha and cried with her. Una cried like Sasha was her sister; like both of them had been slugged in the face by a bully. Maybe they had been.

Sasha did something surprising too. She hugged Una back.

CHAPTER SEVENTEEN
FRIENDSHIP TRIUMPHS

asha felt bad about pushing Sandra, but she hadn't known she couldn't swim. Still, she figured everyone at Una's party thought she was a spaz after that; besides, the girl really didn't deserve it.

Unless she apologized, Sasha knew Kiki would never speak to her again, and Kiki's friendship was important to her. They'd been good friends for a long time.

So before Sasha left Una's place, she told Sandra that she felt bad about what happened.

"It's okay," Sandra said.

"No. It ain't."

"You were just playing, and you didn't know I couldn't swim."

"Yeah, right," Sasha said, hoping for a minute that's what Sandra believed for real.

"It's hard for us," Sandra said unexpectedly.

"What the hell do you mean?"

"It's hard for black girls, whether we have a ton of COH, or not."

"Okay, this is embarrassing; what the hell is COH?"

Sasha scowled. "Cash on hand."

"You think it's easy being the only black girl in my grade at a rich white person's school?" Sandra asked. "Well, it's not. It stinks."

"What's the big deal?"

"I don't fit in there and I don't fit in with you. I wouldn't fit in with the black kids at your school either. I don't even fit in in my own neighborhood. People stare when I walk down to the corner market."

"Oh, I get it."

"Once a county cop pulled into our driveway to question me about opening the front door to my own house. If Dad hadn't been home to show them his driver's license with our address, they might have charged me with trespassing."

When Sandra said that, a buzzer went off in Sasha's head.

"Sounds like a story I heard from a mixed-race girl in my biology class. She said she felt like she didn't fit in anywhere."

"So you *do* understand?"

"This girl was hot-looking and all the guys wanted to be with her, but she had a messed-up opinion of herself. She had dealt with hassles from both whites and blacks."

"See? Now you're getting it."

"You're okay, Sandra," Sasha said, trying to be more generous. "Maybe I just want to be—"

"More like me?" Sandra interrupted.

"Okay, maybe," Sasha admitted. "But you don't know what it's like to have to save all summer just to buy a decent pair of school shoes."

"Good point," Sandra said.

Then she told Sasha something that sounded nuts in a way, but in a way it also made sense. She said that Una called her a *goddess* all the time because she had personality and *style*.

"You have street smarts and exotic looks too," Sandra said. "In fact, you've got so much going for you that I suspect it makes her kind of jealous."

"And you? What about you, princess?"

"Okay, and me too. I admit, at times I'm a little envious."

"Yeah," she said. "I get that. You're cool though, but Una's kind of a hot freakin' mess, ain't she?"

"Yep," Sandra laughed.

"Then how come you like her so much? Don't she get on your nerves sometimes?"

Sandra said Una was so passionate about racial justice that she just couldn't hate her, even though Una often made her want to puke. Besides, Una was doing some cool stuff in the community to help.

"That's true," Sasha said. "Most of these girls out here our age are more concerned with their boyfriends, cliques and shit than they are about things like racial equality and housing. I can include myself in that."

"You've given up, haven't you?"

Sasha didn't care for the way Sandra could put things out there like red darts headed right for her.

"Quit pouncin'," she said.

"But it's true. You've lost your belief that things can change."

"Look," Sasha said. "They shot Malcolm X and King; they screwed up the Black Panthers and murdered a bunch of other black women and men. When do you think someone gonna listen?"

"But I still have hope."

"Why? You think some magic bunny gonna jump into town and make the white power men listen? No. I'm just looking at it realistically!"

"Not all powerful people feel that way."

"The ones that support us usually get messed up. I ain't living my life on dreams, because I've already seen too much."

"But you're strong," Sandra said, "and powerful in your own way."

Then Sandra said something which made Sasha feel like Sandra was passing her a fast football from behind.

"Everyone has some kind of supernatural power," she said. "It just doesn't work the way most people think it does; you've gotta connect with it."

"You're as crazy as Una."

Sandra laughed like Sasha's words were a compliment. "Yeah, maybe."

•••

Despite Sasha's apology to Sandra, Kiki didn't speak to her for several weeks after the pool party. She said she was tired of Sasha's attitude. But Una didn't mention her encounter with Sasha to anyone except Polithia. She said she felt it was a private moment, mostly between the two of them, and she was hoping sometime down the road it might lead to a closer friendship.

However, Sandra shocked everyone with her nonchalant acceptance of the pool incident. She held no hard feelings for Sasha and even asked about her several times in the next few weeks: How was she was doing and had Una seen her lately? It was as if Sandra had some internal spirit knowledge about Sasha. It made Una happy that Sandra was so forgiving in a world where that wasn't looked upon as a popular way to be.

Judy, Una, Jazz, and Sandra had an awesome weekend together. Polithia took them to the mall to see a movie about Harriet Tubman. The girls could hardly believe how strong and brave Harriet was: a *real badass,* they said. After the movie they stopped at a Burger King for sodas.

Judy talked about how her great-grandfather was treated badly when he came to America from Eastern Europe before World War II. This became a double insult after at least six million Jews were murdered by Hitler during the war. The Civil Rights Act of 1964 eased some of the discrimination for both African Americans and Jews, but Judy said that her own temple in D.C. was recently bombed.

"There are still sick people in society who will do anything to express their hate," Polithia said.

"Yep. There have always been a bunch of people around who prefer violence and insanity to brotherhood and peace," Sandra said.

"The hatred of some Americans was so bad that my Navajo ancestors, the *Dine*, on Mom's side of the family were made to walk over four hundred miles when they were relocated by U. S. government soldiers in the 1800s," Judy said. "They were forced to move from their homeland in Arizona to a place in New Mexico called Bosque Redondo."

"I think I heard about it in history class," Sandra said. "That place was like a concentration camp during the Navajo Long Walk of 1864."

"The Navajos were also badasses to have survived," Una said.

Judy agreed, but she explained that when the Navajo people were allowed to return to Arizona, they never fully recovered emotionally. They lost many members of the tribe from starvation, disease, lack of shelter, and outright murder. The children who were left were forced to go to settler schools where their hair was cut, and they had to dress like white people and speak English. They even had to be Christians like the settlers. It wasn't a choice. They'd be tortured or starved if they didn't comply. And the kids were snatched away from their parents.

"People need to be reminded that civilization was born in Africa and the Middle East; and civilization in North America began with Native Americans who came from Mongolia and Siberia thousands of years ago," Sandra said.

Una shook her head. She seldom got a chance to talk like this to friends her own age. It was painful to hear, but she wanted to know the truth. Her history classes at school were so focused on the antiquated classics in the SOLs that not much was mentioned about the history of Native America. Colonial history pretty much skipped over it, and the teacher never went beyond that historical period.

"After so much abuse, my mom says people can suffer from *intergenerational trauma*," Judy said. "It's like low self-esteem passed through generations. Children of victims often suffer from it—when it's the abusers who should have the worst self-esteem."

"Yeah, it's a thing. I've heard of it," Sandra said.

"Just think, Native American, African, and Hebrew cultures span thousands of years, yet some people still treat these groups like they should still be slaves, or not exist at all," Una said.

"I don't fear differences; I like them," Judy said, her face looking luminous.

"That's it, isn't it? Most people *fear differences* and they can't respect others if they fear them," Una said.

As she sipped her coffee, Polithia smiled to see how much and how fast the girls were maturing. "Time for me to drop Sandra off at her place now," Polithia said.

"Bye everyone," Sandra said, waving. "Hope I see you again sometime, Judy."

"Hope so," Judy replied.

...

Una hated for Judy to leave on such a serious note, but it was almost time to take her to the airport. She knew she couldn't resolve the complex issues on her mind in ten minutes. So she started a pillow fight that ended with both girls having ratty nests for hair, but at least they were laughing again. And just before Judy got on the plane, she told Una about the Jewish tradition of *tikkun olam,* acts of kindness to repair the world.

"I'll make a pact with you to set aside more time for social justice when I go home," Judy said, "just as you are doing in here in Roanoke. It's an important part of being a good Jew and a good American Indian too."

"You're lit, girl. I'll miss you," Una said as Judy turned to go through the boarding gate.

"Your turn to visit me next time," Judy said, smiling. "I'll take you to Canyon de Chelly, Mom's old stomping grounds. Oh, and I'll put your birthday present in the mail."

"Wow! Cool!"

And with a wave, Judy disappeared.

Doc was quiet on the way home, sensing that Una needed time to absorb all that had happened during Judy's visit. Una thought that, like her, Judy had known what it felt like to be an outcast. Sandra felt that way, too, sometimes and maybe Kiki did as well. She told Una that she felt pressure to compete for grades because her parents didn't have a lot of cash and she didn't really view herself as a totally competent student. Sometimes other kids even called her dense behind her back and tried to avoid doing labs with her. Still, she wanted to move to a larger city and start her own travel agency one day. Heck, everyone probably felt like an outcast at one time or another.

There were both positives and the negatives about being an outsider or an outcast. As a kid, Una had enjoyed a lot of the positives—like exercising her originality and creativity, but the older she got, the more she saw the tough side of that distinction—like being shunned at lunch when the popular girls walked by and told her she looked better on TV than in person.

"What, Una, did you have a stunt woman stand in for you?" they laughed.

Una had to remind herself that *most* kids got bullied or left out at some point in their high school careers and she, at least, was trying to have fun while doing some good in the community. If that got her negative attention, then so be it. Sophomore year was bound to be better. Besides, a little negative attention or even bullying wasn't comparable to the genocide endured by generations of Native Americans, African Americans, Jews, Palestinians, Asian Americans, and other racial and ethnic groups.

"I can deal," Una said to herself. "In fact, I can do more than deal, I can participate fully in this *free-for-all known as life*. I'll even triumph. And if I don't, at least I'll go down trying."

CHAPTER EIGHTEEN
TAKING THE RAP

On a Saturday afternoon in late June, Doc, her two girls, and Jazz picked Sandra up to do some work on the Grace Street property. Marsha and Rowe had just called Una from Chicago to wish her an early happy birthday. They told her about swimming in Lake Michigan and finding a four-foot-long alligator that had washed up on the shore. Una assured them that nothing that exciting was happening in Roanoke. She expressed her wish that they could all be there in Roanoke helping her on Grace Street and meeting her new friends.

"Maybe someday," Marsha said.

"Ditto," Rowe said. "That'd be awesome!"

"Kiki, Sasha, and Sandra would never believe it if I told them about our tour of the funeral parlor," Una said. "I think Sylvia already squealed about it to Jazz, but she didn't say anything."

"You mean you didn't tell them?" Rowe asked. "I'm insulted."

"Oh, I'm sure I'll get around to it," Una said. "Try not to get into too much trouble, girls."

"You're telling us that? We were just going to advise you to do the same," Marsha and Rowe said, chuckling. "Peace out. We gotta go."

"Peace out."

Una, Jazz and Sandra finished planting pink and white impatiens along the sidewalk in front of the duplex. While they were pulling soil out of a giant bag with eager, dirty hands, a car pulled close to the curb.

"What up, ya'll?" Sasha yelled out of the window, like it wasn't a question.

"Nothin', we were just waiting for you," Una said, lying. She was surprised to see Sasha.

"Droppin' her off, Doc," Mrs. Carter said, "if that's okay with you."

"Sure. Glad to have the extra help."

"Could you bring her by our place later? I've got to get to work."

"No problem."

"And by the way, I'm Annie," Mrs. Carter said. "Sure do appreciate it, Doc."

Una and Jazz asked if Sasha could stay for dinner and Sandra could come over too.

"Of course," Doc said. "I'll take the girls home afterward. I think Martin will let Sandra come."

"Sasha?" Mrs. Carter asked. "You want to eat with them?"

"That'd be all right," Sasha said. "Ain't got no date tonight anyhow."

"Good," Mrs. Carter said. "That's how I like it."

Una had to smile. Mrs. Carter always said exactly what she thought. She thanked Doc and reminded Sasha to behave herself.

Una asked Sasha how she knew they were over on Grace Street right then. She hadn't called.

"You girls are now *hip to the max*," Sasha said with a chuckle. "You were all on the local news yesterday."

"What?" Una asked, looking astonished. "I thought for sure they would cut that piece."

"Yup. Not just Miss Princess, but Miss Jazzy and Witchy woman too; ya'll gettin' a solid rep for building duplexes in the hood. All right now."

"So far, it's just one duplex," Una said.

"For real?"

"Hah, you mean we're actually getting a *good* rep?" Una asked.

"I guess," Sasha said. "At first I thought you, Princess, and Jazz were just all out *boujee,* but now even Roy is sayin' the Bloods are kind of proud of ya'll for at least tryin' to do somethin'."

"And what about you?" Sandra asked.

"What about me?"

"Are you admitting you're proud of us?"

Sasha didn't answer but smiled a sneaky smile and asked for a hoe and some garden gloves.

"Where's a hoe?" Una asked, looking around and giggling.

"Look in the mirror!" Sasha barked, laughing too.

Then everyone got back to work digging and planting. Digging and planting 'till they were bone tired and ready to eat. Slowly but surely, Sasha was being drawn in to the Grace Street project. Sandra and Una, especially, loved it because for so many reasons they were growing to love Sasha.

...

Doc thought Una was satisfied now that the Zipley family and friends were all working hard on the duplex and trying to make a difference in the community. Yet Una began tormenting Doc almost every day about the issue of slavery. She'd read Alex Haley's *Roots* and wanted to know if her family or her dad's had ever owned other human beings. She looked stricken, as deeply troubled as Doc had ever seen her, and she even accused Doc of being complicit in a cover-up due to her refusal to talk about it.

"That's harsh," Doc told her.

"Then why don't you ever want to discuss it, Mom?" Una asked.

Doc told her it wasn't a subject that she had any desire to dwell on.

"But you have to!" Una insisted, looking panicked. "Because if you don't, the *truth of who I am* can't come out!"

"That's *not* who you are!" Doc screamed. "I know I shouldn't have screamed. I try never to raise my voice to you, but slavery has nothing to do with who you are; you're a sweet, caring young girl who had nothing to do with what happened over 134 years ago!"

Doc asked why Una was so angry. Bitsy was having her Lucky Charms breakfast. She must have sensed the tension in the air because she began to cry as if someone were sticking sharpened pencils in her arm.

"It's okay," Una said, gently rubbing Bitsy's little back with the palms of her hands while addressing Doc. "It's an unfair question, Mom, if you don't already know," she said.

"I guess the answer will be unfair to someone, so might as well be me," Doc replied.

Then Doc said that they really needed to move on from bad recollections of those times.

"But you never answered my question!"

"Okay, my great-great-grandfather *did own slaves* and so did your dad's ancestors, but again, that was a long time ago," Doc said.

"Not *that l*ong ago, when some cultures are ancient. The U. S. is still a baby nation compared to other countries and cultures."

"I am sure that if you'd lived then, Una, you wouldn't have owned slaves!"

"How can you be so sure?" Una asked. "I might not have known how to free myself from the cultural customs of those times, so it would have been nearly impossible to have broken away from a societal ailment as terrible as slavery. But I might have tried to teach slaves how to read."

Doc reminded Una that the KKK became active just after the Civil War. If she had lived then and tried to be a social reformer, she could have been hung or shot, right along with former slaves who were accused of getting uppity.

"Couldn't I die trying to be an activist for racial justice today, Mom?" Una asked. "Aren't white supremacist
groups still around? What about the Freedom Riders in
Mississippi who got killed by the Klan in 1964 ... and there
have been so many murders of unarmed black people by
hate-mongering whites?"

"You're right, Una. I agree."

"And what about King and Malcolm X, and all the
others who've died senselessly?"

"I know; the list is too long to recount."

"Yeah, Mom. The list stretches out like a cross-country
highway. It all started with people thinking they could own
each other, but where does the injustice ever end?"

"Una, I'm sorry. I wish I could talk about this with you
now, but my head is pounding. I didn't sleep well."

Doc walked into the downstairs bathroom to splash
cold water on her face. Dark circles formed splotchy ink
wells under her eyes that resembled bruises from being
punched.

"But this oppression is part of who I am, and you can't
remove it from me like you'd take out a tumor!" Una yelled.
"My family was on the wrong side of history!"

Doc told her that was enough; the conversation was over.

"You can't take a scalpel and cut out the horror that my
ancestors caused. It's in my blood!"

Doc didn't respond, but at that moment she wished Una
could just have been obsessed with boys and incessantly
talking on her phone like most kids her age.

"What are you thinking, Mom?" Una pressed.

"I admit, sometimes I just wish you were a *normal* teenage girl."

"You mean a normal *white* teenage girl."

"Well, I see your point. I don't mean to be crass, but life goes on," Doc said. "I'm very sorry about the terrible tragedy of slavery and the cruelty of racial injustice, but life goes on."

Una said nothing more, but she walked away with a look of disgust and contempt. Doc couldn't sleep again that night. But despite the unwanted drama, Una had planted a seed in her heart and mind. Doc knew that she had to change her way of thinking about some things, even if it felt like she had just swallowed a hot pepper whole. She had to come to grips, somehow, with Una's pain. Her own father had once told her that pain was a *holy thing* because God honored it as a way of dealing with the tragedies that humankind often brings upon itself; the pain that people bring on themselves.

Doc picked up the phone and called Dr. Anna. Sylvia happened to be there too, eating a cup of Dr. Anna's *Melktert* milk custard tart, so the ladies engaged in a three-way conversation about racism, trauma, and rearing teens.

"Sweeping trauma under the rug is the opposite of healing," Dr. Anna said. "You can start by allowing for honesty, no matter how difficult that is for you."

"And remember that you're Una's world, Doc," Sylvia said. "She loves you a lot."

"She's not asking you to change the past either," Dr. Anna said. "Just to acknowledge it properly."

"To share in the mourning process."

"And stop asking her to be *normal*. Embrace who she is."

"Remember that few *normal* people ever changed the world."

CHAPTER NINETEEN
SEARCHING FOR ANCESTRAL WISDOM

P olithia had heard about Doc's discussion with Una concerning slavery. She'd seen it coming and it worried her. She told Una she couldn't comment on it because her mom was both a good friend and her boss.

"But you're one of my best friends too," Una said. "It's like having been closely related to a Nazi supporter in Germany during the Holocaust. You have to reach back and touch the monster that's in your blood before the wound can heal."

"Chile, you're asking too much."

"I know," Una said, "but *please* help me understand."

That night Polithia had weird, wild dreams of boodaddies, hexes and haints, roots, powders, and mysterious potions. Black magic. Voodoo. Witches so strange that she couldn't tell if they were demonic sinners or supernatural saints. She had not had such visions in over fifteen years.

She flew back to the Lowcountry in her dreams where she saw dimly lit palmetto trees and Spanish moss. She heard the cicadas and the katydids clicking and buzzing. Gray waves surged onto the beaches. Cotton and indigo grew in the fields.

South Carolina was where Polithia was born; where her parents, grandparents, great-grandparents, and other ancestors were born. It's where her father and mother died and her grandparents, too, all except for Grandma Hatie Dunbar, who took a job as a teacher at an all-black school in Roanoke when she was a young woman. The Lowcountry was also where Polithia's husband Paul's family was from.

She and Paul met in South Carolina when Polithia came back for nursing school. She had moved away for a while. After earning her RN degree, she married Paul and together they moved to Southwest Virginia looking for work. Paul had first looked at the railroad before Norfolk & Southern started laying off hundreds of employees, but Polithia sometimes knew things; she recommended that Paul keep looking. After the couple settled in Roanoke, Virginia, Paul found work in construction. It took Polithia longer to find a good job because she was very picky, but she loved being close to her grandma, so she hung in.

Una began to call Polithia her *root doctor*. She probably didn't even know what that was, but she said she had no one else to turn to. She looked plum sick, kind of like a crisp, dying fern. Not enough light and water.

"My dad told me never to ask a question if I didn't really want the answer," Una said. "But I did ask, and now it's too late to take the question back. It's in the universe and the answer will have to spit itself out, whether I'm ready to hear it, or not."

As far as Polithia was concerned, Una was part sheep bone and part spirit; too smart and real for her own good. She loved the girl dearly, but she saw her as fifteen going on forty-six, and maybe from another dimension. Una insisted that Polithia put her in touch with the spirit world so she might discover more of the truth about herself and her family.

"Maybe I'll find something to redeem us."

"I'll listen to the spirit for two days," Polithia said. "Then I'll do an incantation and a bone reading, but you're awful young and might be unprepared for this, so I'll have to have Doc's approval to let you in on the final reading, my actual contact with the dead."

Of course, Doc *did not* approve, so Una went on a fast that lasted eight days. She drank only juice and dropped some weight she had no business dropping. Doc got so worried about her that she finally gave in.

Polithia questioned herself some, but soon she received the voice of Nelly, a mulatto slave who'd lived in South Carolina near the coast in the 1800s. She was Paul's ancestor, Polithia's only by marriage. Polithia was not sure why she heard *her* voice.

"She's mulatto?" Una asked.

"Yes, a woman born of light brown complexion, often due to the fact that her slave master raped her mother or her grandmother."

Una's eyes widened with disgust, but she stayed quiet.

"Nelly was a house servant, pretty enough to please the master's fancy in the *great house*, instead of being forced to work the fields."

"Wouldn't the slave owner's wife have known?"

"Of course, but at that time wives of powerful men had little say about the sexual habits of their husbands. Her role consisted of being an elegant iron butterfly in a gilded cage."

"What about when children were born of the rapes?"

Polithia explained that some of the children could almost pass for white; some did pass. And those who could were educated at home and treated much like a natural part of the family.

"Those who could?"

"Every situation was different. Sometimes slave owners beat, tortured, or killed anyone who taught their slaves to read, including their own wives, but sometimes the master of the plantation was kinder."

"But what if a slave fell in love with another slave?"

"That was usually frowned upon. Slave lovers and parents were often split apart from each other and from their children. They were sold to other slave owners far enough away that they could not connect."

"What if they ran like those who went with the Underground Railroad?"

"Some made it to freedom, but most didn't make it. Still, many risked their lives trying."

"What about the churches? Didn't they try to do something to help?"

Polithia told Una that some churches in New England and a few other places were *abolitionist* churches. They didn't believe in slavery, and they tried to help, but many slaves had to run all the way to Canada to find anything close to freedom.

Then Una asked about Southern Baptist churches like the one her grandpa and grandma attended in Atlanta. Polithia said that slaves may have been allowed to attend, but for years they were forced to sit in the balcony, away from white slave owners and their families. That's why secret slave churches were organized out in the fields. A song or a hymn might notify other slaves of the gathering.

"Slave owners thought it was okay to buy human beings, yet they still called themselves *Christians?*"

The expression on Polithia's face clarified that answer. Then she turned off the lights in the room and lit a candle. "Nelly speaks now," she said. "Can you hear her voice, Una?"

Una could hear only the beating waves of the Atlantic, 307 miles away. She knew it was the coast of the Atlantic because she saw a lighthouse in the fog. It was Hilton Head. Her mom and dad had taken her there several times when she was small.

"Listen," Polithia said. "It's one of Paul's ancestors, Nelly. If her message is for you, you will hear."

Una heard howling and screams. It sounded like the voices of men, women, and children coming from a cave. Muffled screams. Desperate voices of people caught like animals in a deep cave.

"Help them!" Una screamed. "Help them!"

Then she saw a woman emerge from the darkness. Blue beams of light illuminated her silhouette as she walked slowly toward Una with her arms and hands outreached. There seemed to be a dark shadow behind her, but Una couldn't tell for sure if there were two silhouettes or just one.

"Help us find the light," Nelly whispered.

Una reached for her hands and almost touched them when Polithia blew out the candle and rushed to turn on the lamp. Tears stained her smock and mascara ran down her cheeks like small, blackened streams.

"That's enough," she said firmly. "Let it be."

"Have I intruded?" Una asked, despair engulfing her as though she were lost in the waves.

"You visited the past," Polithia replied. "That takes guts."

"But I . . . ?"

"I know," Polithia said. "You felt helpless, like a mockingbird fallen and crushed on a rock."

"Yes."

"There was nothing more you could do," Polithia said.

"I wanted to know that Nelly was all right and that she was in heaven. And I thought I saw a second shadow . . ."

"Not time for you to know about that," Polithia said. "What you want and what you need are two different things."

"What do you mean?"

"You need to remember what you could not have known, but not all at once," she said. "It's too much."

And as though the candle had flickered on again, Una did remember a glimpse of something. For a moment in time, she remembered the suffering of a great wave of humanity, people who were kidnapped, chained, and brought to this country from Africa against their will. Those people were forced to work in the agonizingly hot fields from sunrise to sundown. The women were made to live in the houses of powerful men who raped them. Their hands bled from picking cotton all day and they were sometimes whipped until they were half dead. Many died on the way over on the ships. Their bodies were simply thrown overboard.

Una now understood why the person who does extraordinary evil takes on the blood of the victim. It's something that time, alone, can't erase. Such crimes will be borne by humanity for centuries to come, because all people are all a part of one ever-beating heart.

Polithia put her arms around Una and rocked her like the nurse she was, rocking the child Una had been just moments before. They both tried to cry out the curse, but there weren't enough tears.

Polithia was right: Una could not have dealt with more during this session. But Polithia was a good medium and Una knew she could help her go back past the gates of time at least once more.

I need to know who or what the shadow was, Una thought.

CHAPTER TWENTY
SOCIAL REJECT

A week later, Una was still reeling from her contact with an actual former slave. She decided to call Sylvia, not knowing that Doc had also recently called her. She hoped the reading hadn't been too traumatic for Polithia, and she was concerned about Doc as well.

When Sylvia answered the phone, Una told her as clearly as she could about her recent trauma and the spiritual event involving Polithia and Nelly.

"Polithia and I have some things in common; the main one being South Carolina and our common Gullah upbringing," Sylvia said. "And, of course, we're both in the medical profession."

"That's true."

"I guess we missed a great deal by deciding to stay in Alexandria for a while."

"No kidding. But you can still change your minds."

"Well, at least Jazz still calls me every night, and you know she's on her way back to our place to visit her Uncle Mat and me for a week."

"Oh, yeah. Sorry, Sylvia. I've missed you, but I've been pretty busy. I should call more often though, and I wish I could have come with Jazz, but I promise I'll do it soon if you'll let me."

"Sure, I will let you, gal. Get it together and come on up soon as you can."

"Looking forward to it."

"'Besides, that boy you met at the pool been askin' about you."

"Oh, you mean Patrick. Really?"

"Yeah, really. Well, let's put that aside and talk about this concern you have with slavery."

"I never told Mom about the spiritual reading with Polithia and my contact with Nelly."

"Maybe that's okay for now. Girls your age have to keep a few secrets. And Doc knew about the reading."

"So you don't think I should feel guilty about it?"

"I think you should apologize for the other things you said."

"Like what?"

"Like forcing her to talk about something she didn't feel comfortable talking about at the time."

"She told you?"

"A little. She thought she'd been a bad mother."

"Oh, no. It was just that—"

"I get it. You don't have to explain, Una, but you do need to talk to her. Tell her she deserves your patience. She does, you know."

"Okay. I'll try."

...

Una woke up when it was still dark to fix breakfast for Doc. She made pancakes with syrup, half a grapefruit, and coffee. She put raisin smiles on the blueberry pancakes to thank her mom for letting her explore the past with Polithia, dangerous as it may have seemed. She also wanted to apologize for rushing a discussion that had been unbearable for Doc.

"I know, Mom, you just want me to be a happy-go-lucky, *normal* teenager, but that's not who I am; it goes against my vision of myself," Una said while munching on her pancakes. "I've never wanted to be *normal.* I want to be *exceptional,* but I am really sorry for putting pressure on you."

"I'm sorry too," Doc said. "It's true that anyone who is willing to fight for change in this world *has to be* exceptional."

"I want to be able to throw off the status quo, which is a powerful, evil rock that presses down on my back until at times I feel that I can hardly breathe."

"I think I see where you're coming from."

"Some people call kids like me *social rejects*, but it's really me rejecting what I hate about society. I can't fit into the accepted mold because my heart tells me that's the riskiest thing I can do."

"You scored a ten with these pancakes," Doc said, trying to gently change the subject.

"Mom, I haven't been happy-go-lucky since probably I was a year old. Even then I sweat dirty diapers like they were a major curse. When I potty trained, I sat on the throne too long. You and Dad had to give me Gummy Bear prizes to get me off."

"You know, you're right. I'd almost forgotten."

"When I was four, a dark-skinned woman named Madonna Adeline often came to me in my dreams. She wore a shimmering blue gown with sequins on it and had a glowing wand that probably interested me more than it should have."

"Oh, yes. You told us she wore work boots and red-striped wool socks with the sequined gown."

"She blessed me so many times that at first I thought she was an angel," Una said. "I'd heard about them from my *Angel Dumplin* book by Mary Anne Saucer."

"I remember that adorable little book. We saved it for Bitsy."

"But she said she wasn't an angel. She claimed to be a life guide with a message. She said God loved me and would see that I was never abandoned."

"Ah, yes. And didn't she assure you that even if you were to fall off the world by accident, you'd still be all right?"

"Exactly," Una said, flashing a resplendent smile full of the rich past, the miracles of the present, and daring hopes for the future.

"You and Dad thought Madonna Adeline was just an imaginary friend."

"I recall that Mrs. Flounderscope, your kindergarten teacher, told me you were gifted, so I should leave you alone. I tried to, but you're forgetting something important."

"What?"

"We thought of the imaginary world as a world as real as myth or fiction. In other words, we knew that myths told REAL stories about REAL people, and fiction was a candle leading people a step beyond what they thought they believed—until it happened to them."

"Cool. I do remember that Dad respected my play in the woods and my imaginary rituals with tree branches and certain special rocks and moss. When I was in the first grade, I asked him if we were related to any fairies or witches."

"'I wouldn't be surprised,' he said. 'Maybe elves on my side.'"

Doc and Una both laughed. Bitsy even chuckled from her highchair. Though she may not have known what was so funny, she heard the words *fairies and elves*, and she knew she liked them because they were prominent in the books Una or Doc read to her before bedtime.

"Look at cutie pie," Doc said.

Bitsy had pancake and blueberry syrup all over her face, and her hands waved in the air as if her cheeks were an abstract art canvas and her fingers were the brushes.

"Better clean up, Little Bitz," Una said, "Don't you want to play basketball?"

"Clean up!" Bitsy screamed.

Bitsy's miniature basketball and hoop were on the patio.

"Get dressed quick so I can pass you the ball!" Una said.

"You're a good big sister," Doc said with a glisten in her eye. "Much as you hated me having another child, you've been wonderful to Bitsy."

Una seemed to ignore her mom's sentimentality. "Bitsy's okay," she said, pulling the sticky girl from her highchair. "Just pray I can forgive her when she gets better than me at basketball."

On a Thursday night after Jazz had gone to see Sylvia and Mat, Kiki called Una in a panic. She sounded bombed. "What's wrong?" Una asked when Kiki couldn't stop choking up with tears.

"My head is spinning, probably from drinking a half a bottle of Thunderbird that I got my brother to buy for me from some guy he knows. My throat also feels sore and hoarse."

"Why did you do that to yourself?"

"Mom has cancer," Kiki said. "I didn't want to tell anyone, but she hasn't been able to work for several months."

"I'm so sorry," Una said.

Kiki broke into a sob so deep she could hardly catch her breath.

"It's nearly 10:00 p.m.," Una said. "Mom won't let me out this late, but I can meet you tomorrow at the coffee shop on Elm; say at two?"

"Okay."

"Is your mom on chemo?"

"Yes. That's what's making her puke all the time."

"Okay, I'll see you tomorrow. Try not to worry too much, and please don't drink anymore alcohol or take any pills."

Una got to the Russian Tea and Coffee Room a few minutes before two. Kiki was already standing there waiting, her usually perfect peaches-and-cream face looking splotched and swollen.

Una bought them both iced coffees and they plopped down in the comfortable red velvet chairs.

"My mom hasn't been able to work because the chemo makes her weak and she throws up all the time."

"I'm sorry."

"My dad has had to support the family, but what he brings in as a maintenance supervisor doesn't pay all the bills, including the tons of medical bills that insurance won't cover."

"What can I do?"

"I don't want money. That's not why I called you."

"I know that."

"Una, you believe in prayer and the supernatural. Could you meet my mom and lay hands on her or something?" Kiki begged.

"I believe in the transcendental, which does include the supernatural," Una said. "Just look at all the miracles in the Bible and you'll see. If they're good enough for Jesus and the disciples, they're okay by me."

"That's why I thought you could help."

"I'd like to meet your mom, but it's more complicated than just praying or laying hands on someone."

"Why? I've heard of it lots of times."

"Does your mom go to church somewhere?"

"No, Mom used to work Sundays and now Dad sleeps late on Sundays."

"I get it," Una said. "I need some time to think."

Una agreed to at least meet Mrs. Rogers and said she'd pray for her. She asked if she could tell Polithia. Kiki said she could if she wanted, but not Doc.

"I don't want this to get around the medical community," Kiki said.

The next afternoon, when Una told Polithia about Kiki's mom, she was advised that supernatural cures probably wouldn't work unless Mrs. Rogers's will and faith were aligned with the possibility of such an experience.

"What exactly did Polithia say?" Kiki asked. "Talk plain, like in my language."

"Polithia warned that cancer cures may go down many layers into the subconscious ground of being and then arch up into other realms. These may be dimensions that are unknown to us, such as parallel universes," Una explained.

"That's not what I mean by *my language*."

"It's complicated," Una insisted. "Polithia said what I'm about to undertake is daunting, at best, and could be dangerous if it were to fail, or if it was never meant to be. Still, she said it was my choice."

"Please, Una. You've got to help us. My family is falling apart over this, and I don't want my mother to die!"

"I'll see what I can do, Kiki. I promise I'll try."

Kiki told Una she'd love her as a friend forever if only she could pull this off, or at least give it her best shot.

"It's not me, Kiki," Una maintained. "It's the *Great Spirit*. It's the healing of supernatural energies that keeps us alive in this world."

"*Whatever.* Just please help."

Una prayed to the Great Spirit for direction. She wanted to ensure that her ego did not interfere with this decision. But that was easier said than done.

How can I be certain that deep down I don't want Kiki or her mom to think I'm some kind of savior? Una asked herself.

Una knew if a healing were successful, there might be talk of avatars and angels, magic power, talismans, and wizardly amulets; yet she wanted none of that. Not now. She just wanted Kiki to be happy again and Lindsay Rogers to walk free of the cancer demon. She also she didn't want Kiki's home to be repossessed, something Kiki greatly feared. The bank had already contacted her dad about a time limit for non-payment of the mortgage. That limit was fast approaching. Kiki's house in Southeast Roanoke was the only home she had ever known.

Even though the yard was small, Kiki and her brother had spent many summers playing badminton out there. She knew most of her neighbors and volunteered once a week at the library around the corner. Her mom had grown a vegetable garden in a section of the backyard. Neighbors were invited to pick tomatoes, cucumbers, and sweet potatoes when they were ripe. Some showed Kiki and her brother how to can cucumbers to make pickles.

The Sunday after Una met with Kiki, she went to a church Sandra had told her about in Northwest Roanoke: Garden of Our Savior Baptist Sanctuary on Olive Street. Some friends in Dr. Davis's bridge club attended there. Una filled out the online form for transport and sure enough, a small green bus marked *For the Glory of Christ* picked her up at exactly 9:00 a.m., in time to get there for Sunday School.

Una invited Jazz, but she was too tired, having just returned from Alexandria.

Although Una was the only white person in the church, she felt much more at home there than at South Roanoke's Peoples' Presbyterian, where her mom attended occasionally.

Three women and two men greeted her during the service; four of them gave her a quick, gentle hug and asked her to put her name and email on a list for the Bishop's Newcomers' Task Team.

The first hymn was "Swing Low, Sweet Chariot." A knock-'um-dead female soloist sang the first verse. Then the whole choir of about thirty male and female singers joined in. Everyone swayed to the rhythm of the music.

The next hymn, "There Is a Balm in Gilead," had the entire congregation clapping to the more contemporary beat provided by the keyboard player. The keyboard seemed to have a voice of its own that rippled up unexpectedly, then deflected back, creating a rich, jazzy sound.

Una found herself kneeling at the altar when the call was given for everybody who wished to commit or recommit their lives to Jesus. He was the Hebrew carpenter who had lived a modest life, healed people, did miracles, taught about love, and was murdered on a tree at age thirty-three.

She asked the *Great Spirit* of Jesus to humble her, guide her, fill her, and use her to help Kiki's family in any way she could, and to protect Kiki and the Rogers family from evil.

"You got a special need?" Bishop Morrison leaned down to whisper in Una's ear.

"Yes," she said.

"Come to my office after the service, young lady."

"I'd like to, but I have to ride the bus home."

"Oh, it won't leave for another forty minutes or so. First, refreshments will be set out downstairs in the social hall."

After a soul-ripping, *call-and-response* sermon on forgiveness, Una's knees felt weak, and her head spun a little. She couldn't tell if she was headed for the gates of hell or the raptures of heaven, but she definitely wasn't going to be spewed out of anyone's mouth for being lukewarm. She tiptoed into Bishop Morrison's office and seated herself in one of his tan leather office chairs. A picture of Dr. Martin Luther King Jr. adorned the wall behind his commodious desk.

"What is bothering you, child?" he asked.

In the next thirty minutes Una poured out her heart to Bishop Morrison. She talked about her desire to heal Kiki's mother and help save the house Kiki's family might lose, about black Madonna Adeline when she was small, about contacting the former slave Nelly, who had spoken to her through her Gullah friend, Polithia. She mentioned the shadow behind Nelly, the Grace Street duplex, and wanting to help save the entire Northwest part of the city from further destruction. She wasn't sure of the order in which she had addressed these concerns, but Una knew she'd touched on each one briefly.

"You sound frantic," the Bishop Morrison said. "And for good reason; you cannot attempt this healing alone."

"Then what should I do?"

"I'm sending my Worship and Praise team out with you to meet Mrs. Rogers, the lady with the cancer."

"You are?"

"Several of them are Geechee, from Georgia, and one is Gullah from South Carolina Indigo country."

"That would be greatly appreciated!"

"Yes, we have a gentleman born and reared in the Lowcountry who is particularly called to this kind of healing."

"You'll send him?"

"Just a few of us will meet with you and Mrs. Rogers first, and then we'll all pack the bus and we'll come whenever it's convenient for your family, Kiki, and her mother."

"Oh, thank you so much!" Una exclaimed, rushing to give the kind man of God a hug. "Wait, Una," he said, looking stern. "I want you to back up a bit before you go."

"Sir?"

"You said something about *a shadow* you saw when you did the spiritual reading of the former slave."

"Yes, there was a shadow behind Nelly. I only saw it for a second, but I'm almost certain I saw something like another silhouette."

"I feel that this riddle has to be solved before the Praise Team comes."

"What do you suggest?"

"First, I'm going to visit you at your home with Shadwell Brooks, the Gullah man on our team."

"But my mom doesn't even know about Kiki's family, and I promised I would only tell Polithia."

"Well, now you've told me, and I'll be sharing it with a whole Praise Team, so I think it would be best for you to let your mother and Kiki's family know right away."

Bishop Morrison supervised the first meeting at Una's house. Everything went well, except that Una still could not identify the shadow behind Nelly. He advised her to invite Politiha and her brother-in-law, Dr. Martin Davis, to the second meeting.

The following Saturday, Jazz went bowling with friends from school and Doc dropped Bitsy off at the sitter's so she could attend a Junior Ladies' League meeting. Before she left, she put out a fresh pot of coffee with lavender napkins. She fetched yellow glads from the solarium to put in on the dining room table. Then Una set out the white china coffee cups and dessert plates with the silver sugar cup and creamer, and a silver serving dish of warm croissants.

Around five in the afternoon, Martin Davis rang the doorbell. Soon after, Bishop Morrison and Mr. Shadwell Brooks filed in. A few minutes later, Polithia, Kiki, Mrs.

Rogers, and the church members arrived and joined them in the dining room. Una made the introductions for about twelve people and served refreshments. Then she lit the candles and dimmed the lights.

Dr. Davis began by explaining to Mrs. Rogers that God often uses the science of medicine for some of His best healing miracles. He asked several questions about her chemotherapy and radiation.

She quietly answered and flashed everyone an uneasy, half-smile.

Then Mr. Brooks asked everyone to stand in a circle and hold hands while Bishop Morrison prayed. His prayer made Una cry, and when he said *Amen*, a heavy weight was lifted from her body, a weight she hadn't known she had been carrying.

"Una, when you called out Nelly's name, who or what do you think the shadow behind her represented?" Bishop Morrison asked.

"I have no idea," Una said.

"Conjure the vision once more if you can," Mr. Brooks directed. "Hold my hand and Mrs. Davis' hand while you pray."

"I will also lay my hand on your back," Polithia said.

Kiki looked dazzled and slightly frightened, but Mrs. Rogers just looked exhausted, like a fragile wounded deer that had run too far in the meadow, trying to avoid its enemy.

Concentrate! Una scolded herself.

"Pray now," Polithia said. "Let go of yourself and pray for Higher Wisdom."

"Help me, Polithia!" Una cried out. "I want—"

"It's not what you *want*, it's what you *need*," Polithia reminded her. "The Almighty knows what we *all* need."

At last, something in Una settled. She sat still with her thoughts, breathed deeply, and closed her eyes. She let her mind drift past the whitewashed rooms of her house, into the yard, and down the street into hundreds of yards belonging to people she didn't know. Then she realized that her feet were bare, and she was running through a distant field, past trees, gurgling streams, and rushing rivers. She was nearing a desert valley with rock formations in the shape of hands. Then she passed the deep, crimson canyons at sunset and down into a vast flat land near an ocean of 600,000 dark bodies.

Then a vision of a tall, shadowy woman came to her. The woman said she was Una's distant ancestor, Ellen. She waved and called her name as if Una were the name of the wind. Her long gingham dress was covered with an apron tied around her waist.

"Go back, Ellen!" a voice commanded. "The master will be seeking thee! Go sweep the terrace!"

"No!" she screamed. "I must tell Una and Polithia that I stand behind the spirit of my cousin, Nelly."

"Your cousin?"

"I must tell them that we are an ancient skein of kinship. We skip the light fandango, twirling and singing our rage and our healing; flying above the earth!"

"God!" Una gasped.

"We have moonbeams in our hair, electricity in our hands. We are the storm before the calm. We walk among the shapeshifters, Proteus, and apparitions of the dead; yet in the morning we fly past despair. We light up the air!"

"Ellen? My own distant ancestor, and Nelly's cousin?" Una cried out.

"Your own, come from the land of shadows and sun, darkness and light."

"Then, am I also the child of a distant rape?" Una asked, kneeling by a chair, her eyes drenched in tears.

"Beloved child of a distant rape, just as the Land of our Fathers was stolen and raped, you are a descendant of our painful past and one whom we entrust with our triumphant future."

"Amen!" cried Bishop Morrison.

"Your African ancestors are healers," Ellen said. "I will show you."

"Hold out your hands, Una," Mr. Brooks said. "The powers of Light will manifest there."

Una felt woozy with the realization of who Ellen was to her, and, since Nelly was her ancestor, too, she realized she was related to Paul and Polithia, Sandra, and Dr. Davis. Then she awoke.

CHAPTER TWENTY-TWO
OVERCOMING INTERFERENCE

The following Sunday afternoon, the entire Praise and Worship team (fourteen men and women) from Garden of Our Savior Baptist met at Una's house once again. Mrs. Rogers and Kiki were there, as, of course, was Polithia. Jazz kept Bitsy upstairs in her playroom as a special favor to Una. Bishop Morrison, who Una had discovered was the Reverend Dr. Charles Herbert Morrison, arrived in time to say hello to Doc before she slipped out the door to meet a friend for tea.

Mr. Brooks suggested that everyone gather on the terrace, a place that afforded more space and privacy as it was enclosed by a stone wall. A long glass and wrought iron table held refreshments. Una served lemonade, ham finger sandwiches, and almond cookies; but just as the group was moving to the terrace, she heard the doorbell. Looking out of the peephole she saw Doc's friend from the Junior Ladies' League.

"Oh, no."

"Hi, Una, you remember me? I'm Clarise Oliphant from the League."

"Oh, hello, Ms. Oliphant," Una said, feeling extremely frustrated. "Mom's not here."

"Well, do you know when she'll be back?" she asked. "I really need to pass something by her about preparations for the yearly Grand Sale at the civic center."

"I'm sorry, I don't know. She said she was meeting someone for tea."

"Well, I can wait if you think it won't be too long. I'll just sit in the solarium."

"Oh, I don't think so!" Una said. "Ma'am, I really think it could be awhile."

"Una, who are all of those people headed to the terrace?"

"Oh, they're friends of mine," she said, looking as though she was right on the fringe of desperate.

"All of them?"

"Yes."

"Does Dr. Zipley know you invited all those people when she's not here?"

"Yes, ma'am. She's fine with it."

"Still, I think I should stay here and wait for her."

"Ma'am, this is my house, too, and I'm afraid I am going to have to ask you to leave."

"You're kidding!" Mrs. Oliphant wailed like a wounded animal.

"No, I'm not. I'll tell Mom to call you as soon as she gets back."

"You do that, young lady!" Ms. Oliphant barked. "I had plans to set up your invitation for Roanoke Junior Socialites' Assembly this year, but now I think it wasn't such a good idea after all!"

"That's fine," Una said, escorting the indignant lady to the door. "I've heard they don't want very tall girls with green hair anyway."

"Good day!" Mrs. Oliphant exclaimed, staring at Una as though she were an insect with bubble eyes and thousands of legs.

"Have a nice afternoon," Una said, trying to be as polite as she could under the circumstances.

She tried to breathe and refocus, but Ms. Oliphant had clearly interfered with what was supposed to be a watershed moment for Una, Mrs. Rogers, and the others, all of whom would be involved in the healing process.

Polithia came into the foyer looking for Una.

"It was Mrs. Oliphant," Una said. "Someone Mom knows," her voice trailed off.

"I can tell by the look on your face that she wasn't a welcome visitor."

"No, not at all."

"Take up the armor of God, Una," Polithia directed. "Take His yoke upon you, for He tells us that He is gentle and humble of heart."

Those words strengthened Una. She pushed back her shoulders, stood tall, and marched ahead to the terrace. "Leave me, devils!" Una commanded.

Bishop Morrison greeted her with a glass of pink lemonade on a napkin. "May I get you anything else?" he asked.

"No thanks, we need to start."

"Would you like me to pray first?"

"Please."

Bishop Morrison asked everyone to hold hands in a circle for a moment of silent prayer. "God's will be done, Amen," he said, surprising Una with the brevity of his benediction.

Mr. Brooks asked Mrs. Rogers and Kiki to sit on two woven floor cushions in the center of the circle. They took off their shoes and sat in the lotus position, holding hands. A gust of wind blew through the magnolia trees, the pines, and the maples, tossing all the napkins off the table and scattering them on the floor.

"I want to light a candle," Una said.

"No need," Mr. Brooks said with the authority of a judge.

Una looked around at the prayer warriors and recognized the first poignant verse of "Amazing Grace." The melody and the words formed a powerful prayer that floated in the air surrounding the group. Una became one with the warriors as they swayed to the music.

Amazing Grace, How sweet the sound
That saved a wretch like me.

Sometime during the song, Mrs. Rogers' tears were unleashed like rushing water escaping a dike. Una knelt behind her, placing one hand on her back, and the other on Kiki's shoulder. Kiki looked small now, and more vulnerable than her mother. The warriors sang louder, holding their hands up to the heavens. Suddenly, Una's fingers felt as hot as burning coals. An electric field zigzagged from her hands, flying across Mrs. Rogers's back, neck, and breasts.

"Kiki, close your eyes tight!" Una cried. "And don't be scared."

"Almighty Father," Bishop Morrison prayed in a booming tone. "We claim the healing of this woman, Lindsay Rogers!"

"We also claim the complete healing of her family," Mr. Brooks prayed. "May they go forth into the world confident in your abiding love and filled with your grace."

"May peace be the sign of renewed life," Una prayed, "and may this peace spread throughout our community—to our schools, churches and other meeting places."

"Amen!" Bishop Morrison intoned.

No one moved or spoke for what seemed like a long time. Then Kiki and her mom slowly rose to their feet and embraced Una, Mr. Brooks, Polithia, Bishop Morrison, and each of the prayer warriors. After mother and daughter put on their shoes, they asked for something to drink. Then they slipped out quietly and reverently as though the day itself was sacred, anointed with a sense of calm and rest: peace.

After everyone had left, a boy Una knew from school named Preston Richards stopped by to ask if she wanted to play tennis. She declined. Ms. Oliphant called several times, and finally, Doc got home. Una wanted to tell her about her links to Ellen, Nelly, and Polithia's family, matters Doc obviously wasn't in the mood to hear. Then Una tried to explain about the healing, but Doc wasn't ready to hear about that. Una hesitated to tell her about Ms. Oliphant's visit, but she knew she'd get in trouble if she didn't, so she nonchalantly mentioned it.

Doc rarely clinched her teeth when she spoke to Una, but she was upset that Una had apparently riled Ms. Oliphant. She said Mrs. Oliphant was *one of the most influential women* in the city. Una didn't argue with her or try to offer a lengthy explanation. Instead, she carefully cleaned up the terrace, put the dishes in the dishwasher, and, after checking to see that Bitsy had not given Jazz any problems, quietly went to her room to finish her homework.

Una realized that night that she'd reached a point in her maturity that signaled the end of a childish kind of intimacy with her mom. Doc might never understand her kinship to Ellen, Nelly, and the Gullah people, nor her desire to assist in healing someone of a devastating disease. Doc thought of Una's choice of an African American church as sweet, but a little perplexing.

"Mom doesn't *get me* anymore," Una told Jazz. "She says she worries about my apathy concerning social customs. She even wonders if I've lost my Southern hospitality."

"But she's a good person, Una," Jazz said defensively.

"I know. Mom tries her best to do what she can to help Polithia's family and to encourage fair housing across the city. I really love her. I admire her and always will, but we are two different individuals and I have to go my own way."

Una believed that Mrs. Rogers' healing coincided with her own. Through that experience she was able to uncover her true relationship with the past, her own strength as a woman, and God's gifts to her. She sensed a radical change in her self-perception—that she was becoming a person she could not only love but forgive. Yet as she described her feelings to Jazz about the healing and her relation to Ellen and Nelly, a question arose in her friend's face.

"What?" Una asked. "Jazz, what is it?"

"Don't get me wrong, Una. I'm happy for you. I am. But this stuff you're talking about is hard for a black person to hear."

"What stuff?"

"The slavery thing and your sense that you could actually be *black* because some distant dead ancestor said so."

"What do you mean?"

"I mean that even if you are some small percentage of black and it's not because you're related to the slave owner; even if you are, you don't know what it's like to walk around with *my* skin. Ask Sandra or any black person."

"What about Polithia?"

"She's different. She's employed by your mom, just like Aunt Sylvia. They could never tell you the whole truth."

"Then I can't ever be free."

"Free of what? For what? You're as free as anyone gets to be in this society."

"You'll never understand where I'm coming from."

"Maybe not. You should talk to Sandra. Maybe by some miracle, she'll tell you the truth."

...

A few weeks after the healing at Una's house, Mrs. Rogers' doctors confirmed that they saw no more evidence of a tumor in her left breast or cancer anywhere else in her body. They were surprised, since she had been diagnosed with metastatic breast cancer that had spread to the bone.

She told the oncologists about her *spiritual healing*, but they chuckled that she had already begun chemotherapy and radiation, so any physical changes were more likely to have been the result of science rather than spirituality or what they called *magic*. But her oncologist, Dr. Davidson, admitted that he'd seen things before that couldn't be explained through science or reason.

Kiki's mom said she was at peace with the healing and very grateful for it, wherever it came from. But she didn't want to go back to the hair salon where she'd worked for the past fifteen years. She wanted to work somewhere that wouldn't expose her to so many chemicals. Unfortunately, Kiki's dad was angry at the thought of his wife attempting to change jobs when the money was so low, and they were still getting threatening notes from the bank.

"It's no time to live in a dream world, Lin!" he yelled. "We're about to go under!"

Kiki's brother, Luke, almost always agreed with his dad, and was beginning to act out, constantly getting an older friend to buy cigarettes and pot for him.

"Shit!" Luke said. "Mom's being picky about where she'll work. Pretty soon we'll all be in a homeless shelter!"

Kiki told him to go get a paper route.

"Why don't *you*?" he shot back.

Mrs. Rogers said she recognized the *fear factor*. She said that before her grandma's death she'd warned that any heavy-duty change would usually cause people to feel insecure and anxious.

"Our family was already shaken by Mom's illness, and now they are having trouble believing that everything will be okay," Kiki said. "But Mom has developed enough faith for all of us."

"Shawn, I wasn't healed from a terminal disease just to drag my family into a homeless shelter," Mrs. Rogers told her husband.

Sure enough, Mrs. Rogers found work as a companion and nurse's aide at A Place for Mom and Dad. They trained her on the job, where she could work with the elderly people who were fragile, but usually kind, funny, and content.

"It's going to take time," Kiki said, "but I believe that eventually the overwhelming pile of medical bills will get lower, and we'll be able to keep our house. Luke agreed to mow yards and I plan to babysit whenever I can. I'm also going to start a savings account for college."

Mr. Rogers wasn't a man to buy flowers, but he bought two dozen yellow roses for Kiki and her mom. They were so touched that they cried.

"I guess sometimes it takes a minute to know you've been saved from an avalanche," Kiki said. "Thanks, Una, for everything. Would you like me and Mom to go to church with you this week?"

"Kiki, I'd love for you and your mom to go with me, but I noticed that your parents have a Confederate flag in the front yard," Una said. "Are you sure they understand that the Garden of Our Savior Baptist Sanctuary is an African American church?"

"Look, Sasha is my good friend, and I like Sandra a lot too," Kiki told her. "So why would I deliberately discriminate against black people?"

"Maybe you wouldn't, but what about the rest of your family?"

Kiki replied that her dad just had this *Southern heritage* thing going on. That was all.

"Well, could you please talk to him about it? That flag is a painful symbol for African Americans."

"Why do you care so much? You're not black."

"That's a long story. In fact, *I am* black."

"Okay, now you're confusing me."

"I did sort of a genealogy search, and I'm black. Not everyone looks black when they are. I've already upset someone else by telling them I was black, so can we change the subject? I just need people to be respectful; that's all."

Una told Kiki she could pick her up before church if her mom didn't mind.

"I haven't been to church for years. But witnessing Mom's healing showed me that God isn't just some old guy sitting on a throne in heaven somewhere playing a flute; he's a real dude who cared enough about us to come to earth."

"Yeah, He gets it," Una said.

Mrs. Rogers and Kiki picked Una up on Sunday morning to go to church. They also invited Sasha. She still thought Una was kind of a screwball, but after she found out about Mrs. Rogers' healing, she decided to give her church a try.

"Hope you don't mind if we brought Sasha too," Kiki said when Una got into the car.

"Of course not," Una replied, reaching over to give Sasha a playful pinch on the arm.

"Watch it, bitch!" Sasha said, smiling.

Then Sasha said she didn't know what to wear 'cause she hadn't been to church since her Grandma Carter took her when she was nine.

"You look good, Sasha," Kiki said. "Can't go wrong with lemon-yellow satin and spikes."

"Hell, that's what I thought," Sasha said, looking pleased with herself. "*Bad*, ain't I?"

Kiki laughed. "Yep, you're always bad, woman. Dangerously bad."

Una had on a navy skirt and flats.

"Guess I don't really fit in with you fashionistas," she said.

Sasha told her she looked tight with her lacy blouse and rhinestone earbobs. "You should have washed that damn green crap out your hair though."

Una shrugged her shoulders.

The 11:00 a.m. service began with the song "He's Got the Whole World in His Hands." It was one of Sasha's favorites.

"That was once sung by the great African American contralto, Marian Anderson," Una whispered. "It was *electrifying.*"

"Shut up," Sasha said. "I don't need to hear that mess. You think I haven't heard of Marian Anderson and her repertoire?"

Sasha sang along with the choir, louder than she'd meant to, until she noticed Una and Kiki staring at her.

"What the hell did I do?" she whispered to Kiki.

"It's your voice! It's so good!" Kiki said.

"Your voice has such perfect and rich tones," Una said. "How'd you learn to sing like that?"

Sasha ignored the comments and kept singing.

"I had no idea you have such a great voice," Kiki whispered when the hymn was over.

"Me neither," Una said. "It's rad! I mean, incredible!"

Some ladies sitting behind the girls tapped Sasha on the back and told her she had an *amazing* voice. After the sermon, the same ladies asked her to join the choir. She told them she'd think about it.

She mentioned this to her mom when she got home, but Mrs. Carter laughed at the idea, like Sasha was telling her a dirty joke. She asked what Sasha's gangbanger boyfriend would think.

"Shit," Sasha said. "A bunch of people think I have a great voice. What so wrong with that? Roy don't have nothin' to do with it."

She called Kiki that night and told her what her mom said. Then, of course, Kiki told Una. The next day, Una asked to come over. Sasha agreed, but she suspected something was up. When Una arrived, the first thing she did was ask Mrs. Carter if she wanted a shoulder/back rub.

"Why you askin' her that?"

"Just bein' nice. It relaxes tension."

"Mom, crazy Una want to give you a shoulder and back rub to relax your tension," Sasha said. "Can she do it?"

She told her to go ahead.

Sasha shook her head. "What next?"

Una rooted for another invitation to Sasha's house the next time Mrs. Carter was on her day off from work.

"Mama, crazy Una want to give you another shoulder/back rub," Sasha said. "Can she do it?"

"Oh, yeah, don't see why not," Mrs. Carter said.

That next day Una mixed up some valerian relaxation tea to offer Mrs. Carter. She also burnt some dried sage and cedar in the incense burner she always carried in her bag. She tossed in some turquoise, too.

She figured Mrs. Carter was uneasy to see Sasha do something as unusual as joining a church choir. At least when Sasha was being her normal unruly and temperamental self, her mom knew what to expect. But if she were to change, their relationship might have to be reevaluated.

"You going to be a doctor like your mama, Una?" Mrs. Carter asked.

"No, ma'am, probably not," Una said. "I'm not sure what I want to do yet; wouldn't mind being a holistic healer, but I've heard that doesn't pay much unless you cater only to rich people."

"Naw, I suppose it wouldn't," Mrs. Carter said. "But plenty of wealthy folks would come out to be your clients. I'd bet on that."

"I know, but I definitely don't want to give my life away to people who think they can *buy* my time."

"I get ya," Mrs. Carter said with a grin.

Una didn't mention Sasha's superior voice, or anything about church. She just fixed the tea while the incense burned, she prayed and rubbed Mrs. Carter's shoulders and back with her hot hands.

"Why ain't you havin' some tea too, Sasha?" Mrs. Carter asked.

Una hadn't told Sasha about the special tea, only that she wanted to give her mom a back rub because she thought Mrs. Carter was under a lot of stress. Still, Sasha didn't trust Una any more than she trusted her faulty alarm clock.

"You must be trippin'!" Sasha said. "I'm gonna drink me a Pepsi."

"Watch your mouth, young lady!" Mrs. Carter said in her shrill, no-nonsense tone.

The following Sunday, Sasha, Kiki, and Mrs. Rogers sat right up on the front row of the Garden of Our Savior Baptist Sanctuary with Una. When the hymn was announced, Sasha got out her hymnal and sang "Kumbaya" more beautifully than an angel in paradise.

But what made Una dry her eyes with a tissue that morning was listening to Sasha sing her unique, jazzy version of "Swing Low Sweet Chariot." Sasha was bound to know she had a gift that only the Great Spirit could have conjured. And although Una was a little jealous that she'd never have that Whitney Houston kind of voice, she felt inspired by Sasha in a way she couldn't quite describe.

After church, Mrs. Rogers and the girls had lunch in the fellowship hall. The fresh hot rolls, fried chicken, collard greens, potato salad, and iced tea made Una forget that she'd ever had a problem in the world. And she got so many hugs for just being herself, that she knew she'd come home to her own church family.

Sasha must have felt the same way; the Sunday after that she was singing on the front row of the choir, wearing a gold choir robe.

Kiki and her mom started attending every Sunday too. Even Mrs. Carter arranged to come now and then. And she said her back and shoulders were feeling better than ever.

Una heard there were some harsh words between Mr. and Mrs. Rogers about the Confederate flag, but Mrs. Rogers said if anyone wanted to stay married to her, they'd take down that eyesore. She also heard that Mrs. Rogers planned to host the Ladies' Mission Society of the Garden of Our Savior Baptist Sanctuary at her house before summer's end. She asked Sasha to perform her rendition of "Amazing Grace" at the first meeting. Mrs. Carter had already agreed to be there.

D r. Candace Jasper, Una's Aunt Candy, never married, but she happily settled into teaching sociology, cultural anthropology, and peace studies at Virginia Tech. She and her sister, Doc, tried to get together about once a month. It would probably have been more often, but Aunt Candy traveled a lot doing research. Even when she was home in Blacksburg, that was an hour away from Doc in Roanoke. She called her one day in early July. It had been almost five weeks since their last visit and she wanted to wish Una a belated happy birthday.

"What's happening, Dotty?" Aunt Candy asked.

She was the only person allowed to call Doc *Dotty*.

"What's not, is more like it," Doc said. "Bitsy is into everything and the rest is too much to tell you on the phone. Anything going on at the university?"

"Yeah, as always. Why don't you meet me for lunch up here this time; Tim's Farmhouse at noon Saturday?"

"Ah, yes. I love their steaks and roasted asparagus. Their mint juleps aren't half bad either. See you then."

"I know when you and Aunt Candy get together, it's usually just the two of you, but I was wondering if you'd mind if I joined you this time," Una said. "Even though I'm just a sophomore, I'd like to discuss universities; something Aunt Candy knows a lot about."

"Well, okay," Doc said. "I'll call Candy, but I'm sure she won't mind. Besides, you and I haven't had a real outing together since the Clarise Oliphant fiasco. I can get the sitter to watch Bitz. Do you think Jazz would want to come along?"

"I'll ask," Una said. "Thanks, Mom. Oh, could I wear skinny jeans with the lavender silk blouse that you gave me for my birthday?"

"Sure, I don't see why not. With your wedges?"

"Yep, the new purple suedes that Polithia and Paul gave me."

"Fine, and you can borrow my diamond stud earrings if you'd like."

"Cool!" Una said. "I might even attract a university man!"

Doc chuckled and told her to watch what she wished for.

That Saturday, Jazz had a date with a boy named Julius Domingo, who she'd met in biology. "Sorry," Jazz said, "but this is like my first date with a boy and my first date with false eyelashes too. Next time?"

"Sure," Una said. "We'll be back before dark."

That Saturday was a red-letter day for Una as well, because she had just had her fifteenth birthday and gotten her learner's permit. She was pretty sure she could convince Doc to let her drive up scenic State Route 450 to Blacksburg. Doc agreed, as long as Una promised to watch the speed limit and keep her eyes on the road. Una promised, but it was hard to ignore the Blue Ridge Mountains partially hidden in a gray-green morning mist. She thought that if ancient natural wonders like the Appalachians (including the Allegheny and Blue Ridge Mountains) could talk, they would surely be dangerous, at least to some people, for the simple fact that they knew too much.

Doc's encyclopedia said Cambrian fossils over 500 million years old could be found in the shale along the roadside, reflecting a time when the sea covered the valley. Trilobites had no idea they'd one day be replaced with American Indians like the Shawnee and later, English settlers, and later still—Civil War soldiers and more modern people.

"A swarm of screaming, hunting, and roughhousing humanity took over these hills in the time it takes God to blow his nose," Una said. "Just think if it, Mom."

"Yep. We're cruisin' history!" Mom announced as if she were in a fast-moving time machine. "But keep your eyes on the road, dear."

Aunt Candy was waiting for Doc and Una at the restaurant and had already ordered their drinks.

"My God, Una, you've gotten to be a year older and a whole foot taller since I saw you last!" she said. "Playing basketball now so you can try for a scholarship to Tech?"

"Tryin'," Una said. "They say I'm an okay power forward."

"I'm sure you're better than just okay, and I've heard your grades are good too."

"They're hanging in there."

"So, did you want to discuss colleges?"

"Yes, ma'am, after you and Mom catch up a little."

"Most of my news is actually related to Una," Doc said. "Like her newfound community activism."

"Oh?" Aunt Candy said, arching her eyebrows. "Details?"

"Una is close to my nurse and friend, Polithia Davis," Doc explained. "So when Polithia, her husband, Paul, and her brother-in-law, Dr. Martin Davis, approached me about fair housing in Gainsboro and Northwest Roanoke, naturally, Una was enthusiastic."

"Isn't Polithia an African American woman?"

"Yes," Una said. "And if you know anything about the history of Roanoke, you know why Mom and I want to help fight discrimination there in any way we can."

"What are you doing to make a dent in it?"

"We're helping to construct a duplex in the Gainsboro area, for starters," Doc said.

"My friends Sandra, Jazz, and I are getting a little famous and a little infamous, too, for our work there," Una added. "We've got clippings from the papers to prove it."

"Is that more *famous* in a good way, or more infamous in a *controversial* way?" Aunt Candy asked, looking over at Doc.

"That's the question of the day," Doc said in a somewhat sarcastic tone.

"So, Dotty, how is this affecting your practice?"

"Business is still okay from the looks of my patient load, but I've had a few odd comments from the hospital administration."

"Anything serious enough to elicit a response?"

"Not yet," Doc said, looking frayed around the edges.

"I never thought about that, Mom," Una said.

"You know, small town. But you do what you have to do."

"What does that mean?"

"Yeah, sounds rather ominous, Dotty," Aunt Candy said.

"Well, I have to live up to being my courageous daughter's mother," Doc replied, smiling mysteriously. "So, whatever the results of this decision, I'm in. I weighed it in my mind before we began."

"Mom, I don't know what to say!"

"Nothing, Una," Doc said. "Walking the walk instead of just talking the talk is part of every parent's responsibility."

"That's commendable, Dotty," Aunt Candy said. "Maybe that's why I'm not daring enough to have kids."

Doc laughed. "You don't even have a husband! Are you daring enough to try out one?"

"Not right now. I'm casually dating a man in the department but nothing earthshaking."

"Casual sex?" Una asked. "Sounds yummy."

Doc and Aunt Candy giggled like eighth graders instead of two professional women.

"*I wish*," Aunt Candy quipped, looking half serious. "Okay, Una, back to colleges; what are you thinking?"

"I'm considering Hollins, the private women's college in Roanoke, or maybe Tech."

"Both great schools. Have you considered a major?"

"Well, don't get all excited; it won't be nuclear physics, law or anything like that. Maybe psychology."

"I respect psychology," Aunt Candy said. "Of course, I'd also like you to look at cultural anthropology and sociology."

"Can you tell me a little more about cultural anthropology?"

"It's the study of cultural variation among humans. *Cultural relativism* is the idea that beliefs, values, and actions depend on an individual's historical and cultural surroundings and perspective."

"Sort of like understanding *diversity?*"

"In a way."

"Interesting."

"In fact, I may have an invitation for you."

"Shoot."

"I'm planning a trip to South Carolina just before school starts."

"Nice."

"Dr. Jim Gifford from the environmental science department and Dr. Tara Solonsky from archaeology are meeting me in Barnham, near Allentown, South Carolina."

"Allentown?" Doc asked.

"Yes, do you know it?"

"That's near where Polithia's husband, Paul, grew up, and Polithia's family is also from South Carolina. Why are you going there?"

"The other professors and I are all doing research," Aunt Candy said. "We want to compare notes for a multidisciplinary symposium pertaining to prehistory, social history, and current social trends in a small Southern town. That will include an exploration of the status of environmental and social justice in Allentown."

"I can see where they each would occupy a crucial piece of the puzzle." Doc said.

"You got it," Aunt Candy said. "There's some evidence that archaeological findings may go back as far as 50,000 years in the area. Yet, we know that there's a raging case of environmental racism going on there today. I'm going to study society and cultural artifacts so I can make a case for *cultural relativism* in the schools."

"Sounds like this will take a lot longer than a couple of days," Doc said.

"We'll make several trips. The research will take time."

Una was giddy overhearing a mention of the Lowcountry, Paul and Polithia's old stomping grounds. Her mind was busy making all sorts of connections that were risky, all leading up to a suggestion that she, Jazz, Sandra, and Polithia go with Aunt Candy on the trip. But she would need to convince her mom and Aunt Candy. The trip had to be for humanity, not just for pleasure.

"Aunt Candy, I'd love to go, but Polithia Davis has special knowledge about the area," she said. "Knowledge that might be helpful to you and the team."

"Una thinks she has a distant kinship with the Davis' ancestors," Doc said.

"Through Squirrel's side of the family?" Aunt Candy asked, legitimizing Una's assertion about herself.

"Yes, his side."

"Actually, it might have just as easily been through our side of the family," Aunt Candy said. "Is there any documentation?"

"No," Doc said, looking at Una with concern.

"Candy, you may recall that Una says she connects with the transcendental; the supernatural, you might say. She feels she doesn't need documents to prove anything."

"Okay, girl of many talents," Aunt Candy said. "Maybe I can help solve that mystery for you, ladies. I'll do a gene-alogical search. Dotty, if there's any evidence for possible kinship, will you consider letting Una go with us and encourage Polithia to come for a few days if she wants to?"

"This is freakin' huge!" Una exclaimed. "So Polithia and I might be able to go?"

"Dotty?" Aunt Candy deferred.

Doc nodded her head in timid confirmation.

"Dotty, look at it as a learning expedition. Una and Polithia might uncover some secrets about themselves or even a few that might benefit humankind."

"Exactly my thoughts," Una said. "And forgive me for being bold, but if Polithia and I go, I'd like to invite Jazz and Sandra as well."

"We'll see, Una," Doc said.

...

Not too long after her visit with Aunt Candy, Doc told Una that a distant kinship with the Davis family might have been possible. She didn't mention Nelly or Ellen by name, obviously uncomfortable with the brutal facts of slavery and Una's identification with a historical reality that Doc wanted to forget. But she did tell Una she could go to South Carolina.

Polithia, Sandra, and Jazz were also invited on Aunt Candy's expedition, but Jazz elected to stay with Doc. She used the excuse that she was too wrapped up in her new man, Julius, but Una knew there might be more to it than that—like Jazz's discomfort with Una's assertion that she was black.

Still, Una was excited about the trip and so was Sandra. She, too, wanted to explore her roots in South Carolina.

CHAPTER TWENTY-FIVE
SOUTH CAROLINA: THE GOOD, THE BAD AND THE UGLY

The day the VW bus pulled off from Tech's Squires Student Center, Sandra and Una looked like they were planning to be gone a month instead of just a few days. They were so giggly in the back seat that Polithia jumped on them for acting like little kids. But soon they both fell fast asleep, their flushed faces pressed against their traveling pillows that were balanced against the windows. When they woke up, they had nearly reached Charlotte, North Carolina.

"Want to grab some lunch?" Aunt Candy asked.

"I'm game," Polithia said, hearing two little echoes.

They stopped at Burger King for Whoppers, cheese fries, and iced teas. Still kind of foggy-headed, Una and Sandra didn't talk much while they ate. Back in the bus, the girls hoped Aunt Candy would flip on some music, but she expounded on South Carolina schools instead.

"Allentown's high school has been taken over twice by the state since the late '90s," she explained, "for performance failure."

"The school is 98 percent African American," Polithia said. "Almost all the white people have sent their children to Barnham, about twenty-five miles away."

"But why?" Una asked.

"I'm guessing mainly racism," she said.

"Recently, they've made a lot of progress in performance," Aunt Candy said, "especially in math and English."

"But they have a ways to go," Polithia said. "They're still at the bottom 50 percent in the state."

"What changes need to be made?" Sandra asked.

"Taking out the drugs would be a start," Polithia said. "Drug lords use the area as a transfer route to larger cities. I've even heard that the power structure wanted the schools in Allentown closed so they could create a highway to Savannah through the town."

Polithia added that friends and family near Allentown reported that the high school kids often brought drugs to school—and officials turned a blind eye because the corruption in the town went right up the ladder.

"They pack drugs in the ceiling, so putting the dogs on them or their lockers won't help."

"I'm not surprised," Aunt Candy said, shaking her head. "It's that way in many school systems across the country and no one seems to care; at least, no one in power."

The first day of the visit, Aunt Candy suggested that they stay at a small motel in Barnham, South Carolina.

They barely had enough energy to unpack, but everyone enjoyed supper at a nice Chinese restaurant in the town. Despite their exhaustion, early the next morning the girls popped up like yellow crocuses on the first day of spring, waking Polithia and Aunt Candy.

Right after breakfast, Aunt Candy met Dr. Gifford and Dr. Solonsky at a park in Allentown, about forty miles away from Barnham. They consulted together, then the trio of docs gave Polithia, Una, and Sandra their assignments. They were to ask Allentown's school and county officials about illnesses and deaths related to chemicals coming from the landfill near the Savannah River.

Aunt Candy gave Polithia the Volkswagen bus so she could drive over and talk to Helena-Dodd Chemical Company officials. While she did that, Aunt Candy rented a car and went to the school administration building to check on student graduation rates, mental health, social gatherings, rituals, mores, and other sociocultural statistics.

That evening, everyone compared notes. The news wasn't good. Aunt Polithia, Una, and Sandra discovered that the chemical company landfill site was operated as a pesticide manufacturing facility from the mid-1960s until the present. What they couldn't get from Helena employees, they got from research at the library in Allentown.

They learned that surface soils at the site and in the area were heavily contaminated with aldrin, benzene hexachloride isomers, chlordane, dieldrin, disulfoton, endrin, and toxaphene. Additional investigations uncovered groundwater contamination with volatile organic compounds in addition to pesticides. Contaminated groundwater migrating from the site continued to pose a threat to a nearby municipal well. Pesticides from the site had also spread to adjacent wetlands and posed a constant threat to the environment (see "Health Assessment").

Nearly every student at the local schools had a family member dying of cancer. The water in the town was still unfit for drinking, despite assurances that the town and the state were doing all they could to correct the problems.

The next day, they were able to visit a few classrooms at Allentown High School, thanks to Aunt Candy's negotiations with the local school system—and the fact that South Carolina started school several weeks before schools started in Virginia.

Sandra and Una chose to go during lunch. They hit the cafeteria, then headed to a few classes after lunch. Polithia walked around outside to see what the students were up to out there. They left just before three o'clock and drove back to the hotel to go over their findings.

"I was hoping that my predictions about drugs in the school based on friends' reports in the past were wrong, but they weren't," Polithia said. "When I walked outside I saw a D.A.R.E. [Drug Abuse Resistance Education] officer smoking blunts with some of the students on the picnic table out back."

"God!" Una gasped. "Did you say anything about that?"

"No use," Polithia said. "As I told you, the corruption goes straight to the top and probably still exists within the police department. The chief of police was fired for drug involvement a few years back, but then, somehow, he became mayor. What does that tell you?"

"My findings were also terrible," Una said. "One student told me he brings *hooch* in his thermos every day and no one checks."

"The students I spoke to wouldn't say much," Sandra reported. "But they laughed when I asked if they thought drugs were in the school."

Sandra asked if the drugs were packed in the ceiling tiles, but as she did so, a guidance counselor came to sit with her. The students snickered and shut up.

"When I visited one English class after lunch, the teacher couldn't get control. Kids were climbing over desks and falling on the floor laughing," Sandra said.

Una said the same thing happened when she visited a science class. The teacher looked like she was turning a pale shade of green, almost like she was one of the frogs they were trying to dissect. The lab looked infected with laughing gas.

Aunt Candy said she wasn't shocked, especially considering her findings.

"What were your findings?" Polithia asked.

"I'll tell you about them tomorrow," she said. "We've got an exciting day planned. Let's grab a bite to eat and hit the sack early."

After supper, everyone passed out right away, as though they'd just run the New York City Marathon.

The next day was to be the group's last full day in South Carolina. It was a Friday, and neither Sandra nor Una wanted to leave. Polithia wasn't ready to go either.

"We've got a special treat in store," Aunt Candy said. "We're going to Sheldon to visit the Yoruba Nation there."

"There's another nation near here?" Una asked.

"Yes, an impressive African nation," Aunt Candy said, "about an hour away."

She explained that the *Kingdom of Oyotunji* African Village covered close to thirty acres but was not considered part of the United States according to King (Oba) Ofuntola Oseijeman Adelabu Adefunmi I, who founded it in 1970. Its residents lived in the woods and often wore colorful, flowing robes.

The five travelers were warmly greeted by the people of the village. They were asked to be seated while King Oba told them a little about the culture of his kingdom. Aunt Candy and Polithia took an opportunity to discuss the school situation in Allentown. King Oba said he felt bad for the school children who lived just an hour away because he suspected that they knew little about their African heritage.

Then the king looked at Una and laughed suddenly, like he'd heard a great joke.

"Sir?" she asked, looking puzzled.

"You are trouble, aren't you?" the king said. It was a statement rather than a question.

"How did you know?"

"'Tis obvious to me; indeed, one day you will be known as the Queen of Trouble!"

"Good King," Polithia said, "you just *intuited* this information about Una?"

"Her ancestors are loud, and they surround her," the king said with a grin. "Indeed, they surround all of you, except the lovely doctor here."

"They speak to you?" Una asked.

"Of course," the king said matter-of-factly. "Just as they speak to you. Now let us discuss the needs of the students in Allentown."

The king proposed to send his drummers to the school if the school system would allow it. Everyone was thrilled with that idea. But when Aunt Candy called to clear the visit, the superintendent refused to approve it.

"Superintendent Gillingham said she would love to have the African drummers visit, but the school board would not authorize it for reasons she could not explain," Candy said.

"There's something shady about that," Una said.

Sandra agreed.

"Something's not right," Aunt Candy said. "The schools should be glad for the students to learn more about their own culture, and African drumming is an essential part of that. It plays a part in the emotional and spiritual life of children, as well as their physical well-being."

"It sounds like drumming would give the kids a physical outlet for their stress and their fears," Sandra said.

Just then Una remembered something else the king had said. He emphasized that the people of his kingdom had to learn to listen to the trees, the plants, flowers, and dirt. They had to love Nature as if it were both part of God and one's own kinfolk. Una wondered if the students at Allentown High were learning the importance of their kinship with nature. From what they had seen so far, she was pretty sure they weren't.

"Even though Allentown is an agricultural community, the kids are probably afraid to spend too much time outside due to the silent pollution they know is killing their land and their families," Sandra said.

The king mentioned that sustainable farming was one of his goals, but Aunt Candy said her research indicated that South Carolina had no comprehensive plan for sustainable food systems, especially in poorer communities. Certainly, there was limited funding for programs to help farmers in Allentown.

"The king is right," Polithia said, "about many things. I am sure the culturally deprived children in Allentown County are not aware of their Gullah heritage any more than they understand broader elements of their African heritage, even though these active cultures and their roots are all around them."

"Their ancestors probably dance and sing to them each night," Sandra said, "but the kids don't recognize them."

"How can they?" Una asked. "How can they know intuitive things when destruction threatens them on all sides, and drugs anesthetize them?" She wiped tears from her eyes with her hand and shook her head.

"I am sorry to say, there is more news that is hard to hear," Aunt Candy said. "Dr. Solonsky and I talked earlier about her findings. They were both fantastic and disheartening."

"What do you mean?" Polithia asked.

"Dr. Solonsky explored an archaeological site known as *Topper,* located nearby on the Savannah River. The artifacts she found indicate that humans lived in the area even before the *Clovis Culture*, so people were in this area by about 50,000 BCE."

"That's cool!" Sandra exclaimed. "What's disheartening about that?"

"It confirms that human communities lived in this area in the Upper Paleolithic Era, the Stone Age," Aunt Candy said. "Yet instead of this land being cherished as sacred, it is treated like a trash dump by the power elites. The children here are rarely taught about the amazing legacy that belongs to them."

"Their rightful inheritance," Sandra said.

Aunt Candy also revealed that white children in the local schools a town away were more than six times more likely to be offered advanced classes than African American children in Allentown. Pass rates were far below 50 percent in all subjects at Allentown High. Some teachers had not even been properly licensed, and dropout rates were predictably high. These figures matched high unemployment rates in the area. Widely accepted cultural practices were largely unidentified or kept under wraps, at least locally. Just over an hour-and-a-half away, near the beaches, Gullah and Yoruba cultures flourished; but again, as all of the group's findings suggested, kids only as far inland as Allentown seemed oblivious to it.

"I feel like screaming; I need to run!" Sandra cried.

"I know," Aunt Candy said. "We all need time to absorb this. We have uncovered so many tragedies and no real solutions. Hilton Head is just another hour-and-a-half away. We could spend the rest of the day there on the beach."

"That's a perfect idea," Una said.

"Maybe not perfect, but I think it might do us all some good."

"Why is it not perfect, Aunt Polithia?" Sandra asked.

"Because there is heartbreak in the air there too," she said, wiping her eyes with a fresh handkerchief from her bag.

"The Gullah people?" Una asked.

"Yes, our people make intricate, sweetgrass baskets and the Gullah have their own language. They practice their own religion: a mixture of Catholicism, Methodism and West African religions, with a touch of Cuban Voodoo mixed in but . . ."

"But?" Sandra asked.

"Their music, rich storytelling, cuisine, folklore, and art reveal strong influences from West Africa and parts of Central Africa," she continued, "but their land on the coast near Hilton Head and on the islands has been stolen for centuries and continues to be stolen today by unfair high taxation, gentrification, and other corrupt practices."

"Many of the Gullah and Geechee people have faced poverty and degradation as a result," Aunt Candy said. "St. Helena Island and many others off the coasts of South

Carolina and Georgia have experienced the same torment and destruction."

"I wish there were some magic spell I could cast that would take away the sorrow of this place and halt the corruption," Una said.

Polithia told her that magic came in many forms. "Listen to the ancestors. You'll find it one day. You'll find it, too, Sandra."

Sandra and Una held hands when they reached the white beach drenched with sparkling sun. "Let's run!" they screamed.

They ran with the wind in their faces for what seemed like an eternity, turning back for a just a second to see Aunt Candy and Polithia not far behind them.

That evening, when they got back to their motel in Barnham, they showered and changed for supper. They stayed there because there were no motels in Allentown.

They were supposed to meet Dr. Gifford and Dr. Solonsky at a Mexican restaurant famous for its meat tacos with mole sauce. Unfortunately, they couldn't find any Gullah restaurants. The girls would love to have tried the cuisine, but tacos would taste good too.

When Dr. Gifford arrived, he shared his environmental findings. He noted that air pollution alone in Allentown County raised the risk of health concerns, including asthma, heart attacks, allergies, and lung diseases. His research also confirmed Aunt Candy's findings pertaining to the toxic landfill and its effect on rivers, streams, and groundwater.

"And that's not all," Dr. Gifford said. "I discovered that Allentown at the Savannah River site was a nuclear weapon stockpiling area for the government."

"That means more cancer," Sandra said.

"Yes, there is still nuclear waste there," Dr. Gifford continued. "Contamination is unavoidable, and no one knows how long the cleanup efforts will take to be successful."

Dr. Solonsky also reviewed her findings pertaining to ancient and even prehistoric cultures in the area, and Aunt Candy concluded that cultural relativism (or the idea that beliefs, values, and actions depend on an individual's historical and cultural surroundings and perspective) had a lot to do with the blight in Allentown; while most children there were aware of the environmental abuse and racism, they were not as aware of their rich heritage. It was never included in the state curriculum.

"In spite of the horrible things we've uncovered, I have a ton of gold here for my symposium paper," Una said. "Perhaps it will do some good down the line."

"I have a treasure trove, myself," Sandra said.

"Explain?" Una asked.

"If the exotic, powerful, spiritual, and creative Gullah/ Geechee, African-inspired culture and the inspiring Yoruba culture were the inheritance of many African American slaves from the South, and if those descendants migrated North, then many of the black kids in Roanoke, Virginia, share the same heritage as the kids in the Lowcountry of South Carolina."

"They just don't know it," Una said, smiling, but smarting with a tinge of pain over the fact that she had not felt comfortable revealing her own blackness to Sandra.

"Yep. It's almost as if a buried treasure chest of gold, diamonds, rubies, and emeralds were buried in the front yards of many African American children, but they don't know it's there," Sandra said.

"They may never know," Dr. Solonsky said, "unless someone tells them. Are you that someone, Sandra?"

"If you could let these kids know how valuable they really are," Dr. Gifford said, "one of those kids just might become a legislator who would put a stop to the corruption, halt the pollution and help to save the environment."

Sandra and Una looked at each other with mutual conviction.

"I have my work cut out for me," Sandra said.

Polithia looked at Una, wondering what she was thinking.

Then she said it: "At least I feel like I'm a part of *a team* now, a whole team of magicians who use different kinds of magic like science and sociology, archaeology, psychology, and technology to explore the earth and its people."

"Those earth people who've been left behind will one day be the leaders," Sandra said. "Doesn't the Bible say something like that? I know the Koran does."

Polithia smiled her most enchanting smile. The two girls she loved as much as her own daughters seemed united in their mission.

CHAPTER TWENTY-SIX

MAMA ISA'S CLAN

B efore leaving South Carolina, at Polithia's request Aunt Candy stopped by Paul Davis's family home in the country just outside of Allentown. Polithia had spent part of her childhood a few miles away from her husband's family after her parents moved from Charleston County to a house near Allentown in Fairfield. Her own mom, dad, and brother had been killed in a terrible car accident when they were driving up to Roanoke to see Polithia and Grandma Dunbar. Still, Polithia said the Davis' place felt like home.

Polithia directed Aunt Candy, Una, and Sandra to follow a dirt road, then turn on a shady lane lined with pines, palmetto trees, cypress covered in Spanish moss, and sweet-smelling white camellia bushes. Polithia told them to look for the Gullah bottle tree—and there it was, a huge oak with hundreds of cobalt-blue glass bottles hanging from its branches. A slight breeze rattled them, making a soft, flute-like noise.

"How whimsical!" Aunt Candy exclaimed.

"They provide protection from evil spirits," Polithia said.

When Aunt Candy pulled up in front of the house, seven members of the Davis family came out to greet them. Paul's grandmother hadn't seen Sandra since Polithia and Paul took her down to South Carolina at age three, just after her mother died. Sandra said she didn't remember the visit.

Isabella Davis (called Mama Isa or Grandma Davis) was Paul's youthful-looking ninety-five-year-old grandmother. She said, "Who dese pretty girls?"

"The most distinguished is Dr. Candy Jasper," Polithia said. "This dark-eyed girl is Sandra Davis, Martin's daughter, and the tall, green-haired one is Dr. Jasper's niece, Una Zipley. Her mother, Dr. Dorothy Zipley, is my supervising doctor. Dr. Jasper is Doc Zipley's sister."

"You may have to go over all that a few 'mo time."

"Nice to meet you, ma'am," Una said.

"Same."

The old woman grinned and eyed Una for a minute, like she was inspecting a strange new product, but her intent wasn't clear. Then she reached up and grabbed Una around the top of her arms for a quick, surprise hug.

"Mama Isa, you saw Sandra when she was just a baby," Polithia said. "You probably don't recollect."

"Give me a hug, girl," she said, and Sandra, who was half a foot taller than Mama Isa, reached down to hug her.

Aunt Candy reached out her hand to shake Mama Isa's. "Ain't no shaker," she said. "I's a hugger."

Then Mama Isa grabbed Aunt Candy and reached up to give her a hug and a peck on the cheek.

"Polithia, ain't seen you an' Paul in gwone on three year when yo' mama, daddy and brother Teddy pass," she said. "So sad to hear dat, but then we thought you two done fell down a hole somewhere."

"Naw, Mama Isa, bless your heart, but I been busy, busy," Polithia said.

"Too busy to hug yo' ole Mama Isa?"

Polithia grabbed the old woman's face and kissed both cheeks. Then she hugged her for a long time.

"So, where my grandson Paul, and how he?"

"Ornery as ever!"

"Well, good. He gots to be to keep up with you, gal!"

"He's workin'. Said to say hello and he misses ya'll."

"Well, alright," Mama Isa said. Then she introduced everyone to her son Malcolm-Lewis, her son Luther, her grandson Belali, her granddaughter Quao, her great-grand-daughter Anyika, and her great-grandson Cuffy. They had all gathered for Luther's birthday. She said Anyika's six-month-old baby girl, Jilo, was back in one of the bedrooms taking a nap.

"We havin' stew and benne wafers; come on an' join us!"

"We don't want to impose," Aunt Candy said.

"Luther, they don't want to impose!"

"Come on, chilluns!" Luther said, waving everyone in. "I gonna kick Paul an' Martin butt fo' not comin' wich ya'll!"

The food smelled wonderful and looked even better: fried bacon, corn fritters, garlic chicken stew on rice, okra, and yam pie in addition to some delicious benne wafers made of brown sugar and sesame seeds.

"I'm in!" Una exclaimed, boldly taking a place at the dining room table before anyone else sat down.

Sandra sat next to her, wide-eyed as a little kid on Christmas Day, but careful not to grab at the food.

"Belali, pour the cold beer from the ice box!" Mama Isa ordered. "An' give dem younguns buttermilk or watah from the pourin' jug."

"Paul grandfather were Bailey Davis Sr.," she said. "Papa Davis die years ago of de cancer. He and I always like Hatie, Polithia grandmama, and all her peoples. Her mama were sweet as muffins. They come from James Island in Charleston County."

"What did you and Papa Davis do for a living?" Sandra asked, "I mean before you both retired?"

"I done basket makin' and done took in laundry," Mama Isa said. "Papa Davis were a farmer on Mr. Beau Jackson farm. Grew cotton and soybean."

"Must've been hard work," Sandra said.

"You ain't kiddin', chile. Work sunup to sundown."

"Schools down the road are in bad shape, Mama Isa," Polithia said. "We stopped by to visit Allentown High."

"I know it. Quao kids done gwone dey."

"Ain't no good schools 'roun here no mo'," Quao said. "Most white folk drive dey kids to Barn evy day but ain't much bettah dey."

"I understand," Polithia said. "Mama and Daddy sent me to live with an aunt in New Jersey when I got to high school age, or I would have been forced to attend Allentown. What are your kids doing now?"

"Don a military man," Quao said. "Station in Beaufort. Betsy in Charlotte doin' some kinda insurance work. Her youngun', Ralph, takin' classes at University of South Carolina. He want to be a doctor someday."

"Your kids and grandson did well then," Aunt Candy said.

"Prayer, daughtah, prayer what done it," Mama Isa said. "Most dese chilluns in Allentown gwone down to work fo' dem resorts makin' no good money 'tall. Some died of cancer 'fore dey even reach middle age."

"Do you ever want to go down to the beaches, Mama Isa?" Una asked, changing the subject to something she thought was more cheerful. "We just came from Hilton Head; so beautiful in the shimmering sun."

"Listen, Una!" Polithia said. "Don't be ignorant, girl. Didn't you hear what Mama Isa just told us? The resorts are taking over and many young people who leave here have to work for them after high school, making pauper's wages."

"Oh! I'm sorry," Una said.

"Ain't no way I'd go," Mama Isa said. "Last time I went near the water, a slip-skin hag pret' near tooken me down. 'Sides dat, the shadow spirits too thick; so many angry peoples pass' down dey."

"Root doctor Goodstone live near dey now, Mama," Malcolm-Lewis said.

"True, but he a elder like me. Ain't done no real conjurin' fo' some year."

"His daughtah do herbs," Luther said. "He okay."

"Herb ain't gonna burn no haint!"

"We believe you, Mama Isa," Polithia said. "We just happened to be near the shore yesterday and the girls felt like a run."

"Sounds like there are just an abundance of bad memories there," Aunt Candy said, forking her last bite of pie.

"Dem dangerous ethereal spirits dey," Belali said. "Put a blue root hex on ya; not only that, but the Gullah culture done took a big hit 'cause a dem resorts."

"Dat true," Luther said. "New roads and highways done tore through dis land on the way to the resorts. Businesses and homes done been torn down so de rich man can gobble it all up. Gullah blood done pave dem roads."

"Top a dat, we always been an oral tradition," Cuffy said. "But it's hard to keep up when kids so depressed nowadays, families torn up, drugs done spread juss 'bout ev'ywhere, and peoples havin' to travel an hour or two to get any kind of work."

"Dat true too," Luther confirmed. "Farmin' ain't like use ta be in de county."

"We still tells dem ole family stories to the chilluns," Mama Isa said, "but most dese younguns got other stuffs on dey mind. Say tales 'n stories don't mean much no mo.'"

"Tourist peoples carry on 'bout our Gullah sweetgrass baskets, quilts, wood carvings and other crafts, but dey ain't understandin' what we been through or what we 'bout," Anyika said. "An' don't nebah stay long 'nough to learn."

Sandra shook her head. "I'm sorry Dad didn't bring me down here more, after I was old enough to remember all of you."

"I'm sorry about that too," Polithia said. "Paul and I should have brought you down more than we did, even if Martin couldn't. You needed to have heard your family stories about survival—just like the kids around here need to know more about this secret family knowledge."

"We were just talking about that before we came to see you, Mama Isa," Sandra said.

"Maybe dat green Geechee gal dat got a runnin' mouth on huh and you, Sandra, our smart chile, can conjure a root or some juju to help dis lost generation."

"Geechee?" Una asked.

"You Geechee, ain't ya?" Mama Isa asked, sounding confident.

"I thought I was Gullah," Una said, "but how did you know that I . . . ?"

Una looked at Polithia.

"Didn't say a word," she said, smiling mysteriously.

"I'm distantly related to a former slave named Ellen and her cousin Nelly," Una proudly confessed. "But I thought Ellen was Gullah, so I thought I was."

"She probably from Georgia," Luther said. "Ain't no Gullah; she Geechee."

"We all cousins," Malcolm-Lewis said. "But de ones gwone to Georgia usually call Geechee."

"Well, I'm just happy that I'm still related to all of you, in a distant way, though I'm not proud of the probable reasons behind our kinship."

"You recall, Mama Isa, that Ellen is Nelly's cousin," Politha said. "Remember, I told you about the reading? And Nelly is a distant ancestor of yours and Paul's."

"Zactly," Mama Isa said. "But I ain't nebah thought I hadda me no green-haired relative! Not sure I gonna claim ya, chile! Look like you *triple trouble!*"

With that, everyone laughed and threw their napkins down on the table. Everyone except Sandra.

CHAPTER TWENTY-SEVEN
I MEANS WE

The supper conversation at Mama Isa's was the first Sandra had heard of Una's newfound racial and familial identity. Her mind was full of questions like puzzle pieces that didn't exactly fit, and she didn't like feeling the way she did.

Quao and Luther picked up some dishes and took them to the kitchen.

"Sit on down, Luther!" Mama Isa yelled. "Yo' birthday cake ain't been serve yet and Quao made it so it meltin' good."

"It Gullah dirty cake," Luther called from the kitchen. "Best chocolate cake in de whole world. Almighty Hisself be my witness, ya'll."

"Cut 'em each small slice; me too!" Cuffy directed. "We 'bout stuffed."

Una looked around at the room full of lanky people and wondered how they ate so much and stayed so thin.

Just then, Aunt Candy got a call on her cell. "Excuse me for a minute," she said. "I apologize, but I'd better take this."

While she went into one of the bedrooms to take her call, the rest of the party sang "Happy Birthday" to Luther. Afterward, Polithia said it was time to go. She and Aunt Candy had whispered to each other earlier that time was getting away from them.

"You gonna sleep right here in my beds!" Mama Isa commanded. "Too late for travel tonight."

Una looked at her watch; it was after 4:00 p.m.

"Can we stay 'till tomorrow, Aunt Polithia?" Sandra asked.

"Let's see what Una's Aunt Candy says."

Aunt Candy got off the phone and walked back into the dining room looking animated, but tired.

"Mama Isa has invited us to spend the night," Polithia said. "Might be a good idea."

"Oh, that would be so great," Aunt Candy said. "You have room for all of us?"

"Sure do," Mama Isa said. "Only Luther live wid me; rest dese chilluns got homes of dey own. We got 'nough beds for all y'all."

Aunt Candy said that the person on the phone was Laura Copperfield Meade, the famous anthropologist/ ethnographer. Aunt Candy had met her at a Harvard conference a few years back. She was calling from Charleston saying she could meet for breakfast in Charlotte about 9:30 a.m.

"Ya'll go 'head an' meet dat gal 'morrow," Mama Isa said. "Luther an' me ain't use to eatin' no breakfast 'till long 'bout 10, an rest a dese folks got things to do too."

"So, I guess we'll say our goodbyes now," Polithia said, hugging each of her family members except Mama Isa and Luther, since they weren't going anywhere.

"One more thing 'fore we go," Cuffy said. "I heard someone mention de ancestors. Would you like to pay yo' respects to dem?"

"We would," Sandra and Una said in unison.

"Of course, we would," Polithia said.

Cuffy guided them out back past the Gullah bottle tree, the bottles now rattling loudly in the wind. "This way," he said.

They walked down a trail lined with purple rhodo-dendron and ivy, past a grove of oak trees and a venerable magnolia in full bloom, the light lemon scent wafting its sweet perfume all over the garden. There at their feet was a giant heart made of white conch shells. Inside the heart were rough gravestones marked with the names of the deceased: Watkins (Sweet Wally) Davis, Olivia (Libby) Walker Davis, Bailey W. Davis, Bailey Davis, Jr., Sarabeth (Sarabee) G. Davis, and Nelly Geneva Knox Davis.

"As I told you in yonder, Bailey were my husband," Mama Isa said. "Libby were his mother, Sweet Wally were his father, Bailey Jr. were our son (Paul an' Martin dad); he die of de cancer when he were still young; Sarabee were my daughter. She die at age four. Nelly Geneva Knox Davis were Papa Davis' great-grandma. We calls huh Grandma

Nelly. Leas' dat what de kitchen records say. Ain't no official record. Hear tell Papa Davis' grandfolk done been sold down Savannah way."

"Past ain't far back as we think," Cuffy said. "Peoples think it is, but it ain't."

Una stared for a minute at Nelly's gravestone. A steel pot sat on it next to a pewter spoon. She didn't know why those things were there, but she felt sure it wasn't an accident. By some miracle tied up in tragedy, Una was related to this woman and her cousin, Ellen. She was part of this family.

"May we be excused for just a minute?" Sandra asked. "Una and I?" Sandra grasped Una's right hand and led her away from the cemetery, not waiting for an answer from anyone.

"Why didn't you tell me about your black kin?" Sandra asked, looking fully evil-eyed and straight at Una.

"I just hadn't had a chance yet," Una replied, trying to shake off the cursed eyes that seemed to be staring into her skull.

"Aunt Polithia was in on this, too, and didn't bother to tell me?"

"It didn't concern you. It was personal."

"Well, it concerns me now. You are claiming to be related to *my family*. That means you're somehow related to me!"

"Okay, I admit, I was afraid of how you'd take it. I wasn't wrong to be afraid, was I?"

"You just can't comprehend how I feel."

"Jazz told me to talk to you. I was going to. Honest."

"Well, you didn't, and now we are here standing in my family's cemetery where you are to be welcomed with open arms even though you're about as black as Snow White!" Sandra said. "Jazz told me something about you thinking you were black, but I didn't know you thought you were related to me!"

Polithia overheard a small part of this dialogue. She came over and patted both girls on the back. "You two will have to continue this later and somewhere else," she said.

"Please tell Mama Isa I don't feel well. I'll be on the porch. Let me know when you're ready to go," Sandra said.

"Are you sure?" Una asked.

"Sure."

Polithia and Una walked back to the group.

"Sorry, but Sandra's not feeling her best. She'll wait for us on the porch," Polithia said.

"Naw, she ain't!" Mama Isa exclaimed. "She gonna come right back over here, right now. Quao, go fetch dat gal."

Quao had seen enough evil eyes for two lifetimes, and she wasn't intimidated. Besides, she liked what she saw of Sandra.

"Sandra, Mama Isa say you come back to the cemetery. Now! She ain't one to take no excuses."

Sandra looked angry, but she was a guest and had no resolve to be an unpopular one, so she came back and took Una's left hand where Mama Isa placed it, while Polithia took her right. Then everyone held hands in a circle that enclosed the entire family cemetery. They stood there together for a minute in silent prayer.

Then Luther yelled: "Hey, Lord, we down here! Hep us, Lord! Sweet Jesus, Hep us in our grief now!"

Mama Isa let out a deafening scream and jumped as high as a kitchen stool. Sandra and Una covered their ears for a second.

Cuffy yelled, "Oh, thank ya, Lord! We hear ya come to send our ancestor spirits, meet us on de light path!"

"Weeeeeee-ooooooo-ahhhhhhhhh!" screamed Belali.

"Jeeeeeeeee-suuuuuuuuus!" Quao shrieked. "Hear us! Hear us, Jesus. Help our precious ancestors an' send us they encouragement!"

"Dance roun' de circle!" Mama Isa shouted, her arms reaching up to the sky, worn hands waving back and forth.

Abruptly, everyone began to gyrate and move round and round the circle they had created. The beat was in the feet while the hands kept a clapping rhythm. In a mystifying jerk, Una felt her body released from its chains of inhibition; a suppression in her chest discharged itself like liquid electricity into her arms and feet, all moving wildly with bursts of rhythmic energy passing through her, around the circle and back. Sweat poured from her head until her hair was drenched.

"We ask for forgiveness, Lord!" Quao called out, "Have mercy on us all in dis generation of sin and darkness! We confused and scattered. Don't know who to slug or who to hug!"

"Bring light now, Lord, we pray!" called Mama Isa. "Light now. Bring it on!"

"Thank you, for these revelations Great Lord of Spirits and Bodies!" Una cried, "Lord of the Universes, of the Dark and the Light together!

"Wooooooooeeeeee!!!! Heal us, Great Spirit!" Sandra cried, shocking herself.

The wind whipped heavy branches and leaves from their moorings, and then a twig swatted Una in the face. She heard a voice rise in her throat like no voice she'd heard before. "We will survive means I will survive!" the voice within her cried. "*Amin!*"

Despite Sandra's rebuff, Una no longer felt like the outsider she had once known herself to be. She was *part of us* instead of just herself, alone. She was part of a great people who survived, even though descended from a man who raped a woman, descended from a corrupt system that allowed the mass perpetration and perpetuation of such crimes against humanity. She was part of a heroic people who'd survived every sort of torture and atrocity.

"You did not earn the right to be among my people here," Sandra said, staring at Una. "Yet God or, say, the universe, allowed me and you to stand here side by side, listening to the ancestors whose voices just filled our heads."

"Thank you, Sandra. That means a lot."

"I admit, there was some kind of grace in that, some mercy that I couldn't have conjured that allowed me to stand here with you against my will or even my better judgment."

Mama Isa squeezed Una's hand and looked up into her eyes with intense concentration. Then she looked at Sandra with piercing dark eyes full of light. "Una and Sandra, *I means WE in Gullah/Geechee*," she said. "Together we and God can overcome anything! Remember that yo' whole lives!"

Probably by some strange coincidence, just as Mama Isa finished her profound proclamation, a thunderbolt cast its blinding light upon the girls' faces, illuminating the delicate heart of shells at their feet.

And then the rain came down in torrents.

...

Polithia got the girls up early the next morning. Aunt Candy was taking them to meet Dr. Meade in Charlotte, North Carolina, nearly three hours away. Mama Isa had given them each a yam to stuff in their pockets in case they got hungry on the way. Una and Sandra again slept in the back seat. They felt sorry for Polithia, who offered to drive even though she must have been sleepy, too, but it seemed like they got there in no time.

Dr. Meade asked the group to meet her at Charlotte J's Cafe, a restaurant known for its Gullah breakfast fare. The shrimp and grits with warm biscuits and homemade strawberry jam were excellent. They told Dr. Meade about all that they had learned: both the terrible and the heavenly, pouring out their hearts to her as if she were some divinely appointed mentor who happened, by the mysteries of what Una called *synchronicity*, to be there for them at this particular time.

Dr. Meade shared stories from her trip to Charleston. She called it *The Holy City*.

"Why is it called that?" Una asked.

She explained that it was once called Charles Town, and was named after King Charles II. In the seventeenth and eighteenth centuries many European immigrants came and brought their diverse forms of religion with them, so the town became known for its religious diversity. But Charleston has always been a big port city, so in the eighteenth and nineteenth centuries it was known as one of the major cotton, rice, indigo, and slave-trade centers of the South.

"I can't understand how anyone could think it was moral to separate families so you could sell them into slavery like the plantation owners did," Una said.

After listening closely to Dr. Meade, Sandra was obviously lost in her thoughts.

"Sandra!" Una screamed, trying to jar her back to reality. "What's up?"

"Music!" she said. "That's it, Una! I was thinking of Gullah music like what was on the radio last night. We can take the healing sounds of South Carolina home with us. You know, the African drums, the saxophone and trumpet. The guitar and the singers!"

Now Sandra and Una seemed to be on the same chapter, if not the same page.

"Dr. Meade, did you by chance get any home movies of the Gullah musicians performing when you visited Charleston?"

"Not the church music, but I did get some of the steppers."

"The steppers?" Una asked.

"You know, Una, the *African gumboot dancers*," Sandra explained. "Aunt Polithia told me about them."

"Oh, yeah," Una said. "The beat steppers. Sylvia and Mat mentioned them."

"And the African drummers," Dr. Meade said. "I've got really good movie footage of them. I'll send it to you if you can get a projector. You remember that the songs and chants were often used as codes that signified when slaves could enter the Underground Railroad."

Aunt Candy glowed with happiness when she heard about that. "Yes. Tech has a projector we can use. This is just what we need in Blacksburg, Roanoke, and the entire valley," she said.

"Do you think the high schools will allow it?" Una asked. "I'm sure I could order more video from the Penn Center on Saint Helena Island."

"Well, I know Tech and all the local teaching colleges will welcome it," she said. "And once a respected teacher gets it in her or his classroom and closes the door, there's no stopping it. We could find a computer tech to create a digital file."

"I guess there's more than one way to step up to the plate," Polithia said.

"I bet the local libraries and community centers will likely support an evening of cultural enrichment," Sandra said.

"And the churches!" Una added. "I know my church will host an evening of inspirational entertainment."

"See?" Aunt Candy said, "This trip empowered us, just as I thought it would."

"You girls could deliver a talk centered on what you learned about Gullah and Yoruba cultures; then Dr. Jasper and the others who accompanied you could discuss their findings," Dr. Meade suggested.

"In layman's terms," Polithia said.

"Of course."

"The findings would make a wonderful project for any student, elementary age up to college!" Aunt Candy said.

"Then these Gullah/Geechee cousins of ours (both black and white) might begin to see themselves through a different lens."

"The history of oppression in America isn't just black or white," Dr. Meade said. "It's yellow and every shade of red and brown."

"That's true," Polithia agreed. "Everyone who has suffered from oppression could get some inspiration from this. Music has a quality that lifts the soul and soothes the spirit."

"Polithia, do you attend church somewhere?" Dr. Meade asked.

"Worship under my own vine and fig tree, you might say."

"Me, too," Dr. Meade said. "Maybe I'm socially lazy, but I feel exhausted much of the time and Sunday is my only day to relax."

"I feel like the folks I meet down at the laundromat near my house are just about as spiritual as anyone in the megachurches I see on TV," Polithia said. "But my husband Paul and I host a small prayer and worship group at our house twice a month. We're reading the Bible and a guide to nurturing diversity through love. Discussions are invigorating."

"Sounds like my kind of church," Dr. Meade said. "If I didn't live in New England most of the year, I'd love to attend."

"I don't live that far away," Aunt Candy said. "May I join you sometime?"

"We'd love to have you," Polithia assured her. "Give me your mailing address and I'll send you a book, a schedule and directions to my house."

"What about you, Sandra?" Aunt Candy asked. "Am I being too nosy if I ask if you and your dad attend church anywhere?"

"No," Sandra explained. "But Dad's Muslim so we go to the Islamic Center when we go anywhere."

"Oh," she said, looking like she was taken off-guard.

"Yep, Islam is the largest organized religion on the African continent, so Dad thought he'd give it a try. He also had a good Muslim friend when he was in the Marines."

"Where did he serve?" Una asked.

"In Vietnam."

"This may be an ignorant question, but do Muslims worship on Sundays?"

"Not an ignorant question, but the answer is no, we observe *Jumah* on Fridays at noon, but we pray five times a day, so we always feel connected to *Allah* (God)."

"What about school on Fridays?" Una asked. "Doesn't it interfere?"

"Dad picks me up during lunch unless he has a special meeting or a surgery, but he tries not to schedule anything on Fridays."

"My friend Judy is Jewish, so her *Shabbat* runs from Friday to Saturday nights," Una said.

"What about drums?" Aunt Candy asked. "Do Muslims use drums in their music?"

"Wind and string instruments such as the *kora* and the flute are preferred in most of the traditional music, but sometimes, we listen to the *talking drum* and the *djembe*. They are West African and would be recognized by our Gullah family."

"So, the African drums and other Gullah instruments would also be welcomed at the mosque?" Una asked, smiling her amazed smile.

"Of course!" Sandra laughed.

"Sounds like we've wrapped up a plan," Dr. Meade said. "I'll have to be leaving for Boston now, but we'll be in touch soon."

Polithia asked Dr. Meade if she would be driving all the way that night.

"I can make it by midnight if I have a mind to," Dr. Meade said, "but I may stop at a motel along the way if I get tired."

Polithia and the others gave Dr. Meade a hug and thanked her for her wisdom and all her creative ideas. Then they packed a few more SC souvenirs in the bus and headed home. Sandra felt mellow and hopeful. Una and she talked all the way to Blacksburg. Doc picked them up at the Tech student center, then dropped Polithia at her car. Una was breathless, explaining details about the trip, but she first had to ask about Marvelous Marvin.

"Aunt Candy, who kept M & M while we were gone?"

"Hah. Marvelous Marvin stayed at my kennel. He has buddies there and a few nice girlfriend types too. But he'll probably be glad to see me when I get there."

"You girls look a little washed out, but happy, and more excited than two rabbits who found their own lettuce garden," Doc said.

Doc was appropriately wowed by the news from South Carolina and the girls' plans to bring African music to the Roanoke Valley. She felt sorrowful about the drugs and corruption in Allentown, but she was facing her own challenges. She didn't know for sure if Clarise Oliphant had something to do with it or not, but the Junior Ladies' League did not invite her to help with its yearly Grand Sale at the civic center, nor was she invited to the annual Fall Ball at Hotel Roanoke. She had hoped to ask Dr. Davis to be her dinner partner and guest. She had always looked forward to both networking events and had even bought a luscious-looking aqua taffeta gown, a real razzle-dazzler.

"Looks like you got the diss, Mom," Una said.

"Yep, rejected and shunned."

"It was my fault," Una confessed. "I'm sure if it hadn't been for the Ms. Oliphant episode that I mishandled—"

"I was peeved at first, I'll admit," Doc cut in, "but if there is prejudice and you stand up against it, someone will pay; in this case, I am proud to be the one if that was the reason."

"But this could seriously affect your career, Mom."

"Then so be it, but we don't know for sure what's behind all this. It could be the mixed news coverage about the Grace Street duplex, or maybe someone just doesn't like my cologne."

"I doubt that, Dr. Zipley," Sandra said. "You smell really nice."

Doc smiled and told Sandra she appreciated the compliment.

"You girls keep right on making goals and working to accomplish them," she said. "I'm really proud of you, and now that I'm feeling a little bit of the heat, I realize that we all may have to make some sacrifices to accomplish things. But if we stick together, we can do it."

"That's right," Sandra said. "We all have something to contribute to the cause of justice and equality: you, Una, Dad, me, Aunt Polithia and Uncle Paul."

Sandra was rarely outspoken, so it was unusual to hear her this excited about coming together as a team. It made Una happy and relieved. She felt sure it was due to the epiphany at Mama Isa's. She wished that Jazz had been there to experience it. In fact, she wasn't sure how to explain it to Jazz—or even if Jazz would want to hear about it. Una decided to pray on it and leave it in God's hands. She even wished for Sasha to understand this new part of her, but she acknowledged that that revelation could be a long way off in the future, if ever.

"Don't forget Aunt Candy, Jazz, Sasha, Kiki, and Mrs. Rogers," Una said, still speaking about those who had something to contribute.

"Agreed," Doc said, smiling her mysterious-lady smile. Then she shrieked, "Ice cream time!"

"I'm getting chocolate chip!" Una cried.

"Vanilla with butterscotch swirls for me!" Sandra yelled.

Doc decided on the cherry bomber, a mixture of cherry and vanilla ice cream with sprinkles and marshmallows.

"What if I ask Dad to take you to dinner at a fancy restaurant, Dr. Zipley, someplace you could wear that aqua dress?" Sandra asked.

"Hmm," Doc said, "I might consider it if you two would dress up and be our escorts."

"Cool!" Sandra exclaimed. "I already know what I want to wear. I've got a pink sleeveless chiffon I can wear with my black patent leather pumps.

"Mom, I have a question," Una said. "Could we possibly invite Jazz, Sasha, and Kiki too?"

"Well, first we have to find out if Dr. Davis wants to go, but if he does, let's ask him about the others coming along."

"Sounds good."

Dr. Davis was affirmative about the date-night idea and even agreed to take Jazz, Sasha, and Kiki. He suggested the Lavender Room at Hotel Benton, which offered both dinner and dancing. They decided to meet at Sandra's house on Saturday night. Doc picked up Sasha and Kiki.

Bitsy stayed with friends and, of course, Jazz rode with Una. The girls glowed in their cocktail dresses and looked more like sexy young women than high school girls on a date with parents.

Doc looked especially radiant. She paid special attention to her hair, blowing it out and straightening it so her chestnut curls curved slightly under her jaw. She wore pearl earrings and silver sandals with her silver clutch purse.

As the group arrived at the restaurant, Polithia and Paul showed up.

"Sweet!" Una said. "Mom and Dr. Davis, thanks so much for inviting my other favorite people to join us!"

Polithia wore a lacy red gown with spaghetti straps that really showed off her figure. Both Paul and Dr. Davis wore tuxes. During the delicious steak and seafood supper, Sandra, Polithia, and Una told everyone about their South Carolina findings and plans to bring some Lowcountry music to the Roanoke area.

Toward the end the meal, Doc whispered something to the waitress. A few minutes later, a gigantic red velvet cake was presented. "Belated Happy Birthday, Una!" was inscribed on it in bright pink, yellow, and green letters. Una was careful to blow out each of the fifteen green candles, making a secret wish on each one. She glanced over at her mom with a clear sprinkle of something in her eye. It was mid-August and her birthday had been in July, but at that time she and Doc had been quarreling and she'd told Doc she didn't want a birthday celebration.

"We wanted to surprise you!" Doc said.

"Well, you did that!" Una exclaimed, wiping her eye with a tissue.

After everyone in the restaurant sang "The Birthday Song," Dr. Davis asked Una to dance.

"Did I tell you that Stevie Wonder and Paul McCartney's 'Ebony and Ivory' was my favorite oldie?"

"Your mom had a hunch."

The song played for so long that Sandra, and then Sasha, cut in. Then Paul asked Kiki to dance, and then Jazz. Finally, Polithia danced with Paul and Dr. Davis guided Doc around the floor like a pro.

Doc and Dr. Davis wanted to give Una a special gift, so they'd arranged to have a local band play some Afro-Cuban pieces, with drums. The Lavender Room was completely accommodating. After several Afro-Cuban numbers that the band had prepared, everyone danced to "Ain't No Mountain High Enough," sung by Diana Ross. By the last song, "Mama Told Me (Not to Come)" by Three Dog Night, another one of Una's favorite oldies but goodies, all shoes were thrown off.

Doc asked if the party wanted to tail her and Una home for a nightcap or coffee. The guests were giddy with celebration, and the night was still young, so everyone accepted. Doc was ready with pink, yellow, and green birthday napkins; pink and yellow roses adorned the kitchen table. Una had asked that no one bring gifts, but that request was ignored.

Kiki and Sasha bought Una a leather diary from the Blue Cocoon. Polithia and Paul got her a year's subscription to *Dreamy Teen Heartthrob,* a magazine Una had always wanted but was afraid to ask her mom for it because it had a few guys in it wearing no shirts. Sandra and Dr. Martin brought Una pink pool floats with five new pink-and-green striped beach towels. And Jazz presented a gift from herself, Aunt Sylvia, Uncle Mat, and Bitsy: a small wicker chest to keep Una's special things in. Jazz had discovered it in an antique store and Sylvia sent her the money for it. Inside was a stuffed dog that looked amazingly like Marvelous Marvin. Jazz said that was added by Bitsy. There were also cards on the veranda from Marsha, Rowe, and Aunt Candy.

"Sandra, are the beach towels a hint that we should go to Virginia Beach before school starts?" Una asked.

Sandra laughed. "I wish; maybe next year."

Doc said she'd give Una her final gift the following Monday because they were on order.

"You've done more than enough, Mom," Una said, hugging her. "This is one of the happiest birthday bashes on record. Thanks so much!"

"You're special, Una," Polithia said. "We're lucky to have you in our lives."

Una's face turned a shade of plum, but Polithia insisted on getting a photo with her anyway. Una was glad Polithia asked; she wanted to remember every detail of this night.

The party all agreed to get together again for a quick supper at McDonald's the following Monday afternoon, then they would head over to take care of finishing touches at the Grace Street property. While they were eating, Doc presented Una with a new pair of gold sneakers wrapped in the funny papers crowned with a yellow ribbon.

"I could warm up to them!" Kiki said.

"I don't even have a pair of those yet," Sasha said, "but I'll be looking for some."

"You'll get spikes on yours," Una teased.

"Yeah, right."

"I already have a pair," Jazz boasted, "so I told Doc you wanted some like mine."

"Thanks, then!" Una exclaimed. "I love them!"

Una and Jazz drove to the duplex with Doc. On the trip over they made a mental list of last-minute details, like checking outlets, HVAC, plumbing, hot and cold water, making sure landscaping chores were complete, and picking up any litter that may have blown around the yard before emptying the trash.

When she popped out of the car, Una was feeling as bubbly as a glass of champagne.

"Oh, no!" Doc exclaimed. "Not this. Not today."

"Well, I'll be a rat's ass," Polithia said as she strode up the front walk.

"Look like someone *is an ass*, but it ain't you," Paul said. "I wish I knew who it was."

"So do I," Doc said. The front door was marred by purple, orange, and black graffiti that said: "DO NOT ENTER: THIS HOUSE IS CURSED: PROPERTY OF A BLACK-LOVING HAG and a WITCH'S MAMA."

Una sat down on the front stoop feeling like she was going to be sick. Everyone stood in an arc partially surrounding her, forming long shadows on three sides.

"I'll call the police," Dr. Davis said. "This has to be reported."

"It's very threatening," Polithia said. "Someone meant to inflict fear in you, Doc, and probably in all of us."

"Let's think," Doc said. "Who would want to threaten us?"

"Plenty of folks," Paul said. "For years the powers in this town have run things exactly the way they wanted to. Then we came along and brought some unwelcome change."

"Looks like the work of thugs," Sasha said. "But just about everyone at school and in the neighborhood thinks what you're doing is pretty cool."

"I think I might know what happened," Kiki said, her eyes filling with tears.

"What?" Una asked.

"It's a long story."

"How could you have known?"

"Please explain, Kiki," Doc pleaded. "We need to get to the bottom of this."

"Well, after Una healed Mom, she told a lot of people."

"But I didn't do that by myself," Una said.

"I know, but Mom told people about the miracle she experienced and said she felt the heat and even saw electricity coming off your hands when you touched her."

"But the church people prayed and—"

"Yeah, I get it," Kiki said, "but Mom was so happy afterward that she ran her mouth. She said you were a powerful supernatural healer. One of the people she told was the son of some lady who knows you, Dr. Zipley."

"Oh, goodness, not Mrs. Oliphant."

"Richard Oliphant is his name. He's our paperboy and Mom pays him to trim the hedges sometimes."

"That may explain it," Doc said. "Did Mrs. Rogers happen to mention what Una and I were doing here on Grace Street?"

"I believe so," Kiki said. "Mom thinks the world of you, Una. You got us back in church too. It was more than just the healing."

"I think I understand," Doc said.

"I guess I screwed up, Mom," Una said, sounding panicked.

"No, Una, you followed your conscience and did what you thought was right, like we're all doing. We're trying to do what we feel is right here on Grace Street."

"This is linked to the shunning, isn't it?"

"Most likely."

"We thought Richard was just a nice boy, Dr. Zipley," Kiki said. "I'm so sorry, and I know Mom will be freaked when she finds out what happened."

"It's okay, Kiki," Doc said. "Please tell your mom not to fret over it. It's just that several things came together at the same time."

"Several negative things," Una said. "But don't worry about it, Kiki. I'm sure it will all work out."

"I hope so. Richard just blabbed something to me and Mom about his mother being over at your house. I guess he saw us together. Anyway, it wasn't very nice."

Just then, the police pulled up and spoke to everyone, taking notes and snapping photos.

"Not sure we can catch whoever did this," Sergeant Royal of the Roanoke City Police said, "but we'll do our best to get our detectives on this as soon as possible. Do you know when this place will be occupied?"

"We were hoping to move into the duplex in late summer," Paul said. "My wife's grandma was going to move in the week after us; we were thinking maybe the third week of August."

"You may want to delay that," the sergeant said, "at least until we get some solid leads. It may take some time."

"I don't think so," Polithia said. "That may be just what the vandals had in mind."

"That's right," Sandra said. "It seems like you'd be falling right into their hands if you gave in that quick."

"Thanks, officer," Doc said. "We'll have to think about this, but we appreciate you coming out to get it on file."

With that, the officer nodded and pulled away without agreeing to check on the property.

"I don't feel too hopeful about getting much help from law enforcement," Dr. Davis said.

"Neither do I," Doc said.

"Guess we'll just have to take this into our own hands," Polithia said. "Paul and I will start by sanding the door down and repainting."

"Sounds like a plan," Una said. "I'll help. How would you like a nice blue door instead of the gray?"

"I'll ask Grandma Hatie," Polithia said, "but I think she'd like blue just fine, and I wouldn't mind it myself, since it brings good luck."

"You in, Paul?"

"Sounds fine."

"I can help tomorrow after church," Sasha said.

"Me too," Sandra said.

"Oh yeah, Sandra and I can be here about 2:00 p.m.," Dr. Davis said. "If that's all right."

"Thanks."

"I'll ask my Mom," Kiki said, "but I think she'll want to come too. She can bring me over after church."

"I'll take care of Bitsy," Jazz said. "If that's okay."

"Thanks," Doc said with a half-hearted smile. "Then we'll see the rest of you all here tomorrow and we'll start fresh."

"Sandra and I will follow you home, Doc," Dr. Davis said. "Since they did this on Grace Street, there's no telling what they might have done to your house on Mountain Look Drive."

"Thanks, Martin."

"Before you go, Doc, I'd like to tell you something," Polithia said.

Doc grabbed Polithia's arm and hung on to it.

"I think I speak not only for myself, but for the entire Davis family; we're committed to seeing this project through."

"Not only this, but other projects here in Gainsboro and Northwest," Paul added.

"And we'll be watching out for you, Doc," Dr. Davis said. "You and Una both, and little Bitsy."

"We'll all be watching out for you," Kiki said.

"That's right," Sasha said. "We got your back."

"And we'll continue to stand up to city council," Sandra said.

"I can make signs and organize a march on city hall if that's what we need to do," Kiki added.

"Amen to that," Sasha said. "Mom and I know a bunch of folks in the community. We'll help in any way we can, and I know the church will pitch in."

"That's right," Kiki said. "Mom and I will call the Praise and Worship team."

"We can set up regular meetings."

"Thanks for everything," Doc said.

"Could we call our organization the CHAG?" Una asked. "It stands for the *Creative Healing Activists' Group*."

"Sounds like a great name," Doc said. "What do you guys think?"

Politha smiled. "Sounds perfect. We'll discuss the details at our first meeting."

Sasha chimed in, "For now, Kiki and I will be on the phone/text committee. Sound good, Kiki?"

"Yep."

Una told Doc she'd call Aunt Candy. She'd want to know what happened, and Una knew Candy would want to be part of the CHAG.

"Thanks again, everyone," Doc said. "Well, Martin, let's go see what we're facing at home."

Una no longer felt sick. She felt revved up and ready for whatever the future threw at her, because it wasn't just her anymore. She knew that the *power of us* was right here where she lived. It had not been left behind in the Lowcountry.

CHAPTER TWENTY-NINE
THE MANIFESTO

When Doc got home, she gave Dr. Davis the key to check the door. Sandra and the others waited in the cars.

"Looks okay!" Martin called from the front door, "but I'll check around the house."

In a few minutes, he came back and gave the all clear.

"I'd like to install a door lock switch and a home alarm for security, Doc," Martin said, "and the sooner the better. I can stop by a hardware store tomorrow and get them. I'll set them up myself."

"What about the Grace Street property?"

"We need the same security at the duplexes too."

Doc said she needed to think about it.

"Nothin' much to think about," Martin said. "We want you safe and we want the duplexes safe."

"Yes, but there are different kinds of safety. If there is one thing my daughter has taught me, it's that you can be safe on the outside when the thief is coming in through the front door of your heart."

Una looked perplexed. "I said that?"

"You did, in so many words," Doc told her. "You see, we want to invite more people to come in, not keep them out."

"Oh, I see what you mean," Sandra said. "Security may warn people to stay away, but we want people to feel like they should come in and come closer instead."

"Okay, then," Dr. Davis said, "but have you got a pistol, just in case?"

"No, I sold my husband's guns when he died, and I don't ever want to own any more. They don't make me feel safer; they make me feel sad and more vulnerable."

"But what if someone tried to attack Una, Dorothy? Would you just stand there?"

"Martin, if someone wants to steal, or vandalize, or try to hurt us, they'll find a way in, and they'll most likely use our own gun on us. Statistics prove it and I know it's true."

"And you feel the same about Grace Street?"

"Yes, I think so. If Polithia and Paul want that kind of security for themselves or for Mrs. Dunbar, it's up to them, but I'm going to suggest we play it my way."

"Thanks, Dr. Davis," Una said. "We appreciate everything."

"Yes, we can't ever thank you enough, Martin."

"Glad to do it. Sandra and I will see you tomorrow."

"Sounds good."

After Doc, Jazz, Bitsy, and Una went to bed, someone hung a paper skeleton with two beady red eyes on their doorknob. Una found it when she got the morning paper. She decided not to tell Doc or Jazz; she knew it would frighten them and take away the positive vibes they were feeling. Una hid it in the bottom of the kitchen trash. But she did say a brief prayer:

For where angels protect
God Almighty will not neglect.

...

Doc woke Una early Sunday morning. "Good morning, Sunshine," she said. "Going to church today?"

"Yes, ma'am, the church bus ought to be here in about thirty minutes."

"Jazz going too?"

"No, she's still in bed. I'd just let her sleep in."

Una wondered if she should tell Jazz, Sandra, or Polithia about the skeleton.

"I wanted to make lucky pancakes for you, with smiles and sprinkles," Doc said.

"Already took care of that, Mom. I got up early to make them for you, then slipped back into bed for a few minutes. The ones I made are blueberry with a dab of purple icing for eyes."

"Hah!" Doc laughed. "Then let's eat. I'll grab the milk and maple syrup. By the way, what would I do without you, girl?"

"Only God knows," Una said, "which is why he put the two of us together."

"Let's cut a half a pink grapefruit each to go with this feast."

"Can I have a banana?"

"Grapefruit."

"Okay."

"Even though you're fifteen now, you're not totally grown up yet, young lady," Doc told her. "When you are, I'll let you know."

"Right," she said.

"Nana!" Bitsy screamed.

"Okay, Little Bit, you can have a banana," Una said. Then her cell buzzed.

"Go ahead and answer. I'll get Bitsy her nana," Doc said. "I'd better get it quick; she's reaching for the purple icing."

"Mom, Kiki called to ask if she and Mrs. Rogers could take me to lunch after church, and then they'll take me over to Grace Street. That okay?"

"That's fine. Take a ten to pay for your lunch."

"Got it."

When the bus pulled up, Doc reminded Una to pack a bag of work clothes and sneakers. Una called Sasha and Kiki to remind them to bring extra clothes too.

"Have fun!" I'll see you this afternoon after church."

"Okay, Mom, see ya then!"

After church Una approached Bishop Morrison. She told him about the vandalism on Grace Street and what may have been behind it.

"Just one step between vandalism and evangelism," he said.

Una had to laugh, but his point was well taken. Then she told him about the CHAG.

"The what?" he asked. "Sounds like one of those crazy new dance moves."

"The Creative Healing Activists' Group. We're a small group of committed and creative activists for social and racial justice," Una explained. "Fair housing is part of our mission. We need you and the Praise and Worship team to be part of this."

"Let's pray on it," Bishop Morrison said, "before you approach the team."

Una thanked the reverend and left, head down, wondering if the team would really want to offer their help. She knew that community support was essential—the kind Martin Luther King got from churches in the South.

When Una told Sasha and Kiki about her conversation with the bishop, Sasha said, "Maybe they'll need a hard sell on this."

"What do you mean, exactly?" Kiki asked.

"Lemme think. I'll come up with something," Sasha replied.

They discussed their ideas over lunch at Mario's Lasagna before driving over to Grace Street. By the time Una and the others arrived, Polithia and Paul had already sanded and painted the front door of the duplex.

"I see you painted it cobalt blue," Una said, glowing with approval.

"Look good?" Polithia asked.

"Looks lit," Sandra said, sneaking up behind Polithia. "Who are they?"

Sandra was referring to two other couples planting sage and white geraniums on the side of the duplex.

"I brought some folks from my church," Polithia said, introducing Kip and JoAnna Coleman, an African American couple from Northwest Roanoke, and Sally and Donovan Woo, a Korean American couple who'd recently moved to Roanoke from Chicago with their teenage son, Brent. They said Brent was in the car listening to the radio.

"Nice to have all of you. I'm Una Zipley," Una said. "Pretty soon we'll need name tags."

"Are these the new members of CHAG?" Doc asked as she walked up behind Polithia. She shook everyone's hand and got introductions from Paul.

The new couples told everyone a little bit about themselves and then got to work in and around the duplex, all except Brent, who was still in the car. Mrs. Woo explained that he was a little shy.

Una walked over to the car and leaned into the passenger window.

"What's up?" she asked the supposedly shy stranger.

"You startled me!" he said.

"Sorry, I'm Una. Maybe Paul and Polithia told you about me?"

"Not much," he said, looking annoyed.

"You getting ready to start back to school in a few?" she asked.

"Not likin' it," he said, seeming like he was trying to be cool.

"You look like a guy who loves school," Una laughed.

"And why is that?"

"You look good 'n smart so you'd be good 'n bored by the end of the summer; that's my guess."

"Good guess. I don't know that many girls, so sometimes I'm not sure what to say."

"Now that's an honest answer."

"Yep."

"Would you like to give us a hand over here? I'll introduce you to my friends, Kiki, Sasha, and Sandra. Oh, and it looks like Jazz came too."

"Okay."

As soon as Una introduced Brent, she could see Sasha's eyeballs getting ready to pop.

"Hello," she said in a *purr* Una had never heard out of her before.

Brent shook her hand and then reached out to shake Kiki's.

"I've been eatin' Gummy Bears; mind if I shake later?" she asked.

"Anytime that's convenient for you, ma'am," Brent said with a weird look that sent Sasha into peels of laughter.

Una thought Brent would be embarrassed, but he must have known he had it coming; he just straightened up his back and smiled the *toothpaste ad smile*. She had to chuckle.

Sandra shook his hand and welcomed him nonchalantly, as did Jazz.

"Brent, we didn't get you over here to play," Una teased.

"Oh, sorry," he said. "What do you want me to do?"

"We want you to carry these petunias to the back; then grab a bag of soil from over there," Sasha ordered with a wink.

Once he got started, Brent was a hard and determined worker. He didn't even stop to take a water break from the bottles Doc brought. Una was wondering who would take the first crack at him; would it be Kiki, Sandra, Jazz, or Sasha? But she decided not to go too far down that road in her mind. Brent looked like a prep and preps didn't usually show an interest in her. Still, she hoped they could be friends. Nerds were a different matter and so far, she hadn't found any who gave her the hots, even though they sometimes seemed hot for her.

A little later, everyone gathered at the duplex. "I call this meeting to order!" Dr. Davis said. "I brought the folding chairs so we can be comfortable here in Paul's duplex. We need to go over some things. Plenty of soap and paper towels in the bathroom to wash your hands."

"You mean, *my* duplex!" Polithia barked with a smile.

"Oh, yeah, Polithia's duplex."

"Sandra will lead us off," Polithia said.

"First, we want to thank Mrs. Rogers for bringing snacks for us today, and for offering to bring packed lunches next time we meet."

Everyone clapped for Mrs. Rogers.

"My pleasure," she said, taking a mini bow.

"This group has decided to call itself the CHAG, which stands for the Creative Healing Activists' Group," Sandra said. "It's open to all members of the community who see themselves as creative activists willing to do Allah's will." She added in an aside, "I call him Allah; you might call him or her God or your Higher Power." She continued: "Now, Una Zipley will talk."

Una suggested that they come up with a manifesto for the group.

"Any coffee?" Paul asked before anyone could answer Una. "This may turn out to be a long afternoon."

Sasha offered to be the recording secretary because, as Kiki said, she had by far the best handwriting. After a lot of what Una called discussion, but some might call bickering, the group decided on the following goals for their manifesto:

1. CHAG is committed to fighting injustice and discrimination in the community.
2. CHAG will try a variety of ways to save the environment and make the Northwest Roanoke neighborhoods more habitable through planting trees, recycling, and writing letters to government leaders.
3. CHAG will set up food pantries in cooperation with local churches, mosques, temples, schools, and libraries for anyone who needs food.
4. CHAG members will share their talents with the community in myriad ways, such as offering free art, yoga, and creative writing courses. CHAG will also offer academic tutoring at local libraries or other appropriate venues.

5. CHAG will welcome people into the group who may look, act, or worship differently than we do and ask them to share their wisdom.

6. CHAG pledges to participate in a variety of social projects, such as building more affordable housing or renovating existing housing through community partnerships like Habitat Homes and others.

7. CHAG will host a cultural diversity program at colleges, recreation centers, and/or libraries.

8. CHAG will create a running list of volunteers.

9. As CHAG's membership grows, it will start a child-care co-op.

10. CHAG will create a Buddy vs. Bully program at local schools and recreation centers.

"This all sounds great," Brent said, "but a few of these things could take a lot of money. Who will be responsible for that?"

"We'll need a treasurer," Una said, "and a damn good fundraiser."

"Someone experienced, objective, and committed," Polithia said.

"I'll do it!" Shadwell Brooks exclaimed. He'd snuck in the door with the Praise and Worship team of Garden of Our Savior Baptist Sanctuary Church. "The Bishop had to take care of other matters today, but he'll be along later this afternoon. He told us your story."

"What story?" Brent asked.

"Why don't you explain it, Una?" Mr. Brooks asked.

Una told the group that the CHAG began as a response to the lack of affordable housing in certain sections of Roanoke. Other missions developed as more people expressed a desire to join with the Davis family and the Zipleys to make the community a better place to live.

"Everyone has brought their own special interests and talents to the table," Una said.

"But simultaneously, my mom, Lindsay Rogers, came to Una asking for a blessing for her healing," Kiki said. "She had cancer. That's when the Praise and Worship Team of Garden of Our Savior Baptist Sanctuary got involved. They came to Una's house to help her pray for Mom."

"Then some mean lady who knows Dr. Zipley heard about both the healing and the push for better housing," Sandra told the group. "That brought about some nasty words plastered on the door of the duplex. Vandalism, plain and simple. We think that uppity lady who knows Una and Dr. Zipley was responsible."

"Bitch," Sasha said.

"I'd hesitate to call her a bitch," Doc said, "even if she is."

"Sorry, but I call it like it is," Sasha said. "Has the Bishop thrown his support in the ring?"

"Totally," Mr. Brooks said. "And after praying on it, I am offering to be the treasurer because I happen to be the Chief Executive Officer of First Peoples' Regional Bank of Martinsville, an hour from Roanoke. I have plenty of experience. Been there twenty years."

"I can help with technology and research!" Aunt Candy chimed in, having just scooted in the door. "Hi everyone,

I'm Dr. Candace Jasper, Una's aunt and Dr. Dorothy Zipley's sister. But you can call me Candy. Nice to see you all here."

"Count me in too!" Bishop Morrison said, throwing the front door open wide as he let in his larger-than-life personality.

The Bishop's presence charged up the room with energy.

"Where are the snacks, ya'll? I always come when there are snacks, and Miss Sasha Carter over there personally contacted me to tell me there would be plenty of food!"

"Right in the kitchen," Mrs. Rogers said. "Pigs in a blanket and Doritos with avocado and salsa dips; said to be your favorites, Bishop."

"Pepsi?"

"Of course," Sasha said. "I brought those."

"We got blue napkins and plates," Polithia said. "I provided those."

"Well, see, I've got a good feeling already about this group," Bishop Morrison said. "Come on and join me, folks."

Everyone packed in the kitchen to load their plates before heading back into the living room to continue the discussion. Paul Davis suggested that Una call for a final vote on the manifesto after they detailed it again for Aunt Candy, Mr. Brooks, and Bishop Morrison.

"All those in favor of the CHAG Manifesto, say aye."

Everyone said aye.

"Sweet!" Una said. "The ayes have it!"

"We will start breaking into committees of interest tomorrow," Dr. Davis said.

"Let's have a circle prayer for wisdom," Polithia said.

Doc looked surprised, but she moved in to grab Polithia's hand. Una grabbed her other hand. When the circle was formed, Una said the following prayer:

Great Spirit of the Circle
We call you to give blessing to our missions,

THE MANIFESTO

Creativity to our thoughts,
Justice to our intentions,
Wisdom to our minds,
Compassion to our hearts.
And bravery to our resolve
To love, as you love.
Your power is in us, so we claim it.   Amin.

After the prayer, Sasha sang her own rendition of "Amazing Grace." Una busted out in tears. Sometimes a person just can't help that. But Sasha knew they were happy tears. Kiki bawled some too. Then Sasha asked if there were any Doritos left.

CHAPTER THIRTY
DANGEROUS PASSIONS

Summer flew by as usual, its death bringing the colors of heaven to earth, at least in Virginia. Hickory trees turned gold-bronze, maples turned scarlet, oaks turned a warm russet-brown, and the poplars took on intense shades of yellow with flecks of gold.

Una and Jazz could hardly wait for school to start. Una was coming up on her sophomore year. She predicted it would be a watershed year. After all, she had learned to drive, even though she still shared Doc's car, and she'd learned how to direct her own life, or so she thought. She felt that if she stayed on a straight-and-narrow course, Doc would let her have a car her senior year. A car like the red Chevy Impala she'd eyed on a used car lot was good enough for her, and the trunk was big enough to load petition posters, fliers, bags of dirt, or whatever she needed to help with the CHAG.

Of course, she'd also need to keep up her grades and babysit either Bitsy or Milton Rhodes (the next-door neighbors' eight-year-old kid) as often as possible to earn money for gas and car upkeep. Some cash also had to be tucked away for college. But with school, the CHAG, and earning money for a car, Una would have a lot to look forward to. And there was something else.

Amazingly, Brent Woo called and asked Una out. He already had his own car and asked her to see a movie. She agreed; he'd pick her up after supper on Friday. She told Jazz but asked her not to tell the other girls yet. She wanted to wait and see if she really liked him.

"I'm going to wear my new Calvin Klein jeans with the holes in the knees, my pink hoodie, and my new gold Adidas," Una told her mom.

Jazz overheard. "Want to borrow my silver hoop earrings?"

"Thanks! I owe you one. How's it going with Julius?"

"He turned out to be a dud," Jazz said. "But I'm okay. That leaves me free to get with other guys."

"That's true," Una said. "This is my first date since Patrick."

"Man, that's been awhile," Jazz said.

"I know."

"I have a question," Jazz said, "if you have time."

"Sure, Brent won't be here for a half hour or so."

"I heard through the grapevine about your South Carolina trip."

"How'd you find out?"

"Heard you talkin' to Sandra one night on your phone. I'm sorry. I didn't mean to eavesdrop."

"No, it's okay. We live in the same house. I wanted to tell you."

"I know. But my question is: If you're black now or, shall we say, of African American heritage, will you put mixed race on your driver's license? And will you put it on your child's birth certificate if you ever have one? In other words, when people ask, will you claim it?"

"I hadn't thought much about that."

"That's the kind of thing black people think about all the time. They'll ask you that on your credit applications—even your job applications. It's often unavoidable."

"Oh, I see what you mean."

"When we go up to D.C. for another Million Man March and the white supremacist groups come, too, will you be marching with us and risking your life? See, that's how you know you're getting closer to being *really black* instead of just a wannabe."

"I get what you're saying. I talked to Mom awhile ago about—"

"Yeah, I know. And when people come right up to you and call you a black girl; well, that's when you know, by the way you answer those questions."

"You mean, do I really want other people to know?" Una asked. "Yes, I do. I'm proud of who I am and what I believe. I wasn't always, but I am now."

"Because you can't change your mind every time the setting changes, like when you're with your mom's rich white friends."

"Now I see exactly what you're saying. And what you're saying are fighting words, Jazz, because I can say yes or I can say no and to you, it's all the same. You don't think I really have the right to call myself black or mixed, or anything of the sort. Sandra said the same thing to me at first."

"Oh, so you finally had that conversation with her? Well, I guess you did since you were with her the whole time on your trip."

"You don't know how I feel, Jazz, or what's in my heart. And it worked out okay with Sandra. Better than okay."

"When they call you the *N-word* like they've called me quite a few times, see how it makes you feel. If you can make it, let me know. And please don't go squealing to Aunt Sylvia about what I said."

"Hi, beautiful," Brent said seconds later as he pulled up in his yellow Plymouth Barracuda.

"I know you're addressing Una," Jazz said. "So I'll say goodbye. Have a nice date."

"What's happening, Brent?" Una said, giving Jazz the half-evil eye.

"Looked like you two were having a deep discussion of some kind."

"It was, but I've got to throw it off for now. I'll think about it later."

Seeing Brent's wicked cool sports car, Una couldn't resist asking him what his parents did for a living.

"Dad is a CPA and Mom is a tax attorney. You might say, that's how they met."

"Nine-to-five hours, or more like ten-to-ten?"

"You guessed it; ten-to-ten."

"Yeah, I was a latchkey kid, too, for a little while after Dad died. It wasn't bad. I guess I threw myself into sports as much as I could. Do you play a sport?"

"Golf and tennis mostly, when they're in season."

"That's cool."

"What about you? You look like a basketball player."

"Yep. I love it. Been on the team since freshman year, but I won't claim to be the best player out there."

"I'd like to see you in action sometime, I mean on the court."

"Do you mind if I ask how your folks got involved with Polithia's church?"

"Dr. Davis, I guess," Brent said. "He's in the Rotary Club and plays bridge with Dad. I think he told him about Mr. and Mrs. Davis's church."

"So, do you go?"

"Occasionally, if I wake up on time. I like to sleep in on Sundays."

"Were your grandparents Buddhist?"

"Yes, how did you know?"

"I'm psychic, didn't you hear?"

"Oh, right."

Una asked Brent why he chose to ask her out when he could have had his pick of her four friends. That was a lame question, but she really wanted to know. He told her she was the most interesting. She liked the way it sounded.

"As you said, I get bored easily and you seem like a girl who would definitely not bore me to death."

"As in, I'm the entertainment for the night?"

"No, you are the best thing that's happened to me in quite a while. How's that for an answer?"

"Sounds good, keep talking," Una said, wondering if she were about to walk through a dangerous tunnel, or stumble into a deep well with no steps or ropes to hold her up.

Una had never had reason to trust boys, and Brent was no exception. Still, that night he smelled like Yves Saint Laurent for Men. She could feel her hormones jetting around wildly and her knees knocking from sudden nerves she wasn't used to. Sweat beads formed on her brow. She wondered where her tissues were when she needed them and if she'd remembered to put on her deodorant.

Brent asked her if she wanted popcorn. She wanted to say yes but was afraid she'd get kernels in her teeth, so she just asked for a Pepsi. The movie, *For Love of the Game*, was so impressive that they went to a greasy spoon and discussed it until almost midnight. Doc had expected Una home by 11:00 p.m.

"I'm toast," Una said. "Gotta get home."

"*French toast*, I hope," Brent said, laughing. He held her hand and asked what the rush was.

"Don't you have a curfew?"

"Hell, no," he said. "I'm a senior this year. My parents trust me."

"Well, get me home NOW," Una commanded. "My mom doesn't trust me at all!"

Brent drove her to a park about two blocks from her house and stopped the car.

"I need a quick kiss first," Brent said.

"I thought you weren't used to girls, but you seem overly familiar with girls to me."

"Don't I deserve a kiss?" he asked. "After all, I took you out to a good movie and—"

Una leaned over in the seat to kiss him, but what she had in mind and what he had in mind were obviously two different things. He grabbed her and thrust his tongue into her mouth. She wished she were the least bit horrified, but his tongue tasted so good, not like milkshake; more like Icy Mints. In a moment they were both breathless.

They smothered each other with hard, but tender kisses. His arms were around her, and from the feel of them he'd been lifting weights at the gym. This was the only time in her life that she'd ever felt this vulnerable; yet she shamelessly luxuriated in the feeling instead of fighting it. She tried to pry her mouth away, but that wasn't happening.

When she finally got home around 1:00 a.m., Doc came to the door and asked Brent if he realized that Una had been given strict orders to be home by eleven o'clock.

"Yes, ma'am," Brent said. "I'm so sorry. We went to get food after the movie, and we were having so much fun we forgot about the time. It's my fault."

"That's right, Mom, we forgot the time," Una echoed.

"Well, this had better never happen again. If it does, Una will not be able to go out with you at all, young man!"

Doc exclaimed. The exclamation included a dragon lady stare in Una's direction.

"Yes, ma'am," Brent said again. Then he flashed his toothpaste ad smile.

"I'll call you, Una."

"All right. Thanks for *everything*."

When she said *everything*, Brent glowed like a silver Christmas ball.

Doc took Una's arm and rushed her up the walk, anxious to get her away from the rake who had violated some unknown part of her innocence.

But Una felt both swooshy and smooth, like the female star of a hit romance. If this was the door to being violated, Una felt ready and anxious to go through it.

I'll find my way out somehow, she told herself.

She called Judy as soon as she got to her room.

"Tell me *everything*," Judy said. "And don't leave out any details."

CHAPTER THIRTY-ONE

HAIL TO THE NO!

Una told Judy that Doc had yelled at her for being late
like she'd never heard her yell before. "I cried, ran to
my room and slammed the door," she said.

But talking to Judy, Una calmed down and remembered
why she'd been so late getting home. "It was both a terrible
and wonderful reason all in one," she said.

"Sounds like it's either a bad crush or you've fallen hard."

"Do you fall just once and land with a thud, or do you
keep falling like you're descending gradually and gracefully
through the clouds?"

"Yep, sounds like you've fallen all right, and with a big
thud. That's my diagnosis. It's a done deal."

"You've made out before, Judy. Didn't you get the ripply
sensation that your chest, stomach and legs were part of
the ocean and you had to lean in and go with the flow of
the waves 'cause you had no choice?"

Judy snickered because Una's description sounded so surreal. She told Una she'd never felt exactly like that.

"I've had sweaty hands," Judy said, "but I never had a whole ocean overwhelm me."

"So, you haven't fallen?"

"Guess not, but you'd better be careful, girlfriend. You're pretty close to the *wild thing*."

"What wild thing? Sex?"

"Sexual penetration. That's the deep well you described; the dark and dangerous tunnel."

"You think Brent is some kind of player, don't you?"

"*Casanova* is a perfect word for him. And if you care about the CHAG, you should be saying *Hail to the No!*'"

"Why? Can't people who care about social justice enjoy sex?"

"Sure. They can have sex and backyard boogie or whatever they want when they're teens, as much as they want, but they have to decide what they're most committed to."

"You mean, I have to decide?"

"Naturally. You have to decide because the fun won't last long unless Brent is in love with you, *for real,* and what do you think the chances of that are when he's just a little older than you?"

"Slim to none."

"Jackpot, genius."

"But it *feels* like love."

"Eating mint chocolate truffles feels like love too, but I'd weigh four hundred pounds if I gave in to my constant desire for them."

"But do your loins get wet when you eat them?"

"No, but they can't get me pregnant either."

"Oh, it's true, I'm not ready for that!"

Judy told Una she might not be ready for *it* but *it* was ready for her. "Do you think Brent will be there hovering over your adorable offspring if something doesn't work out as planned?"

"Hail to the no."

"See, you really are a brain."

"That's why you're my best friend, Judy," Una said.

"I'm sure you'd do the same for me."

"I don't know if I would, but I'm glad you did."

"You have to have a plan."

"What kind of plan?"

"Like maybe double dates or something. Why don't you see if Jazz, Kiki or Sandra can get a date and go with you guys?"

"Or Sasha."

"Yeah, see if another couple can kind of escort you next time. If Brent really cares, he'll deal."

Una said her mind wanted to do it that way, but not her body. Judy said most girls would go ahead and do what they wanted, but Una wasn't *most* girls. She was a girl who had always stood up and fought for what she believed; a girl who wouldn't let anything stand in her way, not even a guy.

"I try, but I'm only human, Judy."

"You need a guy who is as committed to CHAG as much as you are," Judy said. "Brent probably lied and made you think he was *wet behind the ears* when it came to girls.

Well, he was wet behind the ears all right, but likely not for the reason you thought."

"Yeah, I get it."

"Don't be pissed, Una."

"Never. You've given me a lot to think about."

"Call me again soon?"

"I will."

"You're a *mensch*."

"Maybe for now, but my trials are coming. I want it, but I don't. I guess you get my drift."

...

The next afternoon after school, Una called Sasha. She could be loud-mouthed and opinionated, which is why she could probably handle Brent and two more of him. Also, Una figured Sasha could help her laugh her way out of a tough situation. The only problem might be Roy Hunt, Sasha's boyfriend. He was reportedly a member of the Bloods. With Brent attending Roanoke's Geek Academy for the Intellectually Talented, Una wasn't sure the red-blooded dude and the blue-blooded dude would mix. Still, they were both smart guys and probably had a lot in common, like loving cars and trying to get into girls' panties. Una had never talked to Sasha about sex. Never had a reason to, but now . . .

"Hi, Sasha."

"Whaz up?"

"Can we meet someplace? I can borrow Mom's car."

"That's okay. I've got my mom's. Pick you up in fifteen."

"Thanks."

At the Dairy Queen over slushies, Una told Sasha all the gory, delicious details of her night with Brent.

"He a playa," Sasha said with a grin that made Una want to squash it off her face.

"That's what Judy thought, but how do you really know?"

"Sound like he go for a challenge and you definitely that, but he act like he got experience at his game."

"I wasn't much of a challenge last night. I fell right into his plan."

"Ain't no plan. That's just what guys do. Where you been, girl?"

"How do you handle it with Roy?"

"How do I handle what?" she laughed. "I ain't about to tell you my business."

"Can't I ask if you ever wondered if he was *right* for you? You know."

"He got the sparks of Brad Pitt and 2Pac combined. No woman could resist him, but that was the problem. That's why we just broke up."

"He wasn't in love with you?"

"Hell no!"

"So, are you dating anyone now?"

"Josiah Butler asked me out. He our team's quarterback."

"I know. I've seen him. Not bad-looking."

"He creepy lookin' compared to Roy, but he nice enough to talk to."

"I'll get right to my question then: I was wondering if you would double date with me and Brent next time he asks me out."

"Yeah, *if* he ask you out again. That dude sound busy."

"He will."

"Where you want to go?"

"Maybe bowling?"

"Negative. I don't bowl that good. That's out."

"Then let's take the guys to see a movie."

"If you and Deep Pockets buy the tickets."

"No problem. Brent's got the juice."

"I bet. I ought to start calling him *Juicy Fruit*."

"Don't you dare, bitch," Una said, teasing her.

Sasha flipped Una the bird and laughed heartily the way only she could do. Una liked her throaty laugh and her innate style; she had more of it than Whitney Houston, her style icon. She totally forgot that if and when Brent asked her out again, he would already have an idea of where he planned to take her, so the movie would only be a suggestion to compare with whatever he suggested. As long as guys were really in charge of the dating thing, that's the way it would be—at least until there was a relationship carved in cement. Then the girl could make a plan first. Obviously, Una had not done a whole lot of dating, but she was getting the picture of how it was supposed to work. Still, when the phone finally rang after two weeks, she was surprised.

"I'll be having a birthday on the twentieth," Brent said.

"Your seventeenth?"

"No, the twentieth. Just kidding. Yep. I'll be seventeen."

"Cool, do you plan to celebrate?"

"That's why I called. I was hoping you could come to my party. It's at my parents' lake house over at Smithroads

Mountain Lake. I could pick you up about five o'clock on Saturday."

"I'd love to, but I have a favor to ask."

"Shoot."

"I was wondering if I could ask my friend Sasha and her date to come with us."

"Sounds like you already think I'm some kind of wolf. What's wrong, are you afraid to be alone with me?"

"No, it's not that. I just like you a lot and I want you to get to know my friends."

"Okay. No problem. They can meet us out there."

"Oh, no. Sasha doesn't have her own car. We'll need to pick them up."

"Her date doesn't have a car?"

"Nope."

"Then I guess we'll have to. Okay, I'll do it just for you."

"I had thought we could go see a movie sometime."

"Yeah, maybe. I'll see ya Saturday," Brent said.

"Sounds good," Una answered, feeling like the movie idea was a total strikeout.

Una wondered what to get a guy like Brent who had everything. She knew what he really wanted, but besides that.

"What's up?" Una heard a familiar voice say. It was Polithia, sneaking around the corner. "Did you forget that we have a CHAG meeting this afternoon?"

"Oh, I'm so sorry. I've had some other stuff on my mind."

"Like what?"

"Just stuff. I'll get my things."

Polithia quickly figured out that *stuff on her mind* meant a boy, but she was somewhat surprised that the boy was Brent Woo. Mr. and Mrs. Woo were new to her house Bible study/church and new to the community. They said they had moved to Roanoke to lose the competitive life in a large metropolitan city like Chicago. They enjoyed mountain biking and hiking; mainly getting away from it all. But after Una described Brent to Polithia, she felt that maybe the Woo's son had not absorbed his parents' desire for inner tranquility. Instead, he'd soaked up the competitive emphasis that dominated so many peoples' lives in larger cities.

Politha frowned. "Una, you need to be cautious. You're taking on a ton of responsibility right now. This boy could be a definite diversion."

Una said she understood, but what she meant was that her mind understood but her body lagged far behind.

"A man has been the downfall of many a great woman," Polithia said.

"One day I want to have the kind of relationship that Mom and Dad had," Una said.

"But *one day* is at least eight to ten years away. Be brave."

The night Brent picked her up for his party, Una wore a black taffeta dress, cut low enough to reveal a slip of shoulder but not low enough to show boobs; a good thing, since she had none to speak of anyway. She topped the outfit off with black silk pumps and onyx dangle earrings. But she was surprised when Sasha and Josiah showed up wearing jeans.

"Lord, girl, you dressed like you going to a Cinderella ball," Sasha quipped.

As usual, Sasha's keen sense of style for every occasion was correct.

"I thought this was a formal party," Una said.

"I remember telling you to wear what you wanted," Brent said. "But I'm not complaining. You look good enough to binge watch. You look good too, Sasha."

"See? There's a true gentleman," Sasha said, smiling her most mysterious, gushy smile.

She wore black leather sandals laced to the ankles, a slightly revealing green silk blouse, Gloria Vanderbilt jeans, and gold loop earrings. Her hair was brushed out in soft waves. Una figured that Josiah would think Sasha looked good enough to eat. Instead, he kept looking at her while Brent eyed Sasha. The party was mostly just a bunch of guys playing poker, video, and slot machine games in Brent's basement. There were a few girls, but they were all informally dressed in torn jeans or sweatpants with flip-flops, slippers, or sneakers. To say Una felt embarrassed in her fancy black dress was a huge understatement. Brent didn't even introduce her as his date, just as a friend like the others.

By the time Mrs. Woo brought out the chocolate cake with seventeen candles, Sasha was screaming and laughing, playing penny ante poker with the boys.

Of course, she would be *a card player,* Una thought to herself.

Sasha's supposed date, Josiah, and Una sat muddled on the couch, not really saying anything.

"How long have you and Brent been going together?" Josiah finally asked.

"We're not going together," Una said. "And I haven't known him very long."

"How'd you meet him?"

"Long story," she said. "Excuse me. I'm going to get some bottled water from the bar."

No one paid much attention to the cake. Even when Mrs. Woo cut Brent the first piece and everyone sang "Happy Birthday," no one seemed much interested in eating, and there was only one gift, the one from Una.

"Brent, open Una's gift!" Mr. Woo ordered, interrupting the games.

"Oh, okay," Brent said. "Just a minute."

Una wanted to crawl under the couch. She had thought there would be a bunch of expensive gifts, so she convinced Doc to let her buy Brent a leather photo album. She was hoping he would take a shot of the two of them to put in the album. It was engraved with Brent's name in gold letters.

"Nice," was all Brent said. "Anyone else want a piece of cake?"

"I do," said Sasha, who had just won the poker game. "Bring it to me, please, Brent."

Brent sat next to her and handed her a big slice of cake on a plate.

"Why couldn't you cut yourself a piece?" Brent asked. "What, you need me to feed it to you?"

"I wouldn't mind," Sasha purred, the way she had when she first met Brent.

Barf! Una thought.

Then she watched in horror as Brent fed her the cake with his fingers, one bite at a time. She licked her lips between bites and said, "Delish!"

"I'm ready to go, Brent," Una said.

"Please stay a little longer," Josiah said. "I feel like I was just getting to know you."

"Sorry. Later. Brent, I'm ready to go home."

"I'm not ready," Sasha said. "The party is just gettin' started."

"Party pooper!" one of the other girls yelled.

"I'll take her home, Brent," said some girl whose name Una had never caught.

"No, I want *Brent* to take me home," she said in the steeliest tone she could muster.

"Okay," Brent said in a semi-whine. "Wait for me here guys. Be back in twenty."

"Come on, Sasha," Una said.

"I don't want—"

"I don't give a shit. Let's go!"

Sasha must have seen the triple-bitch in Una coming out because she moved. Josiah saw it in her eyes too. And Una didn't care if Brent saw it, or not.

"Let's go, Sasha," Josiah said.

Brent got his keys.

CHAPTER THIRTY-TWO
DATING GAMES AT THE CHAG?

Una called Brent several days after his party and asked him why the hell he was flirting with Sasha at his party. Her green-eyed temper was smoking. Brent must have already figured out what to say because he calmly explained that he was trying to make her jealous and that he seriously planned to call her later that day.

"You ignored me practically the entire time I was there," Una said.

"I didn't mean to freak you out. I really like you, Una. You've got to believe that."

"You probably want Sasha's number."

"Nope. Don't know why you're making such a big deal of this."

"You find her attractive. I can tell."

"I won't deny that, but I find lots of girls nice to look at. That doesn't mean I want to go out with them."

"She's not just nice to look at; she has a great personality too."

"Maybe. She's also got a boyfriend, Josiah."

"You think?"

"Well, she came with him."

"Does that bother you?"

"What bothers me is that you don't believe me."

"It doesn't matter, Brent. You and I have only been out once. We hardly know each other."

"I didn't get a good look at your eyes, but they must be green."

"Aquamarine, thanks to my contacts."

"Close enough."

"Look, Brent. I want to stay friends because you are technically in the CHAG, if you still want to be, and your parents are definitely an important part of the group."

"Same here. I mean, I want to stay friends."

"So, I'm not going to see you anymore as in *going out* together, but I'll see you at meetings."

"Okay, if that's what you want."

"That's what I want."

"It hurts, but I understand."

"I wish I could believe that."

"That I understand?"

"No, that it hurts."

"Goodbye, Brent."

"Goodbye, beautiful. See you at the meetings."

After Una hung up, she texted Sasha and Sasha texted back immediately saying she was mad at Josiah for paying so much attention to Una at the party. Una didn't really believe her, but it was somewhat comforting, all the same. She had a hunch, though, that Sasha had developed a bad crush on Brent. However, she'd have to find out on her own that his game could sting in the end. Ironically, *she* had warned Una that he was a player, and now she was probably getting ready to prove it to herself. Una felt sure that eventually Brent would display his true colors.

Anyway, Sasha's stronger and wiser than me when it comes to street smarts and boys, Una told herself. *Well, that's not exactly true. She did date Roy for a long time, a risky proposition in anyone's estimation.*

In the end, Una was at peace about letting Brent go. Still, she'd never forget his sweet, juicy kisses and his hot embrace. And she certainly wouldn't get his cologne out of her head, either; not for a long, long time.

The next CHAG meeting was scheduled for Friday afternoon at the downtown library meeting room. Una asked Sasha if she wanted to go with her, wanting to get the rough part of seeing her and Brent together again over.

"Damn straight," she said. "I'll meet you there in parking A, on the side of the tennis courts."

Una told her she'd see her there after school at four o'clock.

"Hey, girl!" Sasha said at 4:03, jumping out of the car she'd borrowed from her mom. She was wearing a tennis skirt and a short-sleeve white blouse with a collar. Was this her version of sexy prep? Una wished she didn't have a tendency to analyze everything, but this might be tougher than she'd originally thought, like *dating games* at the CHAG. Shitty.

But she knew this thing would just have to play itself out. Her passionate, unsteady reactions would only make it worse for her and would not affect Sasha's relationship with Brent, should they develop one. She needed to be strong now more than ever.

Una prayed for herself, asking the Great Spirit to give her the strength of a band of super-strong, loud-mouthed angels. She didn't want to be taken for a schnook; yet no one could have prepared her for what would happen next—no one except Shadwell Brooks from her church.

Just an hour before the meeting, Mr. Brooks had called. He told Una he'd dreamed about her the night before and he thought she should hear about the dream ahead of the meeting.

"There were four girls in my dream: you, a straitlaced-looking black girl about your age, a pretty white girl with long hair, and another black girl," Mr. Brooks said.

"Was she wearing lots of makeup?" Una asked. "The last one?"

"Yes, more charismatic perhaps than the others."

"Okay. That was me, Sandra, Kiki, and Sasha."

"Then there was an Asian boy about your age."

"Dark and good-looking?"

"Yes, but his aura was as dark as his hair."

"I think that was Brent Woo."

"Maybe."

"Please, go on."

"The boy who manipulates was playing *mind games*, trying to toy with the sentiments of the people in the room, especially the lovely girls."

"Yes?"

"But the one he chose to light upon was not the one you expected; it was the straitlaced girl."

"Sandra?"

"I think so, from what you've said. Of course, not every dream is prophetic, but often they are meant as a warning."

"That son of a . . ."

"No, Una. This boy is a very nice young man. He's probably just trying to get attention. He knows he is attractive and intelligent. This type of person is primed to assimilate evil spirits until he matures a bit more."

"But that's terrible. Sandra is so sweet and good. She's a lot more innocent than the rest of us. He will hurt her badly if this happens as you saw it in the dream."

"I think I may have a strategy," Mr. Brooks said. "I'll be at the meeting. What if I give Brent a special mission he must accomplish right away, something to pull him out of the group?"

"But what about when he comes back, and what happens at the next meeting? Aren't we just postponing the inevitable?"

"No. We can nip it in the bud."

"I don't know, Mr. Brooks. What if we're messing with karma?"

"Perhaps we are, but doesn't your mother *mess with your karma* when she has a gut feeling that you should turn right instead of left while driving in the car?"

"I guess."

"And what if her feelings warned her that a deer was in the woods getting ready to leap into the road; wouldn't she be messing with fate if she insisted that you take a detour instead of the earlier planned path?"

"I see what you mean."

"So, is it justifiable?"

"Yes, if you look at it that way."

"That's why we pray and ask God for wisdom before we act. Let's have a silent prayer now, shall we?"

Una knew then that Mr. Brooks was a true guide, at least on this particular day. If Brent was allowed to toy with Sandra's feelings, it could not only hurt her, but it could injure the spirit of the whole group. It might even paralyze the group, as such inexplicable things sometimes do. Sandra would probably consider quitting.

When the CHAG members were gathered in the community room of the library, Mr. Brooks said he had forgotten his wallet. He diplomatically asked Brent to accompany him to his place to get money; then they'd stop by McDonald's to get the snacks. It was clear that Brent did not want to go, but his parents insisted that he be helpful. Sasha offered to accompany them, but Mr. Brooks said he wanted to get to know Brent a little better, man to man, so they would ask for her help another time.

Meanwhile, the meeting began with a review of the CHAG Manifesto. Sandra offered to approach the city about planting trees in various urban areas. She and Dr. Davis said they would take care of some of the costs, but she would also do some research and learn how to write grants so the work could be continued throughout the fall.

Kiki, Mrs. Rogers, and Sasha wanted to oversee volunteers. They said they would devise a flier with names, phone numbers, and addresses of everyone in the group. They'd also welcome each member with a packet of inspirational literature, a box of homemade chocolate chip cookies, and a resource guide to the community. In addition, they wanted to hold bi-monthly discussion groups at their homes on topics such as bullying, understanding diversity, developing character, and meditation.

Polithia wanted to take charge of a Saturday childcare co-op to allow young mothers of all colors and cultures to have some free time away from their kids. She would make sure it was properly licensed. The recreation center had agreed to host the co-op if some of the mothers exercising there could use it. Paul said he'd take care of advertising for the co-op using a multimedia approach.

Doc, Paul, and Dr. Davis said they'd stay in touch with Habitat Homes for Humanity (HHH). HHH agreed to assist in building more duplexes in Northwest if the structures were designated Habitat Homes for Humanity. It would also work with CHAG to renovate houses in need of repair, primarily in the Northwest area.

Doc also planned to attend regular city council meetings and speak to local and state government officials concerning the need for affordable housing.

Mr. and Mrs. Woo agreed to chair a committee tasked with contacting local churches and other places of worship about starting food banks and possibly a clothing bank. Presumably, Brent would assist them. He agreed to also help Paul, Polithia, and Mrs. Dunbar move to the new duplex.

Kip and Joanna Coleman said they would start a free art and yoga class at the county library and one creative writing class at the Gainsdown Library. Kip happened to be an artist and a writer, and Joanna could teach yoga.

Mr. Brooks was designated treasurer. He'd produce and regularly share statements of the group's financial activities.

Bishop Morrison and the Praise and Worship team would cover the group in prayer and put on monthly concerts to raise money for CHAG. They planned to recruit musicians who played the African drums They'd also be responsible for advertising in the local papers, a dream come true for Sandra and Una. Church members would also put signs up in public places.

Aunt Candy decided to visit schools and colleges to recruit a team that would possibly create reading theater dealing with the topics of bullying, depression, and drug abuse. Because she had contacts at Tech, she'd start there and work with her friend Alissa Merton, the head of the drama department.

Jazz had taken yoga in Alexandria and dabbled in watercolors. She agreed to start a free yoga class in the projects and a summer art program just for middle schoolers in the Northwest area of the city. She would see if she could raise money with bake sales for the art supplies and she'd ask that yoga mats be donated.

Una had a hard time narrowing down her commitments to one or two, but she landed on a mission she felt would fully express her personality. She'd write and publish stories about African American, Asian American, Native American, Hebrew American, Hispanic American, and Muslim American heroes and heroines. She'd call her platform *Diversity Heroes*. She'd also write and publish *Lunchbag Books*. They would be colorful softcover books about the meaning of diversity, small enough to fit in a purse or a lunch bag. The proceeds would go toward low-cost housing in Northwest and Gainsboro.

Brent and Mr. Brooks returned about five minutes before the close of the meeting. Brent cheerfully announced that he was excited about helping Paul, Polithia, and Mrs. Dunbar move to their new homes the following weekend.

Everyone clapped.

CHAPTER THIRTY-THREE

WHEN PUSH COMES TO SHOVE

The first several weeks of school had been a little confusing for both Jazz and Una with new classes, new teachers, and new classmates. Una had been promoted to eleventh grade, but she and Jazz had mostly different classes. They also had new lunch periods, so the same old familiar groups were no longer accessible.

But at least Sylvia and Mat had given Jazz a white 1999 Honda Accord. They said they wanted her to see them more often, and it was really a gift from her dad. A few weekends after school started, Polithia and Paul drove her to D.C. to pick up the car. They wanted to visit the museums and were able to have a nice meeting with Sylvia, Mat, and Dr. Anna over lunch at the Olde Towne Inn in Alexandria. The NOVA group promised a visit to Roanoke later in the fall.

Una was still perplexed about Jazz's comments concerning her African American heritage, but she'd been asked not to squeal to Sylvia, so she vowed not to. She needed another way to resolve the issue, and she needed it quick if she was going to continue living with Jazz and perhaps catch a ride to school with her. Jazz was also in the CHAG and they shared a class or two. Una thought long and hard about this and realized that despite her promise to not tell Sylvia, she'd never promised not to tell Dr. Anna.

One night, she timidly called Dr. Anna.

"Una, is that really you, girl?" Dr. Anna said, sounding surprised. "I thought you'd be caught up in all your social and mission networks tonight. Jazz told us about the CHAG. How enterprising you are, *wild child*."

Una had never heard herself referred to as a wild child before, at least not by Dr. Anna, and she was flattered.

"Thanks, Dr. Anna. I have a situation to discuss with you. It's confidential, if that's okay."

"Of course, is there a problem?"

"Sort of," Una said. "You see, I discovered not long ago that my family (distant relatives) owned slaves in the South and that obviously disturbed me," Una said. "I mean, it made me want to puke."

"Yes. It's very jarring to think about your own family being involved in a kind of genocide. It was more than a business that big landowners conducted. They were responsible for the deaths of millions of people."

"Yes. So I asked my friend Polithia, who is Mom's nurse . . . well, I asked her to do a bone reading to help me seek out some truth about my ancestors."

"And?"

"And I discovered that I was distantly related to two black slaves."

"I see."

"But that's not all. I found out that I was also related to Polithia's family through her husband Paul's line."

"Interesting. What a strange coincidence!"

"That makes me related in a distant way to the same Gullah people I visited while I was in South Carolina recently, that is, Polithia and Paul's relatives, and even to my friend Sandra Davis, Polithia's niece."

"Do you have a problem with this?" Dr. Anna asked.

"No. In fact, it made me very happy to know it and to be able to claim that connection."

"Go on."

"The problem is that Jazz is unhappy with my new-found identity. She doesn't seem to think I deserve to call myself black or mixed race. I even feel that a part of her hates me for it."

"Do you blame her?"

"Of course not. But she lives with us and goes to school with me and—"

"I understand. You are together a great deal of the time, so you don't want disharmony. What about your other black friend, Sandra?"

"She went with me to South Carolina, so we were able to repair our issues. But I have not been able to do that with Jazz. She asked me if I was willing to tell others that I was black, like my mother's friends or when I fill out a credit application."

"How did you answer?"

"I guess I didn't, really. I had a date the night she asked, and I just told her she didn't understand me."

"So perhaps the problem is that you have not answered that question for yourself. You must do that before you can give Jazz a truthful answer."

"But I don't want to. She shouldn't ask."

"Why not? She has been your good friend for a while now. And I imagine that she reminded you of her own experiences of being a young black woman. There is great pride, but also discrimination and pain."

"Yes, she did say it could be hard."

"How hard do you think it will be for you?"

"Maybe harder than I want to admit."

"Okay. Now we're getting somewhere."

"But what can I do to resolve this?"

"You've just answered that question. Don't you see?"

"Not really."

"No. You don't see because, again, you don't want to see."

Una thanked Dr. Anna and put down the phone. Then she flung herself on her bed and cried. Doc heard her sobbing and came up to ask what was wrong.

"Nothing!" Una yelled. "Please leave me alone!"

Fortunately, Jazz was out with some friends and didn't hear the evidence of Una's misery.

Later that night Una again called Judy in Arizona and explained her heartbreak, briefly detailing Dr. Anna's advice, which was more like a call to evaluate her own mind and heart before she responded to Jazz.

"I have to agree with Dr. Anna," Judy said. "Una, the last lecture at my temple was on the topic of anti-Semitism, but it quickly moved to a discussion of the next race war. Our country has been showing signs of a major race war for a while now."

"Judy, please. I don't even want to think about that."

"But you have to. If you want to claim mixed-race status, will you stand on the African American side of the line in a race war?"

"Why is there always a million-dollar question?"

"What if something happened to your mom and you became responsible for Bitsy? These are things you have to think about."

"Okay. You're making this harder, not easier."

"Good, because these are difficult decisions. You know there is no such thing as a scientifically backed racial construct, don't you?"

"What do you mean?"

"I mean there is virtually no difference genetically between a white person and a black person. That was proven in eugenics experiments. But socially and culturally, there can be loads of differences."

"So?"

"So, you have to decide what world you want to live in. And will you still want to be black when being black is getting people killed? By the way, you know that's already happening. Will you want to be black when that means adopting a culture that's different from yours?"

"Like?"

"Like the extended family rule. Many African Americans live in extended families, just like a lot of Asians and Hispanics do. I guess a house as big as yours could hold at least four or five families, or from sixteen to about twenty people."

"Wow. I knew my house was too big, but I never thought about it being large enough to hold all of those people."

"And you hadn't really considered the possibility of an all-out race war, had you?"

"No, I hadn't."

"Do you know how many fully armed white supremacist militias are out there now?"

"How many?"

"Too many to count. So, still want to claim your black heritage?"

"Would you want to claim your Jewish heritage if you were a teenager in Nazi Germany?"

"Yes. I would because it's who I am, body and soul."

"Even if your hair was blonde enough to allow you to pass as gentile?"

"Yes. I believe with all my heart that I would, even if I knew it would lead me to the gas chambers."

"But you can't know for sure unless you're in that situation."

"That's right."

"And I don't know if I'd run through a fire to save Bitsy, but I hope I would. And I pray that claiming my heritage wouldn't jeopardize my little sister's future in any way, but I have to believe I have the character and the guts and the heart to stand up for what I believe and for who I am—always."

"Okay. I like your answer."

"History will tell the tale."

"That's right. History will eventually reveal what we were all made of when push comes to shove."

CHAPTER THIRTY-FOUR
THE FIGHT

Sandra called Una to ask to meet for coffee after school on a Tuesday. Sandra outlined her eyes with kohl eye pencil and applied a dab of pink lip gloss, unusual for Sandra, who had never worn makeup before. Over coffee, she told Una that a guy from Tilbury Academy had asked her out. Would Una mind her bringing him to a CHAG meeting if she decided she liked him?

"That would be great!" Una said. "What's his name?"

"Rory Schmidt."

"I may have heard of him. Does he live in South Roanoke?"

"Yes, I think he does."

"The only problem is that he could be one of the guys who hangs out with Richard Oliphant. I've kind of had my eye on Richard lately. He plays basketball in the evenings at the cul-de-sac hoop near my house. I've seen several boys with him. They call one of the guys Schmidt. Is he blond?"

"Yes. I guess I shouldn't go out with him then."

"No, just because Richard might be a jerk doesn't mean Rory is. I'd go out with him; see what he's like. Just be aware that Richard can be sneaky, and now that Mrs. Rogers fired him, he may want revenge."

"I thought he got it when he vandalized the duplex."

"That's partly why she fired him, but we can't really prove it was Richard. Even if we could, that may not be the end of it. Still, there's not much we can do unless we catch him in the act."

"Sounds like I'm getting myself into a possible mess," Sandra said.

"Just be careful. You'll get vibes. See if they're good vibes. Besides, Richard and Rory may not be close friends; maybe they just shoot a little basketball together."

"Glad I passed it by you. You've become my BFF ever since South Carolina; did you know that?"

"I love you too. And I appreciate you telling me about Rory. It wasn't necessary though."

"Things can be so complicated sometimes."

"You'd better believe it!" Una laughed. "Like my short romance with Brent."

"I didn't know about that."

"He asked me out, but I got bad vibes; well, mixed vibes. I was really attracted to him."

"I can see why. He's cute."

"Yeah, but I think he's a player and I didn't want him to distract me from the CHAG if it wasn't going to work out."

"So, you ended it?"

"Yep. Now we're just friends. Actually, I think Sasha has a crush on him, but I'm not sure."

"She's not dating that guy Roy?"

"No, they broke up. She never has any trouble getting a date, but we'll see how it works out with her and Brent. For me, the important thing is that he's not on my radar anymore. Now I can throw myself into the group and my missions."

"Brent worked really hard on landscaping around the duplex the first day we met him. Maybe he will end up pulling his weight," Sandra said.

"I hope so," Una said. "Yeah, I remember that day, but he may have just been flexing his handsome set of muscles for our benefit. Who knows?"

"I'd like it if Brent and Rory were friends someday. That sounds silly, doesn't it? I haven't even been out with Rory yet."

"Not at all. No one has too many friends, and I'd love to see Rory get involved."

"But Una, I get that not many kids our age take things as seriously as we do, especially social missions and stuff like that. They're more interested in cars, sports, and getting high."

"True, but there are good and balanced people out there of all ages. We just have to scent them out."

"Well, Brent smells really good, whatever his scent is."

"Oh yeah. Now it's Yves Saint Laurent for Men; the best! But that's also one of the most dangerous smells on earth!"

"Why?"

"It's so totally enticing that it covers up blemishes in his personality."

"Oh, right."

"I'm sure Brent is an okay person; he just isn't right for me."

"He's not my type either."

"You don't know how glad I am to hear that, Sandra."

Sandra didn't ask Una to explain what she meant by that, but a week later she brought Rory to a meeting and he hit it off with everyone right away. He volunteered to plant trees and start a recycling campaign at Tilbury. The city already had the big green recycling bins, but many people still didn't use them. He even thought of a *clean our streets* program for an eight-block section of his neighborhood. He envisioned the program spreading to other neighborhoods in the city.

Bishop Morrison and the Praise and Worship team scheduled their first concert for the second of October. Sandra asked Rory to go, Una asked Jazz, Kiki, and Mrs. Rogers, and Sasha asked Brent, who accepted. Since Sasha was going to sing "My Sweet Lord," she had to sit with the choir. Brent sat on the other side of Sandra; flattering to her but probably annoying to Rory, who kept trying to steer her attention away from him.

Fortunately, Mr. Brooks was also in the choir, looking down on the scene. He shot out of the choir loft and told Brent that he was needed backstage.

"Why?" Brent asked without getting an answer, but he went, reluctantly.

After the concert Brent turned to Kiki and asked if he'd get a box of chocolate chip cookies for helping Mr. and Mrs. Davis and Mrs. Dunbar move into their new homes.

"Maybe," she said with a docile smile.

The following Saturday morning Brent did not disappoint. He showed up at 6:00 a.m. along with Dr. Davis, Sandra, Rory, and all the other CHAG team members. Doc, Polithia, and Paul brought drinks and snacks for the moving crew. But as soon as the last piece of furniture was carried into the duplex, Una spotted Richard Oliphant in the yard with his slightly greasy mop of brown hair. He had the nerve to walk up to Polithia in front of Rory, Sandra, and the rest of the team.

"Nice digs, lady," he said. "Too bad there's a lot of crime here in the hood."

Una knew what Sandra must have been thinking. She had neglected to warn Rory about Richard, probably hoping the situation would resolve on its own.

"What are you trying to say, Richard?" Rory asked. "What are you doing here, anyway?"

"Ask the witch," he said. "She knows."

"Who are you calling a witch, asshole?"

"The tall one with the green hair. Ask her."

"Richard, your mother is an old friend of mine," Doc said. "I'm sure she would not want you over here being disrespectful."

"Not anymore, Dr. Bitch," Richard said. "Ask her. She's not your friend, lady."

"That's all right, I can handle this," Rory said. "Get your ass out of here *now*, bonehead!"

"Stick your head up your ass, Schmidt!" Richard yelled.

Then Rory punched Richard in the face with swift and powerful force, knocking him to the ground and bloodying his nose.

"Stop!" Sandra screamed. "Please stop!"

Dr. Davis and Paul rushed to try to intervene, but Rory took another punch before they could pull the boys apart.

One of Richard's eyes was full of blood and his nose was bleeding. The other eye was black underneath. Doc called an ambulance. Then she called Mrs. Oliphant and asked her to meet the ambulance at the hospital.

The CHAG members trailed the ambulance to the emergency room.

"If my son is seriously hurt, I'll sue you and your daughter's little group for millions, Dorothy," Mrs. Oliphant warned.

"I'm sure Richard will be okay, Clarise," Doc tried to assure her.

"Are you really? Well, as I said, he'd better be."

On the way to the hospital Sandra apologized to Rory for not telling him sooner about Richard Oliphant. She explained the situation as Una had described it to her, back to when Mrs. Oliphant insisted on waiting for Doc against Una's wishes during Mrs. Rogers' healing, the shunning Doc suspected was connected to her push for affordable housing, and Sandra and Una's small-town fame, that is, being on TV picketing city hall. In short, the Zipley and Davis families became *notorious* to people like the Oliphants.

Graham Oliphant, the city manager, was a notable proponent of the use of *eminent domain* to accomplish the city's broad financial goals. He was a member of a coterie of men who ran the city with an iron fist. Ironically, Graham Oliphant was an attorney from Raleigh, North Carolina, who'd lived full-time in Roanoke for only about five years. He also had vacation homes in two other states. He seemed to know little about the African American community's rich, yet tortured history in the valley.

As in many small cities across America, highly educated young men and a few women were recruited from around the country to filter in and assume leadership positions. There appeared to be a one-sided formula for leadership in communities like Roanoke: the rich versus the poor. According to the professional class, the poor were okay if they stayed out of sight and in their places. Doc and Una recognized this pretty quickly after moving to the area. Historically, the formula was black versus white, and although that had been changing gradually, systematic racism and overt discrimination continued to thrive.

When Gainsboro was a famous African American entertainment center, white businessmen in Roanoke were jealous. At least, that's what Paul and Polithia believed, and there was evidence this opinion was justified. Otherwise, why would a city remove one thousand African American bodies from a cemetery and throw them in a mass grave out in the country (twenty miles outside of town) just to construct an interstate through the exact location where the dead had been buried? The old cemetery was a few miles from the center of Gainsboro (see "Family Notes").

This was a secret that many white people didn't want to talk about. If it weren't for the remains of what Polithia called *oral tradition*, the general public might never have known about it after a generation.

Una's mind drifted and circled these harsh realities on the way to the ER. She felt that Rory unknowingly got caught in the middle of something far more evil than an angry kid calling her and Doc names. Polithia held Una's hand on the way to the hospital, praying with her that Richard's injuries were not severe. She also slipped a good luck amulet into her hand.

"It's tiger's eye," she said. "It will help you release the anxiety so a sense of wisdom and balance will replace the fear."

Una knew the talisman was from someone Polithia loved, but she believed in passing along important gifts to others as needed.

By the time all the CHAG members had gotten to the hospital, Rory's dad and Richard's parents had also arrived. Leland Schmidt shook Doc's hand and asked her and Dr. Davis to explain what had happened. Rory wanted to explain, but since he was accused of being the perpetrator of a crime, Mr. Schmidt wanted to hear from the adults who witnessed the incident firsthand.

"I've put in a call to our attorney," Mr. Schmidt said. "If one of you could meet with us next week, I'd appreciate it."

Una and Doc agreed to be present at the meeting.

"I called my lawyer, too, just in case," Doc said.

It turned out that Doc's lawyer and Mr. Schmidt's were in the same firm, which would make it easier to consult with them as a team. After two hours, Richard was still in the emergency room. The hospital had called their top ophthalmologist into the ER. After several more hours a doctor came out to address Mr. Schmidt.

"I'm Dr. Mills. Mr. and Mrs. Oliphant wanted me to let you know that we found a corneal abrasion and hyphema, an accumulation of blood, in Richard's right eye from the punch he took."

"Will he be okay?" Rory asked.

"I'm going to treat it with medication and keep a watchful eye on it," Dr. Mills said. "He'll have to wear a patch over the eye and stay in bed for a while. At this point, we don't know if the damage will be permanent."

"Thank you," Mr. Schmidt said.

The CHAG team waited to try to talk to the Oliphants, but by suppertime, they had not come out of the ER. Rory's face looked gray with worry and stress.

Doc suggested that everyone leave and meet as a group the following week to discuss the fallout. Una, Jazz, and Doc went home and relieved the sitter who was watching Bitsy. They ate cereal for supper. No one slept well for the next several nights. Doc was unable to reach her lawyer, Ron Rupert, until the following week. He agreed to come to the CHAG meeting to discuss the case that Friday. Naturally, he expected to be well paid.

Mr. Schmidt had already met with his attorney, so he'd been informed about the possible complications involved, but he and Rory also attended the meeting.

Mr. Rupert introduced himself, then got right to it. "If the Oliphant family decides to bring a lawsuit, they will likely have to sue the Schmidt family since Rory Schmidt has admitted to perpetrating the injury to their son."

"So they can't try to blame the CHAG members?" Paul asked.

"Highly doubtful, since they have no proof that other members of the group had anything to do with influencing Rory to commit the offense."

"We're so apologetic, Rory and Mr. Schmidt," Dr. Davis said. "We will assist on paying any damages and court costs."

"Yes. I'm so very sorry, Rory," Sandra said.

Mr. Schmidt just nodded, and Rory kept his head down.

"The trespassing committed by Richard Oliphant the day of his injuries was obvious, but it's just a class 1 misdemeanor if he is found guilty," Mr. Rupert said.

"How might he be punished?" Aunt Candy asked.

"Richard could possibly do a little time in a juvenile detention center and his family could be slapped with fines, but the law will likely be more focused on Richard's injuries than on his crime."

"What might Rory's punishment be?" Sandra asked.

"That's a sticky call in Virginia," Mr. Rupert said. "The court will examine whether or not the use of force was reasonable. You're lucky the property was posted. That makes a difference."

Mr. Rupert said that the Oliphant family might ask for a settlement; perhaps a large out-of-court settlement. They would be aware that their son was trespassing, and they probably also knew he was guilty of an earlier act of vandalism.

"How much?" Martin asked. "What's a ballpark number for what the settlement might be?"

"Could be thousands. That depends on the judge, but if it goes to trial, the consequences could be much worse."

"What if the boy's eye heals?" Paul asked.

"The court will consider that as well, but his doctors say they may not know what his prognosis is for weeks—or even months."

"Richard's father is a powerful man in the city," Una said.

"Yes. That may be considered as well, though it shouldn't. I'm not speaking against any one judge, but judges are fallible human beings, just like the rest of us."

Bishop Morrison and the others from Una's church sat motionless and speechless. Mr. and Mrs. Woo also sat quietly, showing no emotion. Brent Woo did not attend the meeting. Kip and JoAnna Coleman looked deeply troubled, as did Paul and Polithia, but no one said much.

Aunt Candy put her arm around Doc. She whispered that she was concerned about how Doc's medical practice could survive this. The concern had not escaped Doc either.

The look on Dr. Davis' face matched Sandra's: bleak and full of terror, mainly terror of the unknown. But the person who took it the worst was Rory. He must have felt responsible for Richard's injuries. He may have been somewhat responsible, but in a more profound sense, it was Mrs. Oliphant's racism and impatience that led to the fight.

"I think we'll go now," Mr. Schmidt announced. "Come on, Rory."

Neither of them said goodbye. Their failure to communicate made Una nervous. They rushed out the door and did not look back.

"I feel light-headed, Mom," Una said. "Chills are running up and down my spine like I've been hit by lasers."

"Una, none of us expected Richard to show up when he did, so unexpectedly. It was a diabolical chain reaction, a domino effect," Polithia said.

Doc ushered Una into a seat. She had chosen to stand during the meeting, but with business wrapped and the group sitting in stunned silence, Una looked faint. Doc asked Polithia to get her medical bag out of the car.

Aunt Candy got some cold water and a washrag. She held the damp cloth to Una's neck and forehead.

"It will be all right," Paul said. "We've got to believe that."

Doc listened to Una's chest. Her heart was racing, but Sandra looked pale, too, and her eyes were slightly dilated. Doc took her pulse and found it to be weak, but fast. She suggested that Dr. Davis take Sandra home right away and get her to rest.

"I'll do that and make her some chicken soup," he said. "That's what I'll do. I'll make her some soup."

If only chicken soup could actually relieve this problem, Una said to herself.

CHAPTER THIRTY-FIVE
MORE QUESTIONS THAN ANSWERS

Sandra felt she should have told Rory about Richard; she should have prepared him. Una also felt horrible for not warning Rory that he might be walking into a quagmire, but Sandra believed that since she was the one dating him, she should have been the one to warn him. Rory thought Richard was his basketball buddy and his friend. Sandra would never forget the look in Rory's soft blue eyes when he left; he was the innocent in all of this, just trying to protect her, Doc, and Una.

About a month after *the incident* on Grace Street, the Oliphant family threatened the Schmidts with a lawsuit, confirming the CHAG's fears. They were never told the exact charge, nor did they know how much money the Oliphants had in mind. They didn't even know Richard's final prognosis. Dr. Davis and Doc Zipley tried repeatedly to reach Mr. Schmidt. They called, wrote notes, and even sent him signed receipt delivery letters through registered mail. The letters were eventually returned unopened. Sandra also tried to reach Rory. She knocked on his door several times, wrote letters and called every day, but he never responded, nor did he return to school.

One day in early November, members of the CHAG read in the obituaries that Rory Anderson Schmidt had died suddenly at age sixteen. Details of his death were not revealed, except to request that in lieu of flowers, donations be sent to the Roanoke Valley Mental Health Association. Rory's interment was to be held in Greenwich, Connecticut.

Sandra found it in the paper first. She was devastated. She couldn't speak and refused to leave her bedroom for over a week. Dr. Davis, Doc Zipley, and Polithia found an excellent therapist for her, but she wouldn't talk to anyone, not even to Una. To ease Sandra's pain, Dr. Davis applied for home schooling with a tutor for her.

The CHAG members were in mourning too. They temporarily suspended all meetings.

"I have tried to understand, but I don't," Una told Polithia. "I don't understand why this happened. I don't understand now, and I don't think I ever will. Where is the Great Spirit? Where is the magic and the light that I've always believed in?"

Polithia also felt brokenhearted, but she put her arms around Una and held her close. She would do the same for Sandra whenever Sandra would let her in. Una remembered the way Sylvia used to rock her when she was younger when she felt depressed, but now she was hours away and Una's guilt grew more intense by the hour, increased by the knowledge that Sandra probably suffered from terrible guilt too, even though it wasn't her fault.

Jazz stayed quiet in her room and even Bishop Morrison did not call for several days. The only person shouting their feelings was Bitsy. She didn't understand why everyone was in such a sour mood. She was always super sensitive about the vibes around her.

"Mama!" Bitsy screamed with desperation, but Doc was with her patients, so Una took a day off from classes to play with Bitsy when she came home from preschool.

While her little sister napped, Una found time to write to Sylvia, asking her to call her when she could. Sylvia finally did call, and Una poured out her heart to her, explaining all the gruesome details of the fight that led to Rory's suicide.

"Child, I want you to do something that may sound kind of strange to you now, but it will make sense later," Sylvia said.

"Okay. Anything that will help."

"I want you to write a skit or a brief play about Rory going up to heaven. I want you to imagine that he's there because you know he is."

"A play?"

"Yeah. I think this imaging will help you connect with that boy's spirit and then you will feel so much better."

"I see what you mean. Okay, Sylvia, I'll try."

"You don't need to tell folks what you're doing; just go ahead and do it."

"After that, it might be good to ask Doc if Marsha could come down from Chicago for Thanksgiving."

"Oh, that's a great idea. Maybe Rowe could come with Marsha."

"I know it's a lot to ask of their families, but just this once maybe."

"I could try. I'd love that and I think Jazz would enjoy meeting them too."

"Naw, now Jazz is coming up to see me and Mat for the holiday; she can meet them another time."

"Okay. I'll get started on the skit right away. Or the play, whichever it turns out to be."

"Good. And remember, Una. Don't hold the burden for this on your shoulders."

Una thanked Sylvia and clicked off her cell. She wondered if Bitsy would stay asleep a little longer so she could have time to write. She did.

···

I guess the way I ended up here makes no difference—because life isn't a straight line, and sometimes you find yourself heading in a new direction. Sometimes, in fact, the journey takes you light-years away from where you were in the beginning. But that's okay.

So, is this death?

I suppose so in the way you think of it, but we don't call it that here. It's more of a transfer of energy from one place to another. Actually, it isn't a place as you would think of it. It's a dimension.

So, am I in heaven?

Sort of, in your way of looking at it, but it's not called that here.

Honestly, if I had it to do again, I wouldn't have left Earth plane so violently. So tragically. I wasn't really that type of guy.

I never wanted to stand out.

Never sought revenge.

Hell, I was rarely ever angry enough to squash a fly, yet . . .

But I must say, as soon as I walked through the door here, there were people I'd always wanted to meet; always, meaning since ninth grade when I had Ms. Shirley Lucas (made-up name) for History of the United States. She had a library in the classroom, so we didn't even have to walk down the hall to find a good book.

The first actual person to greet me when I got here after my grandma, Mrs. Jenny-Jane Berry (made-up name), was Mr. Frederick Douglass.

When I shook his hand, I asked what I should call him.

"Frederick Augustus Washington Bailey" (his real name), he said. "Not Fred or Freddie, please. But Frederick is okay, or Augustus; they are names my mother gave me."

"Augustus, then."

I asked if he had a few minutes.

"An eternity, if you wish, young man," he said.

I found him to be very cool and polite. He's a middle-aged African American man with a black beard and a distinguished-looking mustache. High cheekbones. Serious eyes and mouth. A deep worry line on the bridge of his nose. Looks like he's seen a lot of torment, but miraculously, he has a good sense of humor. Still, he has the demeanor of a judge. A prophet.

"You were really a kind of prophet in the America of your day," I commented.

I wasn't trying to flatter him, just stating a fact. He had no response.

I wanted to say something brilliant, but I was still a kid compared to him and hadn't earned his wisdom.

"They usually kill the prophets," I said, knowing that to be true.

He told me he had survived literal murder on Earth plane, but his transcendental heart had been crushed many times.

"Sometimes the body survives the heart, but not always," I told him, not knowing where in the hell that came from.

"You see?" he said. "The young have wisdom too."

I asked him what he would say if he were able to speak to the people of the Earth today—say, standing on the steps of the Lincoln Memorial.

"That kind of a hypothetical question is difficult to answer in light of the infinite, a place where I

can look a thousand years into mankind's future,"
he said, pulling a lit mahogany pipe out of his vest.

"Well, how do you feel about what you see?"

"I feel many ways at once. I feel saddened, of
course, by dying civilizations."

"Dying?"

"Yes, at their own hands."

"Like I died?"

"No, you died like a martyr, for a cause. You were
just too young to understand the ramifications of
your decision. I mean that people sometimes engi-
neer the death of their own spirits. That, in turn,
destroys the spirit of Earth."

"So, will human life end before time?"

"The life of the human spirit, the human soul;
that is my concern."

Augustus told me that time is just a human con-
struct. He suggested that I speak to a man named
Albert about that.

"I believe Einstein was his last name. Fascinating
man. You may have heard of him. He surfaced on
Earth plane after me and before you."

"I know of him. He was a famous scientist and
a mathematician."

"Yes. You see, humans are rapidly destroying
Earth and all its life forms as they eagerly destroy
each other, so what will remain is incomprehensible
to me."

"But God says His word will remain forever."

"Yes," Augustus said. "That is why I have faith that the Heart of the Earth and its inhabitants will heal someday. The two will flow together."

Augustus told me that he had a monumental faith that there will always be some brave hearts in each generation who will participate in the discipline accessible to them and who will find the will and the faith available to them to carry God's cross.

"God's cross?"

I knew about it, but I still wasn't sure what he meant.

"That is, to fight injustice and inequality, bigotry and hatred in all of its myriad forms. The cross is a metaphor for the dreadful burdens of God."

"I get it. And I mean no disrespect, but doesn't God ever laugh? Like you, I know he's very loving, but I haven't seen him laugh."

"Oh, yes. He laughs all the time, and he needs people to spread that laughter too. Humor is one of his greatest gifts. Humor and love are the stuff that make life worth living. And music. Don't forget music."

We talked on about many things. Augustus said that although he loved to laugh, he didn't find anything funny about W. L. Garrison's hardhead-edness when he wanted to start his own abolitionist newspaper.

"Garrison started his paper first, The Liberator, but mine was The North Star, a much better rag," he said.

MORE QUESTIONS THAN ANSWERS

"So there was rivalry?"

"Yes, but we renewed our friendship when the Civil War broke out, and in the end, we were the best of friends. You should have seen us dancing a jig the night they emancipated the slaves!"

"Was it God's gift of forgiveness and stuff?" I asked.

"That and some good port wine," he said with a gigantic smile.

If his smile had been a bench, I'd have sat down right there for eons. But I would have missed the family picnic. And shy as I still found myself to be, I looked forward to striking up a conversation with Mr. Einstein.

—Rory Schmidt

CHAPTER THIRTY-SIX
TRYING TO CARRY ON

After Rory's death, Sandra rarely spoke for months, Sasha stopped singing in church, and the CHAG stopped meeting. Mrs. Rogers and Kiki brought cookies and casseroles to Doc and Dr. Davis several times, with little notes saying they were so sorry for telling Richard about the healing, which led to other things that were nobody's fault.

Bishop Morrison and the Praise and Worship team continued to preach, pray, and praise, but healing was slow to come. Mr. Brooks visited the Zipley family a few times, but Una didn't usually wake up in time for church anymore. Brent Woo and his parents brought flowers and even distributed a few plants to Una and her four girlfriends. Brent was no longer the player they once knew. Judy kept in touch and hoped to visit Una again sometime in the spring. Polithia continued to work at Doc's clinic and prayed daily that her practice wouldn't lose any more patients, but Doc did lose a handful of her regular patients after the fight and the lawsuit.

Polithia, Paul, and Mrs. Dunbar visited Doc often. Doc and her daughters visited them too, but Jazz became ever more distant, as though she didn't belong at Doc's and was no longer Una's friend. No one heard much from Kip and JoAnna Coleman immediately after Rory's death. Aunt Candy came by when she could and stayed in constant touch with Doc and Una. Graham and Clarise Oliphant dropped all charges against Mr. Schmidt. According to the paper, they moved to Omaha, Nebraska, for some unknown reason. A man named John Giles Harrington took Mr. Oliphant's place as Roanoke City Manager.

Even though Una didn't know Rory that well, she thought about him every day. He represented innocence, the *violence of innocence;* the violence that sought to protect honor and yet had led to a young man's death.

CHAPTER THIRTY-SEVEN
THANKSGIVING

Bishop Morrison called the week before Thanksgiving to ask Doc if he might come for a brief visit. When he arrived, he said he'd intended to ask how she and Jazz and Una were doing, but their faces said it all. Doc had shadows beneath her eyes. Jazz looked worn out, too, and Una looked as if she'd washed her face in bleach. Even little Bitsy looked frustrated and exhausted. She had never been much of a whiny child, but she'd whined a lot over the last month or so.

The Bishop said he and the church wanted to do something to get the CHAG members breathing again. They wanted to sponsor a Christmas concert and dance. His nephew, Brian Morningsong from Georgia, agreed to perform. He had a group that played African drums. They knew how to do the South African gumboot dance—in which the dancers wore boots embellished with bells—too. In fact, they could teach it. He suggested renting out the Ruritan Club for the event.

"Invitations could be sent out and CHAG members could advertise it in the papers," Bishop Morrison said. "Naturally, the Praise and Worship team will host and participate."

"Sounds fantastic," Doc said. "And maybe Sasha would agree to sing."

Jazz merely shrugged her shoulders. "Whatever," she said. "I'll be with Aunt Sylvia and Uncle Mat."

Then the Bishop admitted that he'd already gotten commitments from Brian and Sasha, as well as the Praise and Worship team. He'd also taken the liberty of reserving the Ruritan Club. All that was left was to send out invitations and announce the dance at church and in a press release for the papers.

"It's exactly what Sandra and I dreamed of after returning from the Lowcountry," Una said. "We wanted to bring the music and culture of South Carolina to Roanoke and the valley."

Jazz rolled her eyes and went back to her room.

"It may be just what we need to boost our spirits, and the spirit of the community too," Dr. Davis said when Una called to tell him about the plans. "Neither Sandra nor I have had the heart to deal with the CHAG since Rory's death, but perhaps the Bishop is right; maybe this will inspire us to connect with our roots again."

■■■

The morning before Thanksgiving, Polithia and Doc picked up Marsha and Rowe from the airport. As Una had prayed, they were able to come for the holiday. But she stayed behind to say goodbye to Jazz, who planned to drive back to D.C. in her new car.

"I'm all packed," Jazz said, whistling a happy tune for the first time in ages. "See ya later, Una."

"Can you spare a few minutes?" Una asked. "I want to tell you something—something I need you to know before you go."

"Make it quick, please. Aunt Sylvia expects me by three."

"I've thought a whole lot these last few months, even before Rory's death, about my claim to having black heritage."

"Oh no, here we go. I don't think I have time for this."

"What I realized is that my greatest source of pride is that instead of being ashamed of my past because I'm related to some asshole who owned slaves, I'm proud of my past because the better part of me, the darkest part, fought to overcome oppression."

"Okay?" Jazz said with a question mark in her voice, like she knew Una's epiphany wasn't done.

"What I'm trying to say is, if I could be connected in any way to Rosa Parks, M. L. King, Malcolm X, W. E. B. Du Bois, Marian Anderson, James Baldwin, Gwen Brooks, Ralph Ellison–"

"Okay. I see."

"Not finished. Maya Angelou, Jesse Owens, Paul Robeson, Nikki Giovanni, John Coltrane, Zora Neale Hurston, Romare Bearden, G. W. Carver, Ben Banneker . . . the list goes on into infinity; if I could be in their camp in any way, then I'd consider myself the luckiest girl on earth."

"I'm not sure what to say."

"But I still didn't answer the question you asked months ago. You asked if I would stand up for black instead of just talking about it when the heat was low, and the answer is *yes*."

"Yes?"

"Yes. Of course, no one knows what they would really do if someone were to put a gun to a loved one's head or something like that, but yes, at least I pray that I will always let the real me come out."

"So, you'll put it on your license?"

"Affirmative—and on every other form that asks for my racial identity. I can't change my skin tone, but I can change my status to fit my self-image."

"Then I claim you," Jazz said, hugging Una. "At least for the time being. Don't make a fool of me."

"I won't."

"Happy Thanksgiving."

"Same to you."

...

About an hour after Jazz left for D.C., Marsha and Rowe arrived with Doc and Polithia. Una smiled so big her face hurt.

"I guess you guys got introduced to Polithia," she said.

"We sure did," Marsha replied. "Now please give us a tour of this mansion you've got here."

"First, let me show you to your rooms."

"Our rooms . . . you mean we each get our own room?" Rowe asked.

"Yeah, but I know you. You'll probably end up in the same room pillow fighting and listening to music all night," Una said.

"Oh, no you don't!" Doc exclaimed. "Thanksgiving is tomorrow, and you girls are going to get some shut-eye."

"Okay, Dr. Z.," Marsha said. "I know I'm gonna have some jet lag anyway."

"That's right," Doc affirmed. "So visit for a few hours after supper and then call it a night."

"I'd better get on home," Polithia said. "Got a turkey to put in the oven late tonight."

"Tonight?" Doc asked.

"Oh, yeah," Polithia said. "I baste it all night the way my mama done."

"Hey, that sounds yum," Doc said. "I've never been the greatest cook. You know that."

"Yep. I do," Polithia said bluntly. "Why don't you and the girls head on over to our place tomorrow for some *real* turkey and fixings? My place is kind of small, but the kitchen is the largest room in the house!"

"Oh, we couldn't impose!" Doc said.

"No, you couldn't, but it's not imposin' when a friend invites you, and that's what I just did. Besides, Una is family, so I guess you are too!"

"But Bitz is a mess."

"She's my favorite of all! I think I've got Paul's old highchair folded in the back closet."

"Well, then, if Ms. Dunbar and Paul won't mind, we'll be there. What time did you say?"

"Along about noon would be fine."

The next day, Rowe carried the potato salad, Marsha carried the rolls, Bitsy got the napkins and her bib, Una carried the green bean casserole, and Doc got the Cokes with a bag of ice. The rest was in Paul's hands, since Polithia specialized in the turkey and gravy, but Ms. Dunbar brought sweet potatoes with marshmallows, green bean salad, and collards. Paul decided on mashed potatoes with brown gravy, old-fashioned cornbread with onions, and pintos. In short, there was enough food to feed a battalion of Marines. Bitsy couldn't decide what to eat first, so she tried to cram everything into her small mouth.

"Watch her, Mom!" Una yelled. "She's eating so much she'll explode like Marvin Delany's pig!"

"You mean Roberta," Marsha said.

"Yeah."

"But Roberta never exploded."

"And neither will Bitsy," Paul said. "Looks like ya'll been starvin' the poor baby."

"Now all we got to do is pray over the food!" Ms. Dunbar said.

"Oh, sorry," Una said. "I'm ashamed to say that I've already begun eating."

"Then you say the prayer, girl."

"Okay," Una replied.

She gave thanks for her friendships with Jazz, Marsha, and Rowe, for the food, for the heroes that had overcome so much, and for her *family in Christ* that included every-one at the table and beyond. Gone at least temporarily from her mind were the painful moments of the last few months and the shadow days that had made her question everything.

"Now let's eat!" Paul shouted, plunging his fork into the turkey.

And everyone did.

ive days before Christmas, the concert and dance hosted by Garden of Our Savior Baptist Sanctuary was held at the Ruritan Club in Roanoke. Brian Morningsong and his African Stompers were great; the music was just as inspiring as everyone expected it to be. Local schoolkids received special free tickets. The Praise and Worship team even threw in some gospel, and Sasha sang her unique version of "Jesus Is a Rock in a Weary Land."

Mr. Brooks said almost $3,000 was raised in cash donations from the event, but just the inspiration it provided was worth its weight in gold. Alissa Merton, the drama professor at Tech, came with Aunt Candy. They enjoyed the concert so much that they told Una they had decided to start the reading theater program spring semester. They wanted to recruit Brian's group to perform at Tech as well as some other local schools.

After the performances, Sandra took the microphone to tell the crowd a little of what she knew about Rory. It was the first time she had spoken about him since his death. She talked about his volunteer activities, his reputation at school, but mostly about his big heart for people. Then Dr. Davis came up to the microphone. He said he had a surprise announcement: The Davis family was giving a hundred trees and a new bench to the Roanoke Greenways, the part located in the Northwest section of the city, in memory of Rory.

A bench would be engraved with Rory's name and a favorite passage he'd once quoted to Sandra from Alice Walker's book, *The Way Forward Is with a Broken Heart*: "Healing begins where the wound was made."

Then Sasha sang "I'll Fly Away." There wasn't a dry eye. It was as special as any memorial service Una had ever seen. Many of Rory's friends and his parents weren't there, but everyone knew Rory would have loved it. Dr. Davis and Bishop Morrison had both tried to reach Rory's parents but couldn't. Nevertheless, the message that stuck that night for most in attendance was that love doesn't end with death. Sometimes it even increases after someone dies. Una felt that way when her father passed. She sensed his presence, strong and true, and she continued to feel it.

When the gumboot dancers performed their last number, Una felt the presence of Ellen, Nelly, and so many others gone before. She felt as though they were reaching out through time and space to bring comfort and to remind the CHAG that their mission here was far from over.

Sandra said she felt it too. And she felt Rory's presence. It was an unexpectedly joyous feeling. A peaceful feeling. She smiled for the first time in many weeks.

"I think he'll be okay now," she said. "And I think he forgives me."

"Of course he does," Una said. "And you'll be better than okay. You'll be *great*."

"And you; he forgives you, too, Una."

"I hope so. I believe he does."

"And you'll learn to forgive yourself, Una, for all the things you can't name right now."

Doc, Una, Jazz, and Bitsy asked Sandra to go Christmas shopping with them. They bought arts and crafts supplies with which to create things: Finger paints for Bitsy. Clay birds to paint. Small houses that looked like the duplexes. Tiny canvases to display. They created collages and watercolors and sachets and plaques with special messages like: "Injustice anywhere is a threat to justice everywhere."

They each bought a real miniature pine tree on sale and filled their trees with twinkly white lights, strings of popcorn, and little red bows. They also added ornaments made from poster board, glitter, and ribbons with two-inch photos of loved ones pasted in the middle. That night the church choir, including Sasha, sang *Handel's Messiah* at the Christmas Eve service. Una sat to Doc's left, with Sandra on Doc's right. Kiki and Jazz were on Sandra's right, followed by Sasha's mom and Jazz. Polithia, Paul, and Dr. Davis sat behind them, along with the original members of the CHAG—except, of course, Rory. Polithia passed the Kleenex.

"Mama, it's too beautiful to be real," Bitsy said, her eyes aglow.

On Christmas Day Una and Jazz fixed pancakes with green frosting eyes and hats like elves, cheese omelets, grits, bacon, strawberry parfaits with cherries, and mull cider—all their favorites. Doc, Bitsy, Jazz, and Una listened to Nat King Cole's Christmas album while they had their coffee milk (a little coffee with loads of milk and sugar). Then they each read their new Christmas books. Una gave Doc *The World of Frida Kahlo: The Blue House,* published by The Houston Museum of Fine Arts, and Doc gave Una a copy of *The Biography of Malcolm X, as told to Alex Haley,* published by Ballantine Books. Jazz gave Una Maya Angelou's book, *I Know Why the Caged Bird Sings,* and Una gave her *The Source of Self-Regard* by Toni Morrison. They had shared their wish lists before the holidays, so they were all ecstatic to unwrap their special gifts.

It was a peaceful Christmas, but it bubbled with gaiety too. Sylvia, Mat, Dr. Anna, and James drove down in the afternoon. Dr. Davis and Sandra came over, too, and they all went for a hike in the mountains after a huge lunch prepared by Doc with the help of the new cookbook that Jazz gave her for Christmas.

The weather was chilly, and the morning was overcome for a time by a dense fog; but after noon, a brilliant marmalade sun emerged. It broke through the clouds and lit everyone's spirits.

D oc Zipley moved both her home and her practice to the Gainsboro section of Northwest Roanoke City. Sylvia and Mat Leonard eventually relocated to Roanoke to assist Doc with her clinic and participate in the CHAG. Dr. Anna and James Ozzina moved back to Africa to continue their work there.

Una Zipley changed her name to Yuna, the Nigerian spelling. She became a journalist, an English teacher, and fiction writer. Despite years of concentrating on becoming a superior occultist, she finally admitted that she was better at putting her magic on paper. She moved to Chinle, Arizona, where she teaches high school English on the reservation with her husband, Miles Begay, a math teacher. She has published seven books of fiction and twenty-one poetry chapbooks.

Dr. Candy Jasper eventually founded Concerned Citizens for Environmental Justice in Rural America (EJRA). She does a weekly podcast and when she's not teaching, she travels across the country speaking about EJRA.

Polithia and Paul Davis founded Jubilee Clinic in Northwest Roanoke for medically underserved adults and children. They still live and work in Gainsboro.

Dr. Martin Davis became the Mayor of Roanoke City. He and many others were able to build new housing, restore old housing, and put a stop to the destruction of the black community in Northwest.

Sandra Davis became a civil rights attorney and public speaker. She married Clay Fettersing, Chief Judge of the General District Court in Richmond, Virginia. She kept her maiden name after discovering in a dream that she was a distant relative of Harriet Tubman Davis. The Davis-Fettersing family has three children.

Kiki Rogers married Brent Woo. She joined an accounting firm in Sarasota, Florida, where Brent started his own franchise, *Spice on the Run.*

Jazz Jones created *Backpack Books,* an idea passed along to her by Yuna when they were teens. Her company, *Jazz for Young & Old*, has published more than ten million small books about diversity and inclusion. She married Patrick Cox and moved back to Alexandria, Virginia.

Sasha Carter never married. She moved West and became a United States Senator from the State of California (after establishing a successful singing career).

Judy Light moved to Flagstaff, Arizona, with her husband, Peter Goldberg. They own and manage two retirement communities for indigent adults. Judy and Una see each other once a month for lunch. Sasha joins them whenever she can.

Bitsy Zipley lives in Washington, D.C., where she is working on her doctoral degree in environmental engineering at Howard University. She hopes to work with a firm in Detroit, Michigan, one day.

Marsha Plimpleton and Rowe Riley never married but Marsha adopted a little boy named Riley. Together they own and manage a successful bed & breakfast in Chicago.

Sasha said Roy became Lieutenant Commander Roy Hunt in the navy. He was stationed in Norfolk, Virginia, last she heard.

The two-hundred member CHAG started by Yuna Zipley, Sandra Davis, and friends won the Congressional Medal of Honor for their committed mission to secure social, racial, environmental, and economic justice in areas of Virginia, North Carolina, Georgia, and Kentucky. The group recently enjoyed a reunion supper at Trader Vic's in D.C. At the supper, all the original members confessed that they had enjoyed a visitation from Ms. Rosa Parks. In each of the spiritual contacts Ms. Parks was wearing a handsome red taffeta suit with a red hat and a beguiling smile. Yuna happened to be wearing red that night. She took a selfie with the CHAG and, somehow, an image of Roberta the pig was seen in the background. She was licking the leftovers.

"Where's Marvin Delaney?" Yuna wondered.

...

Gainsboro, the oldest section of Roanoke, Virginia, became a vibrant neighborhood again. In fact, it has become a major tourist attraction for Americans of all races and a paradigm for urban development *of the people and for the people.*

WORKS CONSULTED

Campagna, Mary E. "Family Notes."

Chourey, Sarita. "Input Sought on Allendale Landfill." *The August Chronicle* (2014). Web.

"Corona." *Merriam-Webster.com Dictionary*, Merriam-Webster, https://www.merriam-webster.com/dictionary/corona. Accessed 5 Apr. 2020.

Friday, Raymond L. *The Book of the Navajo.* New York: Kensington Publishing Corp., 2001.

Grossman, Pam. *Waking the Witch: Reflections on Women, Magic, and Power.* New York: Gallery Books, an Imprint of Simon & Schuster, Inc., 2019.

Haley, Alex. *The Autobiography of Malcolm X: As Told to Alex Haley.* New York: Ballantine Books, Random House, Penguin Random House LLC, 2015.

"Health Assessment for Helena Chemical Company Landfill, Fairfax, Allendale County South Carolina,

Region 4. CERCLIS No. SCD058753971. Preliminary Report." *CERCLIS No. SCD058753971* (2016). Print.

"Health Assessment for Helena Chemical Company Landfill, Fairfax, Allendale County, South Carolina Region 4. CERCLIS No. SCD058753971 Preliminary Report." *CERCLIS No. SCD058753971* (1991). Web.

"Low Country Gullah Culture, Special Resource Study: Environmental Impact Statement." United States Park Service and Northwestern University. (2005). Web.

Roots: 30th Anniversary Edition, by Alex Haley, Vanguard Press, 2007.

Stone, Nic. *Dear Martin*. New York: Penguin Random House, 2017.

Helpful Website:

Perry, James A. "African Roots of African-American Culture." *The Black Collegian*.

Online. Archived from the original on March 5, 2007. Retrieved July 3, 2020.

ABOUT THE AUTHOR

Mary Ellen Campagna was born and reared in Northern Virginia. She earned both her undergraduate and graduate degrees in English and Liberal Art Studies at Hollins University in 2000/'02, and did graduate work in education at the University of Virginia. For several decades she was a school teacher and a freelance journalist. Campagna taught in three states and served as lead foreign teacher at a private school in South Korea. During that time, she traveled to China and Japan, as well. After returning from Asia, she became a QMHP; she counseled both adults and teens with mental health problems and won the Media Award from the Montgomery County

Mental Health Association for a fictional short story she wrote for the *Roanoker Magazine* about her own depression under the pen name, Anne Pryce.

In 2005, Campagna wrote and published, *Unalet P. Zipley*, a Y/A novel that is still for sale on Amazon. That book became a collector's item and was translated into French and Chinese. In 2019, she wrote and published a memoir titled *The Blue Velvet Glove*, no longer for sale on Amazon. She also produced *Sammy Gales, an unlikely witch*, a book that is no longer for sale.

The author's history of covering city council and community meetings for newspapers in the Roanoke and New River Valleys of Virginia led to her research on racism in the area. She had marched with Dr. Martin Luther King, Jr. as a child and was there in 1963 to witness his "I have a Dream Speech." She also researched environmental racism while teaching in South Carolina.

CPSIA information can be obtained
at www.ICGtesting.com
Printed in the USA
LVHW100054250522
719681LV00020B/230